JOHN ROBERT RUSSELL

"Russell's science fiction is first-rate. It has that most important attribute of any purely imaginary work: it is consistently believable."

—The Japan Times

"Jack Russell can take you to unknown worlds and unfold fantastic adventures—always thrilling and sometimes horrifying. His novels are finely woven and thoroughly entertaining."

—The Daily Yomiuri

"If you think you've seen everything in sword and sorcery fiction, try TA by Russell. He's got an exciting new kind of action-adventure science fiction. If you liked De Camp's *Viagens,* you'll love Russell."

—Jerry Pournelle,
Co-author of *The Mote in God's Eye*

TA is an original POCKET BOOK edition.

Books by John Robert Russell

Cabu
Sar
Ta

Published by POCKET BOOKS

TA

John Robert Russell

PUBLISHED BY POCKET BOOKS NEW YORK

For Sueko

TA

POCKET BOOK edition published April, 1975

L

This original POCKET BOOK edition is printed from brand-new plates made from newly set, clear, easy-to-read type. POCKET BOOK editions are published by POCKET BOOKS, a division of Simon & Schuster, Inc., 630 Fifth Avenue, New York, N.Y. 10020. Trademarks registered in the United States and other countries.

ONE

Hoso slowly and cautiously felt his way in the darkness along the narrow, slippery field dike. He took one hesitant step and then another. One careless step sent his foot skidding into the black silted water. He withdrew his foot in near panic and took off his boot quickly to dump out the water, hoping that none of the flesh-eating red worms had attached themselves to his skin. He had not walked on field dikes or even in the country since he was a child, and that had been forty years ago. It was an unusual and unpleasant adventure. His rank and importance kept him in the capital most of the time, directing his extensive and vital operations, and the capital had paved streets that were lit at night by torches which cast a sputtering, bright light. But the special nature of his mission required that he walk alone and at night. He had left his agents back on the canal boat at sunset, explaining nothing to them and knowing no one would dare question him upon his return. But he was sure they would guess whom he was visiting in the darkness.

One of Ta's surprisingly bright moons began to rise, illuminating the green shafts of tabo in the square, water-filled fields. "Tabo, the life giver," he said aloud in mock reverence. "And the red worms, the life takers. The give and take of the eternal balance." The red worms, however, only ate the flesh off the limbs of careless farmers, and farmers after all were a class of little consequence on Ta. He had no compassion for them since he saw them as they were—the least skilled and least productive of all of Ta's workers. They were also good breeders and replaced themselves. There would never be a shortage of farmers.

The tabo fields ended abruptly at the edge of a high, strong dike which held back the desert sands. He climbed to the top panting and looked out over the desert while he rested. It took more than a month to cross this sea of sand, if the winds were fair and if the desert ships did not break too many wheels on rocks in passage. As he watched, he saw the sails of the sand ships. Their masters were taking advantage of the moonlight to sail toward eastern Ta where men—inferior men—lived and bartered with the traders of Ta. Sailing craft were still used on the desert although the canal boats now were propelled by efficient steam engines. This technological gap between desert and canal craft did not trouble him. He was an administrator and administrators did not concern themselves with technical matters. His eyes sought out a wind-and-sand-battered mesa at the edge of the desert and he began walking toward it.

He climbed the stone-littered path toward two towering pillars of stone from between which came a faint pinkish glow. As he approached, he noticed that the pillars were pitted by centuries of sand-seeded winds, and he was happy the night was still without a desert storm. He stopped before this massive portal and shouted.

"Tanee, it is Hoso." There was no answer from within so he called out again.

"I hear you, brother. Even the distant stars can hear you."

"You sound much the same."

"And look much the same, Hoso." The voice was closer.

"Are you covered?" he asked nervously.

"In a moment, Hoso. I will not offend your eyes or horrify your mind." The voice was edged with bitterness, but Hoso only shifted his weight from one foot to the other in impatience.

"You honor my home," Tanee finally said with flat, cold formality and Hoso entered.

Home was a high-vaulted cave done in good taste by nature. The polished crystal rocks were a deep red in the wavering light of the torches stuck into wall sockets. They seemed to radiate warmth against the rapidly cooling desert night. Along one stone wall, shelves had been installed to hold hundreds of scrolls. His sister had always been a reader. In niches here and there, desert jewels of sparkling greens, blues, and pinks were displayed to each stone's best advantage. His sister also had always had good taste. A white slab of stone that served as a table was set for two. Tanee watched her brother as he surveyed her cave home. Her heavy black hair fell over her shoulders almost to her waist. Her eyes were wider than most on Ta and a deep brown in color. Her skin was a perfect shade—light beige with a touch of pink. Hoso, who was twenty years her senior, saw that his sister was beautiful, beautiful as long as her robe which hung loose to her ankles covered her abnormalities. These he could not forget despite her beauty.

"You are the same," he said.

"Not quite the same," she said flatly. "And the changes that have occurred in the past ten years will not please you." She sat down at the table.

"Your favorite food and drink are ready."

"You knew I was coming?" She did not answer. She did not have to. He knew it had been a foolish question the moment it slipped out of his mouth. He was well informed about her powers. He joined her at the table and sniffed first and then cautiously sipped the black liquor offered him in a bowl. He could smell or taste most poisons and he never took chances. There was no man on Ta who had more enemies than he. But there were no traces of poison and he began to drink greedily.

"Excelllent! But how did you acquire the black grass wine of eastern Ta?"

"Sand ship crews dock here sometimes. They ask favors from me and pay in wine or stones."

"Smugglers?"

"I do not ask. I'm no longer a member of a trading family. I am an outcast without loyalties."

"You have been protected, Tanee."

"I have been permitted to live and I know that is not a gift of small value, for living even here, and particularly here, I have learned much."

"You enjoy life then?"

"I enjoy other people's lives." Hoso shuddered inwardly, but his training from infancy kept him from exposing the revulsion he felt toward his sister. His expression was bland. He even forced a slight smile and then took an unusually large swallow of black grass wine. Tanee understood what his forced smile and silence were saying.

"What I've become is not my fault. I was exiled shortly after puberty and in my loneliness, I acquired or better discovered the powers you detest. They do give me my moments of freedom and of pleasure. There must have been strong, wise women in our bloodlines, brother, for the powers I have are very strong. They are ancient and frightening even to me sometimes. But they do not belong to our ancestors now. They belong to me."

"Ta faces a crisis of great magnitude," he blurted out.

"Save your rhetoric for your underlings. I know of the crisis and it interests me not at all."

"You shall listen to me." He raised his voice and she fell silent.

"Since you knew I was coming, perhaps you know who sent me?"

"I know. The Director of Ta."

"And do you know why Mako sent me to you?"

"I was not that curious. Mako and his plans bore me."

"Mako is not a man you should insult. He holds great power in Ta, and he is aware of your strange pleasures. You should be informed that the Committee of Five recommended that you be prevented from taking your immoral trips. The members were right. Any good man who knew your secret would be incensed. But Mako is tolerant and willing to overlook your disgusting behavior."

"For his own reasons and advantage. I know Mako. But what right do they have to accuse me of immoral conduct? They—Mako and the rest of you men of Ta—behave like animals. Any girl born of a family that has not touched the sword is your plaything, your victim for any bestial sexual act that your imaginations can conjure up. I have seen too much of your good men. They have no right to condemn me as immoral."

8

"Silence! If Mako had condemned you, you would have been strangled."

"He prefers that I not be strangled."

"He wants your help and the services he asks from you are not for his personal benefit. We are concerned about the survival of Ta as we know and love it, and it is your duty to help save Ta. You were born of men and women of the swordholder class. You are a woman swordholder and you have obligations."

"You're not wearing it," Tanee said.

"What?"

"Your sword. Good for you."

"It is too heavy for a long walk in the dark. And stop diverting me."

"I won't, but wouldn't your mind be less troubled if Mako did order me strangled? As the chief of the Institute for Human Perfection, I must be a terrible embarrassment to you. They must whisper behind your back: 'Did you know the chief's sister is a freak, a woman who could not pass the Institute's standards, even when they were stretched by family influence?'"

"You have been removed from the people of Ta. You are no longer permitted to reproduce, if truly any man could possibly want you after seeing your deformities. That is sufficient under the law. It is unfortunate for you but at least you live."

"My deformities became apparent only after I reached puberty, and I, as you say, am born of swordholders. It is the law that I be exiled and not killed."

"It is the law. But your unnatural acts, your unnatural promiscuity are crimes against every moral man or woman on Ta."

"No law has been written to cover that so-called offense, Hoso."

"There is no law because it has never happened before, at least in our time, which makes your offense outside the law and therefore you are unprotected by the law. This is why the Committee of Five could vote for your execution. The vote, by the way, was four to five for strangling. Then Mako intervened and another vote was

9

taken and there was a unanimous decision to pardon you. But at any time another vote can be cast."

"The threat is clear. Now tell me what you want from me."

"You know of our problem with lower Ta?" Tanee did.

For a thousand years, the swordholders of upper Ta had lopped off the arms, legs, and heads of the barbarians, and the barbarians had run their spears through the swordholders and cut off their heads with the barbarian long knife in a war for possession of the fertile land between the deserts of sand and the wind-sculpted rocks and mesas. Slowly over the millennium, the barbarians were dispossessed of their lands, retreating always southward. The fighting ended five generations ago when the men of upper Ta held all the arable land and the base men took final refuge among the islands in the mists and swamps of lower Ta.

With the lands thus divided according to the desires of the men of upper Ta, the swordholders turned to farm management and industry. Already during their long march southward, the men who had never touched the sword had been put to work cultivating tabo and less significant crops, freeing the swordholders to engage exclusively in their bloody work. With peace, the swordholders built big houses in the countryside and cities. They drank fermented and powerful tabo wine and prospered and turned their energies toward manufacturing. Once there was a surplus in tools and gadgets, they became traders to seek new markets.

They went east across the sea of sand and found other men with perfumed woods, jewels, black grass wine, and precious metals. Demand for these luxuries from the east grew, and the men of Ta dug into the ground and cut down forests to provide their factories with raw materials. What they manufactured was eagerly sought after in the east. The men of Ta were clever, energetic and talented in the ways of making things and the ways of making money, which was their own invention. But the land below their feet was poor in resources and therefore uncooperative, and the men from upper Ta became desperate.

The barbarians sweated and suffered in the smothering, damp heat of the swamps. In the first years, many succumbed to the fevers, which were given such names as speckled fever, pink button fever, two-day fever, and head-cooking fever. The swamps were selecting and discarding, and those who survived grew strong and adjusted to their new unpleasant homeland. The men of upper Ta were unconcerned with the struggles of the barbarians. They were happy after so much war to ignore their former enemies for several generations. Their indifference would have continued for many more generations if the barbarians had not discovered a great natural wealth in their otherwise stingy and hostile swamps.

The barbarians learned how to milk the Takusa plant that sank its roots deep into the wet, spongy islands, and they learned that this sticky white fluid could be heated into the hardness of steel, spun and woven into thin cloth for comfortable tropical wear, molded into hulls for boats, flattened into building boards, scraped and polished into strong tools, and converted into slow-burning fuel.

Once the secret of Takusa milk reached the north, the swordholders boarded boats and primitive landing craft and seized, with surprisingly little resistance, some islands on the fringes of the swamps where Takusa plants grew. The barbarian captives were forced to milk the plants for worthless trinkets and the milk was shipped to the factories in the north. But suddenly, the Takusa plants on the occupied islands withered and died. The men of Ta sent three military expeditions to gain control of Takusa plants in the deep interior but the expeditions were defeated by ambushes and fevers.

A switch in tactics became necessary. Smiling traders with sheathed swords went next to lower Ta offering manufactured goods in exchange for Takusa milk and a bargain was struck. The barbarians agreed to trade Takusa milk for the products which upper Ta made from processed Takusa milk. They abandoned their own primitive industries and reverted to the idle life that the terrible heat encouraged. But they allowed the traders to

11

land only on designated islands on the fringe of the swamp.

As time went by, the manufacturing enterprises grew and flourished but remained completely dependent on Takusa milk. For years all went well, but then the trouble began.

The barbarians seemed to lose interest in the products of upper Ta. The barbarians began trading for fewer waterproof boots, swamp knives, bowls and spoons, and timekeepers designed by upper Ta craftsmen to mark the passage of the hours and minutes by the flow of a fluid in a fancy oblong case that could be suspended around the neck on a chain. Even the popular small steamboats, which were propelled by engines that turned paddles on either side of the craft and were powered by Takusite fuel, went untraded. Less and less Takusa milk was collected by the barbarians and the men of upper Ta were puzzled and worried.

The men of upper Ta began to hear tales of a new leader among the barbarians called Lornz, who preached nonsense according to the sophisticated men of the civilized north. But it became apparent to Director Mako and the Committee of Five that Lornz and his religious converts were gradually cutting off the supply of Takusa milk. They supposed that the barbarians wanted to boost the trading price. Mako tried to negotiate with Lornz but he remained inaccessible and hostile to his approaches. Mako knew there would be a political upheaval in the north unless the supply of Takusa milk was secured. The swordholders would not willingly give up their civilization and return to a simple agrarian society. It seemed that Mako had no choice but to launch another campaign against the south to convince the barbarians that only through reciprocal trade could there be peace on Ta. However, Mako remembered the military failures of the past and hesitated.

"I'm not going to lower Ta," Tanee said breaking the silence. Hoso heard the fear in her voice and studied his sister. So she was afraid of the south. Her horrifying powers had their limits after all. This pleased him.

"Do you fear this man called Lornz?"

12

"Lornz is a man and I fear no man. But there is more to fear in lower Ta than Lornz."

"What?"

"I do not know. I don't want to know."

"Your fear surprises me, sister. But Mako somehow knew that you would not journey in your strange way to the south to help us against Lornz and did not suggest this. I wondered then why and still wonder, but neither you nor Mako will enlighten me."

"He cannot," she said tensely. "And Mako only feels uneasiness about the mysterious swamps while I feel dread." Hoso sipped his black grass wine and thought about Tanee.

She more than any other had the old powers. A few like Mako could send their minds on short, stealthy trips into the minds of others, ferret out secrets, and depart hastily before the host mind became aware of the invasion and began to resist. This was remarkable. But what Tanee could do was horrifying. As chief of the Institute for Human Perfection, Hoso would have liked to have some of her powers. His duties were to keep the race standardized—no one too big, no one too small, all male bodies more or less the same and all female bodies more or less the same.

The Institute had strict limits on variations from the norm, and its agents had their tape measures, their weighing scales, and their charts showing the acceptable skin and eye colors with which to enforce the law. They were vigilant and energetic in hunting down the freaks and disposing of them when this was possible under the law. But there were those families who concealed the imperfections of their children, hoping they would reach puberty before discovery and then the law permitted only expulsion from the community of man and not death.

At least this was so for the families of swordholders. Other men and women who had never touched the sword were subject to the full penalties under the law at any age. If Hoso could mind-travel, he could find the offenders who hid the malformations of their children. Too many freaks were already living in the deserts in

13

exile or had fled to the south. Yes, a little of his sister's powers would go a long way toward helping him to maintain better standards among the people of Ta. But he only wished for a little of his sister's powers and no more. His sister could take possession of a mind and this talent repulsed and frightened him, and Mako was certain she could do an even more despicable thing.

"Why do you do it?" he blurted out and immediately regretted exposing his emotional preoccupation with Tanee's activities. Tanee laughed. "Are you worried that I might possess one of your women, Hoso? I would never do such an unpardonable thing. I am after all your sister and the daughter of a swordholder and consequently have morals. Things like that are not done among our best families."

"Why do you do it at all? Women of your rank are not promiscuous, at least not blatantly so."

"Hoso, I am a woman who has desires like any other woman. Under your laws, I am forbidden sex in the normal way, so I take what enjoyment I can from other people's sex."

"Do you feel, I mean do you experience everything?"

"When I possess a woman's mind, she becomes nothing or almost nothing. I take over completely. I feel and think and function in her place. I experience her love if there is any. But it is harder and harder to find the existence of love on Ta. I learn much more than one woman possibly could learn. I possessed the mind of a pillow house girl for many nights. I gave her a rest, at least mentally, and she was grateful. I was amazed at how many men she had to accommodate over a few days. Bad lovers for the most part too. I experienced quantity if not quality with her. But swordholders are not the best men on Ta."

"Who are then?"

"There was a strong farm boy up the main canal."

"You allowed a man who has not touched the sword to touch you?"

"He touched a farm girl and I just happened to be there."

"Disgusting."

14

"Yes it is. I've had more experience than twenty of your pillow house girls and yet I'm still a virgin. That's disgusting. But this is the life you condemned me to."

"You were rightly exiled to the desert. You were not condemned to live the life of a harlot."

"You can get very lonely in the desert, very lonely. I am still human even if your laws deny me the rights of a human."

"Then why don't you permanently possess someone and escape?" Hoso sneered.

"Because even though I have deformities in the eyes of the law, I like myself. My trips are diversions and nothing more, and they do no harm to anyone. In fact, I often leave those whom I have possessed better off. Oh, they're terrified at first but we communicate in our way and there is soon affection between our minds. I've often been invited to come back. It is sometimes helpful, if someone else takes over your being for a while. You get a good rest. No problems. No responsibilities. And once I check out a mind thoroughly, I'm the perfect person to give good advice and sympathy."

"And men. Do you possess them too?"

"I tried that a few times when I first discovered my powers and was experimenting. But I prefer being a woman. Women are capable of giving far more even in quick, unimportant encounters. Men too often just take, close their robe, and walk away. I can be very uninhibited, emotional, and yes even wild. And I can be loving if love is wanted."

"It is a crime."

"We discussed that. It is an act outside the law. And who has complained except the Committee of Five? What woman revealed willingly that she had been possessed by me? None. It was Mako's mind-spies who found out."

"It is unimportant how Mako found out. He knows."

"He is a sickening snooper."

"Silence. Do not slander the Director of Ta."

"All right, I won't." She drove her two-pronged fork into the food and soon was chewing noisily. Hoso refused her food because he despised her. A possessor who openly admits she uses her powers for cheap pleasure.

15

Women as well as men who are born of swordholders should bear misfortune without whimpering and certainly without trying to escape their fate. Where was the pride of the race in this woman? How could she be his sister? Tanee ate hungrily and then lifted a bowl of black grass wine to her lips and drank it like a man, allowing some of the black juice to dribble down her chin. She carefully collected these drops with her finger and then licked them up. She looked at her brother and his revulsion vanished from his face. The face became smooth and untroubled and his shrewd eyes looked into hers.

"This visit is very unpleasant for you brother."

"It is my duty."

"Tell me what Mako desires."

"It is the belief of Mako that despite your behavior, you are still a woman of Ta, a daughter of a swordholder, and therefore loyal to Ta. It is his conviction that you will help us, help Ta. And I am sure you will. The loyalty and obedience bred into you cannot all have vanished."

"You seek help from a person who is no longer a person. I am an outcast, deformed according to your laws and despised by all men of Ta. Why should I help you? How can I help you? I already have told you I will not travel south and in the south is the cause of Ta's misfortune. Only there can a solution to your problem be found."

"We . . . Mako is convinced you have greater powers which you have never tried. When our race was young, there were women who could send their minds anywhere . . . anywhere. These possessors brought us the knowledge to defeat our enemies and to build Ta's only true civilization. No woman with these powers has appeared for centuries, and it was assumed that the race had lost this art, except in diluted form—the mind-penetrating power of Mako and a few others. But Mako believes that the ancient powers have been bestowed upon you, and Mako knows the old legends well and Mako is never wrong. He has sent his request in writing. As a scholar of the old ways, you may appreciate his classic

16

style, the style of address of our race when it existed in the far north."

From the sleeve of his robe, Hoso drew forth a scroll bound by a ribbon and sealed with the impression of Mako's family crest—a jagged ice mountain and a broken tooth.

"It is Mako's order that you try very hard. I shall return soon, hoping to hear of your success."

"I have no choice but to try hard."

After her brother left, Tanee read Mako's instructions, written in the pedantic ancient style. She had guessed already most of what he wanted from her, but was surprised and troubled by the object of her mission. She then went out into the darkness and climbed the path to the flat top of the mesa where she wandered among the boulders in thought. Ta's moons had vanished over the horizon and the stars were left alone and dominant in the sky. The constellation called Goro's Sword hung menacingly overhead, and the three daughters of Goro were huddled together to the south in their star cluster, giving each other what comfort they could in their cold, distant exile. The old legend said they had been banished to the south for opening the door of Goro's tower to the ice god. Once inside, the ice god froze Goro stiff in his sleep and only in the spring do Goro's eyelids thaw enough to allow his tears to pour forth and form the rivers of Ta.

Some versions of the legend said he cried over his daughters' treachery and some said he cried over his icy imprisonment. When the ice god burst into the tower, Goro's magical sword escaped his cold breath and flew from the tower into the sky where it awaits the day when Goro will become completely thawed out and will be able once more to wage war against the ice god. The legend said that the ice god deflowered the three daughters one after another and then sent them shivering into the far south, where they weep over their stupidity or loss of virginity or for the ice god, depending on what text one reads. However, all the texts agree that they do not weep for Goro who was a rotten father.

There were many legends from the old days when the

17

men of Ta lived in the cold north and battled the ice god and his blue warriors. Those were the days when heroes fought knee-deep in the rapidly freezing blue blood of the ice god's army, and the women of Ta cast their heat spells to save the men from being trapped in their own victories. Few believed the old legends now. But Tanee knew better than to scoff at all of them. One legend she believed was about Aka, the most powerful of all the female possessors, who went away and returned with the knowledge of steel making. The men of Ta armed themselves with swords after that and with this technical advantage pushed the barbarians farther to the south. Aka went away again and returned with the knowledge of agriculture, including how to build dikes and use excrement for fertilizer, and the men of Ta were no longer dependent on hunting the white furry caterpillars which dwelled in ice caves for food.

Thereafter, they spent more time fighting and less time hunting. And then for a third time, Aka went away and returned with the knowledge of tools, production-line techniques and the eight-hour work day. The legends said that Aka had visited the star gods, and let it go at that. But Tanee knew more precisely where she had gone. Somehow she had always known. The legends said Aka had brought some star gods home with her. She had great powers and Tanee knew these powers were now hers.

Her brother's visit had disturbed her more than she had shown in his presence. He was chief of the Institute for Human Perfection and, although her sibling, her worst known enemy on Ta. But it was really only the office he held and what it represented that was truly her enemy. Hoso, as he liked to say, was only performing the duties imposed upon the race after the legends ended and men became practical and political. The men of Ta wanted a uniform race—hair all black, skin of a light, pleasing beige color with pinkish highlights, eyes set in a narrow cast, legs not too long nor too short, and the other parts of the body complying with the standards based on the bodily structure and appearance of the few

18

leading swordholders who decreed that uniformity must be achieved within the race.

Uniformity set the men of Ta apart from and above the barbarians who came in all sizes and shapes and colors. Only a few of the barbarians now had the almost white hair and pale skin of their ancestors because of the interbreeding during the One Thousand Year War. A lot of raping can go on in a millennium and many today resembled more the men of upper Ta than their tall, thin ancestors. But still they lacked perfection or even the desire to perfect themselves. It was the belief in upper Ta that the barbarians had lost the fertile lands because of their careless mating habits. It was only natural, the men from upper Ta thought, that they had been doomed to survive in the mists, heat, and mud.

Tanee was imperfect too; a freak outcast, but a valuable freak. Mako had been forced to come to her for a favor, asked politely enough in the ancient style, but her brother had delivered the threat if she decided not to help.

Tanee brushed her black, soft hair back with her hand and tears formed in her eyes. She knew she was beautiful and it was all wasted. Even the few sand travelers and traders who visited her to seek help came with eyes that never looked directly at her. They feared contamination. They saw nothing. She always wore a long loose robe. And she helped them willingly. She had talents at matchmaking between men and women. She could convince a wayward son to live a better life. She settled minor land and contract disputes since she could always learn the truth. It was all so easy once she had slipped into someone's mind and had begun communicating with that being in her unique way. But Tanee had never used her powers to do harm. She was careful about that.

She became aware that her mind was slyly wandering to postpone the inevitable. She looked deliberately up at the swirling cloud of stars twisting like a vapor across the night sky and she shuddered. Tanee closed her eyes and concentrated and then the journey out began. She felt very lonely, very cold and very far away. Her disembodied mind searched for human warmth in the great emptiness, detected it, and hurtled toward the target.

A month later, Hoso came to her cave doorway, blowing his nose and calling her name. He again had stumbled into a wet tabo field and was shivering. Inside, he peevishly accepted a bowl of black grass wine and gulped down its tingling warmth.

"Mako is growing impatient," he finally said.

"It is you who is impatient. Mako knows the problems."

"Have you succeeded?"

"Yes."

"Another world?"

"Yes."

"Humans?"

"As human as we are."

"So you say."

"Oh they would not pass the Institute's standards."

"Never mind that."

"Never mind indeed. Ta has a crisis after all."

"How often have you gone there?"

"Almost nightly."

"No difficulties in your traveling?"

She laughed. "My traveling cannot be compared to a canal trip or a walk in the desert. There were no difficulties, only terror all the way there and all the way back. Tell Mako I have found another world, the world that Aka found so long ago. But not the islands Aka discovered or their people. A different people."

"Do you like this other world?"

"Immensely."

"You're not doing that there too, wherever you've gone?"

She giggled. "It is an interesting world with interesting men in it. Violent men."

"Violent men are what we seek."

"I mean they're violent in . . ."

"Never mind that," Hoso broke in. "We have more serious things to discuss. The barbarians are giving us less and less Takusa milk. We've been forced to close some factories and reduce our trade with eastern Ta. Again we have tried to communicate with Lornz and

20

again he spurns us. He will not accept our messages. Of course, he may be illiterate. But he also refuses to confer with an emissary. He squeezes and squeezes and will not tell us what he wants. We cannot understand Lornz. We cannot understand any of the barbarians. But they understand us only too well. Mako and the Committee of Five are cautious men and take into account all the risks and dangers before reaching a decision."

"Like good traders and manufacturers."

"Yes. And Mako has come to a decision forced upon him by the stubbornness of Lornz. We must wage war to assure our supplies of Takusa milk."

"Three times the men of Ta have invaded lower Ta and three times all but a few of the invading swordholders have perished in the swamps. The men of upper Ta prefer to blame these disasters on swamp fevers. They refuse to admit that they are no longer the warriors of the One Thousand Year War. They are merchants and traders and only wear swords as ornaments. They no longer want to use them. We are not now a people capable of waging a successful war. We are no longer fighters. The spirit of the race flickers only dimly in commerce."

"These things are not for you to say, Tanee."

"Then what does Mako say?"

"Mako believes that to conduct a successful military operation against lower Ta, a great general, a warrior hero, is needed. He must be a man with knowledge of superior tactics and he must be incomprehensible to the barbarians. He must be greater than all the heroes of the past."

"There is no such man among us."

"That is unfortunately correct. That is why Mako wishes you to find and bring back a hero from this other world."

"I know what he wishes, but I cannot. Please don't make me."

"Tanee! It is against our code to kill a blood relative, but if I leave this cave now without your agreement, two of my agents will enter immediately. Both are skilled

21

poisoners and stranglers, and both have been drugged to resist possession."

"It would be a cruelty to do as Mako demands."

"It is work you must do. Ta's survival depends on it. You have no choice but to do it."

"Ta might have a healthier future without Takusa milk. I have learned much in my travels."

"There is no substitute for Takusa milk. Bring us back a hero."

"I have never snatched a mind before, and you are asking me to take an alien mind without any practice. I could fail."

"Mako tells me that if you fail, you will destroy yourself. If you do not subdue the other mind, you will perish in the struggle for dominance of your own mind. But if you do not try, you will die most certainly."

"Do you have a transplant candidate?"

"We are so certain of your success that we have one ready. He will be delivered here when the moment is right."

"The candidate dies you know."

"The survival of Ta as we know it is worth more than a single life, and anyway the candidate is a criminal who was sentenced to death before Mako intervened to spare his life. He should have no complaints since his body shall live on even if his being is destroyed. That's better than nothing. But this must be done quickly Tanee. Our new hero must be assimilated and trained and all this will take time and we have very little time. Any day Lornz may decide to cut off Takusa milk entirely. When will you be ready?"

"I must search more in that world. Even there, heroes are not plentiful."

"Choose well but do not be too long in doing so. I will return in five nights and I hope you will be ready then." Tanee did not reply.

Hoso's two poisoners were sitting on a rock outside swinging their legs and whispering to each other like children. Both were high on the antipossession drug. Both looked disappointed when Hoso did not motion them into the cave to strangle or poison Tanee. They

22

were prepared to do either, depending on their mood. Hoso felt they enjoyed their work too much. Few agents volunteered for such assignments but these two always did. They followed Hoso down the path to the desert floor without speaking.

Hoso never questioned the Director of Ta's decisions openly and seldom even secretly disagreed with him. But he believed the plan was dangerous. After all what kind of a creature was about to be brought into their midst by Tanee? Mako had sensed his disapproval yesterday and had tried to assure him the risks were minimal. Mako had said that professional soldiers anywhere in the universe must be the same and the one Tanee imported from the stars would be manageable.

"They lust after power and glory but are children when it comes to politics," Mako had said, winking. "Flatter them, heap honors on them, and get rid of them as soon as they are no longer of any use. We know how to be clever. They know only how to shout orders which are obediently obeyed by those like themselves. Blustering children. That's all they are. Don't worry Hoso. I'll control this hero." But Hoso did worry. He worried most because the selection would be left to Tanee. Of course, there was no other way, and true she was the daughter of a swordholder who should know how to choose a warrior-hero. Even if she now did live separately from the people of Ta, she still must know what duty is and she knew the consequences of failing to choose correctly. He thought he heard Tanee laughing or was it a wail? No matter. She would get Mako the man he wanted—a superb killer of other men. But then he began worrying again. What kind of monster hungry for battle and blood would soon join the men of Ta?

TWO

Kenneth O'Hara had good looks and a man-child charm and a relaxed approach to life and the challenges of life. He was a cheerful opportunist who pleasantly beguiled rather than outrageously cheated his victims. He was no spider in the web waiting for prey but a fly who somehow always managed to enchant and seduce the spider. But even an enchanted spider sometimes has its bad moments and a fly caught in such a relationship must learn to be an inventive lover and a good conversationalist. The fly also must know when to tactfully fly away. O'Hara's women, like spiders, made poor longterm companions.

Kenneth was out of the web for the night and on his own. He was free to choose species other than spiders and had chosen the less predatory girl sitting beside him in the speeding taxicab. He could enjoy this freedom for five more nights with this girl or others. Debbie would not be in the apartment waiting for him. Debbie was an absurd name for a woman of almost fifty but she adored her name as she adored everything about herself. Her figure remained firm and her face had aged well— a bit battered, he thought, but the lines were sexy rather than repulsive. Her blue eyes were little girl's eyes but there was no innocence in them or in herself, except for the innate innocence of all humans.

Debbie had decorated and furnished Kenneth's present apartment to his tastes. There were expensive Danish furniture and expensive carpeting and an expensive stereo. She had paid for it all and she paid for the rent and she loaned him money each week which was never repaid. In return, he called her "Debbie baby" and made love to her, practically on command.

24

Debbie had gone south to the sun and sands of Florida. Kenneth suspected that his spider was on the prowl for a new young man. When she did return on the sixth day, she very likely would loan him some more money, a larger amount than usual, and say goodbye. She would leave him the apartment, rent unpaid, and its decorations. He would smile and kiss her on the cheek without hard feelings. It had happened before.

The taxi stopped abruptly at a red light, and the blonde took advantage of the incident to throw herself against Kenneth. She did not withdraw when the taxi accelerated down the street in a futile, weaving race to the next light which blinked red as they approached the intersection. If you get one red light, you get them all. Kenneth felt that it was stupid to fight the world when it was against you at the moment, but the taxi driver was made of tougher stuff.

The blonde was a dancer with coiled, hard muscles in her legs. She was, in fact, a better athlete than dancer. Kenneth could judge since he considered himself a dancer also. Once he had even danced on television with six other men. They all had gyrated their pelvic intentions toward the girl singer who had treated them with contempt on and off the stage. Now he danced only in his apartment and only when he was alone. He had taught himself how to dance long ago for practical reasons.

He took up dancing to develop the supple muscles and good timing which he felt would be helpful in his career as a thief. Charlie had thought the idea bizarre but did not object. Charlie was growing too old for the profession without a partner and he took Kenneth into his company as it were and taught him the trade. Kenneth made his living for an entire winter by stealing from New York's better apartments. They did not make a very good living, and this was one reason why he gave it up, much to the disgust of his teacher who argued for hours in an attempt to dissuade him from abandoning a promising career for which he had great talents. There had been another reason why the young man had thrown up a perfectly good job.

He had been caught. Before the break-in, they had phoned the apartment twice without an answer. Charlie waited across the street at a phone booth to warn him if the occupant returned, and Kenneth casually trailed another tenant through the door and up the elevator. He got the door open without difficulty and confidently began to search the rooms, knowing the woman was gone. But the woman was not gone. She was only sleeping off too much booze and she woke up and sobered up the instant he entered the bedroom. She held in her hand an automatic, illegally possessed and very small in caliber —one of those lady's guns. Nevertheless, it could still put holes in a body and he promptly surrendered. He turned on his brightest boyish smile. A half hour later, he stuck his head out the window and shouted to Charlie to go home. He and the woman spent the spring and half the summer together. He discovered in these few months how to make a safer and more profitable living. Stealing was out.

"A titty for your thoughts." The girl laughed brightly.

"A what for my thoughts? Never mind. I think I heard you right the first time. Sorry, I've got business problems."

"I like deep, deep men."

A deep man to her, he thought, was someone who could read the headlines of the New York *Daily News* with comprehension. He squeezed her thigh but when she tightened her muscles, he hastily withdrew his hand.

"How's your job going?" he asked to say something.

"Six more weeks. They like me. But I should be more than just a dancer. Martin says I should study acting."

"Who's Martin?"

"He's an electrician. He lives in New Jersey."

"Martin is right."

"Do you think so?"

He nodded his head slowly twice. Between women and when he could, Kenneth had acted. He had been on television three times in small parts and tried out as a nightclub comedian. His jokes were joltingly dirty but not very funny. They offered him a job as a bartender, and he did that for eight weeks. He also had been a sand-

26

wich man in a bad restaurant and a doorman in a good apartment house.

"Martin has a ship."

"An oil tanker?"

"No. A sailboat."

"Do you like sailing?"

"I threw up."

"Sorry."

He wondered why she was with him instead of Martin. An electrician who owned a sailboat and believed she had talent seemed like a dull person. And obviously this girl with the mind of a twelve year old and this electrician were well bedded. Kenneth often wondered about girls who went out with other men and spent the evening talking about the man they didn't go out with.

"Martin's selling his boat."

"Why?"

"To help pay for the house when we get married."

"So you're going to marry Martin?"

"No. I can't. I have my career right now."

"Have you told Martin?"

"No. I don't want to spoil our relationship."

Martin's girl shifted even closer to him and Kenneth sighed. The taxi stopped at his apartment building, and the driver flipped back his hand and Kenneth slapped down the bills. They exchanged grunts, and the couple got out. A security camera scanned them in the hall and Kenneth waved at the motionless eye as they headed toward the elevator. No privacy. He wondered if Debbie had bribed whoever was watching the screen to report on him. Once in the apartment, he flipped switches and pushed buttons. Subdued music and lights went on and his small bar slid forth from the wall noiselessly.

"Whee," shrieked the girl as she began flipping switches and pushing buttons. The music changed to a raucous beat, the lights became bright, and the television screen flickered to life.

"Stop that," he shouted. "This setup cost plenty." She made a face and walked away as he hurriedly rebuilt what he honestly admitted was a pretty cheap seduction mood. But it usually worked.

"Martini?" he asked. She made another face.

"What do you want?"

"Chilled white wine."

"There isn't any."

"Martin . . ."

"To hell with Martin."

"You're jealous. But don't be mad. I'll drink one of your dumb martinis."

He began to mix two dumb martinis, and the girl began to dance. Drawing up a leg, she pirouetted and then started waltzing to some music playing in her head. The stereo throbbed another beat. She stopped briefly and downed the whole martini.

"Dance with me, dance with me, Kenneth." Her arms drifted toward him but he shook his head.

"You're deep. A deep queer." She then sat down abruptly on the floor and began trembling. Her mouth seemed to form into a scream but nothing came out but a little air smelling of gin. And then she relaxed and smiled at him warmly. Her wide, brown stupid eyes had narrowed a bit and, for the first time, Kenneth thought he detected intelligence in them.

"Maybe martinis and dancing don't mix," he said grinning at her.

"Let's talk," she said. "Let's talk about all those books on the shelf. Are they all yours and do you read them, or were they just here when you moved in?"

"They're mine and I've read all of them."

"I thought you might be the intellectual type."

"Oh sure."

"You've been wasting your life. With a little help you could develop, develop into a really fine person."

"You know I liked your dumb act better. Martin was right though. You should take up acting and I don't think you need lessons, Mildred."

"Call me Tanee."

"That's not your name."

"It's my name all right, Kengee."

"Look, you are Mildred and I am Kenneth and no more games."

"Kengee, do you want to go to bed with me? We have time."

"Go home."

"It's a long way, Kengee, and I don't want to go alone. Were you ever a warrior?"

"A what?"

"A soldier, I mean."

"I was in the war everyone wants to forget, so let's forget it."

"What did you do in the war, Kengee?"

"Avoided it for the most part." Kenneth smirked.

"You are clever. I sensed that about you right away."

"I was an assistant to a chaplain, answered his phone, filed his papers, and carried his junk around. He was an up-tight guy with the bad breath that comes from not smoking, drinking, or enjoying what you eat. But he and I shared the same views toward the war and religion. It was his belief that sermons were more dignified and effective if held in chapels on base and not in the jungle someplace and that a man of God should not get involved in killing. He stayed at the base camp as much as possible next to a deep bunker we talked the engineers into digging for us. We saw as little of the war as possible and therefore developed no un-Christian hatred of the enemy. He and I were sort of like the Swiss and the Swedes—neutral. For me, it was a boring and depressing war, but then wars are not supposed to be cheerful affairs, and as I said, I avoided the excitement."

"Who won the war?"

"Who the hell do you think? I won the war. I came back."

"Do you know anything at all about military tactics—how to win battles or even a war?"

"Sure. I do a lot of reading and thinking. My work schedule is very light. War is clever tricks employed on a massive scale. And in war all the rules respected in peaceful life are kicked under the table proving they were only temporarily convenient and without any deep significance anyway. You go forward like a savage with the cunning of a savage. Our greatest military leaders—our great generals—were bloody bastards who knew how

29

to use dirty tricks and were good gamblers and often crooked gamblers. Most of our great generals would have been just as successful at holding up gas stations, looting corporations, or selling girls on the street, only they were lucky enough to find jobs considered respectable."

"Did you ever sell girls on the street?"

"Yes, but only for a short time and I'm not ashamed of it. You can do worse things in this world. And the work isn't as wicked as it's made out to be. There are more girls who want to become whores than the profession can comfortably accommodate. You are sort of a middleman, doing everyone a favor for a damn small percentage when you consider operating expenses and the risks. Anyway I gave it up because my friends then kept telling me it was a low-class job, and—before I thought long and hard about it—I believed them."

"Have you ever sort of wished to become a general?"

"I never considered it. I hardly gave generals a thought when I was in the army and only really learned something about them after I started reading some military history. My afternoons are long. I don't have such ambitions. I'm just an ordinary guy trying to get by and I cause little grief to anyone by doing so."

"I think you're an extraordinary guy who could do much better in another environment where your talents and philosophy toward life could have free play."

"First it's a dumb act and now it's flattery. You want something from me. O.K. Tell me about it. I'll listen to any proposition if there's profit in it."

"I'm glad you're being so reasonable, Kengee. I do need you and we'll talk it all over later."

"Good. Now let's have a little belly to belly communication. I hope you don't mind hard mattresses. I like them, and anyway you'll never notice the mattress because I'm very good. We can talk business in the morning. But please stop calling me Kengee. It sounds too damned cute."

"Kengee is easier for me to say. All words that end in open vowels are easier for me to pronounce and you'll have to have a new name anyway. I would very much like to go to bed with you but there just isn't time now. We've got traveling to do and Mako is waiting."

"I don't go anywhere in the middle of the night and I don't go anywhere unless I know where I'm going, and this Mako sounds like a foreigner. I think you're a little off and I shy clear of screwed up women. You can turn me on and off quicker than any woman I've ever known. Now either we go to bed or you go home alone." Tanee looked hurt and he felt sorry for her, but only for a few seconds.

"I like honest and direct men like you. There are so few like that where I come from. I am truly sorry that I have to take you with me but I have no other choice. And you just might like it, although I can't imagine why. I'm sorry, but I had to select someone and I liked you so much the moment I saw you in the taxi. I knew it had to be you. It won't be so bad going home with me, really it won't."

"Get out." He grabbed his head. She wasn't hurting him but she was inside his head and that was frightening.

"Kengee, Kengee. Don't struggle so. It's much easier if you don't."

"Bitch."

He tried to call her a bitch again but could not say it nor even think it. He had the sensation that he was being rolled up and shoved into a bag where it was very dark. He tried to escape but he had no hands or feet, and Tanee was there seemingly touching him everywhere with warmth and love. He felt like a two-year-old child again being led by the hand. But they were not walking on a sidewalk. They were soaring into great emptiness. He tried to scream and Tanee hugged him closer or so it seemed. Then he began to melt into her. He obeyed her command to sleep.

Hoso looked down at the powerful man sleeping soundly in the hammock.

"The transfer is a success then?"

"It's done," Tanee said. "I'm exhausted."

"The hero of Ta," Hoso said in a noncommittal tone. "He won't like it."

"What?"

"This man's body. He won't like it."

"It's a very good body. The boy was from a poor but honorable family of swordholders. I admit the body's a bit outsized but certainly well within acceptable limits. He's a good-looking boy, too."

"You never saw his former body," Tanee said with a long sigh. "It was beautiful."

"Two heads and a childmaker as long as an arm no doubt. You would think a monster beautiful. And I suppose you did it with him. Did it with a monster. How could you?"

"I'm a monster too, remember."

"Let's not argue. When will he be functional?"

"He'll naturally suffer from postpossession shock for a time and probably depression once he gets a good look at his new body. He'll have to adjust to his body and this world so new to him, but he can quickly absorb this man's recorded memories. It shouldn't take more than a week, maybe less."

"Will he be dangerous?"

"Are you worrying about my safety, Hoso?"

"I am worrying about the security of Ta. After all, he is a military man, a great conqueror, and those types are always dangerous." The conqueror in the hammock threw out his arm violently in his sleep and Hoso leapt backward.

"Even in his sleep he's becoming aware. But he won't wake up for hours yet."

When Hoso was gone, Tanee slipped into her own hammock intending to rest only but immediately fell into a deep sleep. The mind-snatch and the transplant had been tiring work and she slept on as one by one the torches on the wall sputtered out and the orange dawn slowly invaded the cave. She did not hear the aerial giants of the desert—the birds the color of graveyard headstones and with a wingspread three times the length of a man—screech as they dove from a circling glide on the six-legged reptiles. The reptiles died so that the giant birds could live another day. It was a type of murder acceptable to all. In the fertile lands behind the big sand dike, farmers waded in the chilly morning water of the tabo fields. The cold water locked the flesh-eating red worms in sleep. On the canals, the boats with barges trailing behind headed toward the capital as commerce came to life. Ta was waking up and so was Kenneth O'Hara.

His first sight of Ta were the stalactites overhead and these were foreboding enough. They were blood-red in the morning light, resembling daggers wetted in human blood. He quickly closed his eyes and reached out to touch his mattress for reassurance. His hand flapped in the air and the hammock began to sway, rocking him in terror.

His head hurt too but that was the least of his worries since this was a familiar morning torture and it was almost comforting. He thought of his mother—a beautiful woman with narrow eyes, slim waist, and long, shiny black hair. His eyes popped open again. His mother had been a redhead with round green eyes and pleasantly wide hips. He quickly rejected the mother of the beige skin, but he had to accept the fact that he was in a cave. This was certainly disturbing, but not as disturbing as the realization that he was thinking in a foreign language. He reverted to English in confusion. He decided to take up one fact at a time. I am swinging in a hammock. I am in a cave. I am breathing dry, warm air. There was a girl named Tanee who last night got into my mind. "You go to my head like the bubbles in a glass of champagne." He sang pitifully and stopped almost immediately. No time for bad jokes.

Tanee must have drugged him, he thought, and automatically searched for his wallet. No wallet and no pants. He was sleeping in a robe and his arms looked like they had picked up a suntan overnight. He slowly lowered his legs to the stone floor, feeling the coolness on the bottom of his feet. A reality. His body felt thick and heavy. A very strong drug. He tried a few dance steps but his feet were grotesquely clumsy. "Drugged," he said aloud. "But I'm coming out of it." He saw the other hammock across the cave. The bulge at the bottom suggested a female body. "That bitch Tanee." He stiffly shuffled across the floor toward the hammock and then looked down at the sleeping woman.

Her long black hair fell carelessly across her beige face. It was a beautiful face but it did not belong to Tanee. He now was truly frightened. The woman's eyes flickered open and closed and opened again.

"You're awake, Kengee."

"I don't know, and who are you?"

"I'm Tanee, your Tanee. Do you like me this way? This is the real me."

Kengee tried to say "like hell" but some other strange words tumbled out instead. They meant the same thing and he understood that.

"You speak Ta very well, Kengee. But that's only to be expected. I know you're bewildered and that's only natural. You're frightened of course. But please don't be. I'll explain everything and please promise not to get angry. You are much stronger than you used to be and you must be careful. What was done to you had to be done to you or at least to someone. You must understand I had to bring someone back. I chose you."

Kenneth O'Hara was slowly growing aware that he was not Kenneth O'Hara or at least not the old Kenneth O'-Hara. He was O'Hara and someone else. He did not have the courage yet to examine the body he wore, but he suspected it was very different. He stood there rigidly as Tanee gracefully descended from the hammock and worked her toes into desert scuffs. He saw a shapely leg and Tanee with alarm in her eyes pulled her loose robe securely around her body. "Go look into the mirror on the cave wall," she said.

He peered into the mirror with a good deal of interest. The face, as he already had suspected, did not belong to O'Hara but the face obeyed O'Hara's commands. One eye at a time winked and the nose wiggled. The mouth curled into a nasty smile and then opened wide, exposing strong, gleaming teeth, undecayed and unstained by pipe smoking. His skin was darker than Tanee's with a bit more pink in it. His hair was black and long and tied in a ponytail in the back like some third-grade girl's. The eyes were brown and set in narrow folds

34

of skin, the cheekbones were high, the general shape of the face was triangular. It wasn't a bad face, but it belonged to a foreigner. He opened his robe. The body was muscular and he knew those arms had twice the strength of O'Hara's arms. It was an athlete's body and powerful but not graceful. He looked lower down and to his disappointment discovered that it was about the same size as O'Hara's. He turned and twisted, deciding that his left profile was better than his right. He concluded that it was a good body and nodded his approval into the mirror. And then the totality of the metamorphosis struck him and he screamed.

Tanee rushed to him and began hugging him and patting his cheeks now wet with tears.

"It's all right, Kengee. It's all right, dear. You are considered very handsome on Ta, and it's a much better body than I had dared hope for. I know you prefer your other body and so do I, but it's gone now and there's no sense in wanting something you can't have." His sobbing went on and she looked distressed.

"I know it's a shock, dear, but you simply must adjust. It's time to bite the sword hilt and go on."

"You damned witch. Give me back myself." He was speaking English and so was she, but both of them had atrocious accents.

"Please try to understand that I can't take you back to Earth or yourself. And I'm not a witch. We don't have witches on Ta. I consider myself something like a scientist. Now doesn't that make you feel better? And I'll help you. I really will. I'll help you as much as I can."

"I could never dance with this body. People would laugh."

"You're not supposed to dance here."

"Then what am I supposed to do? Stud for you?"

"No." It was a very sad no. "We can't make love on Ta. It's against the law. You are supposed to be or you already are or at least you most certainly must become a hero." He pushed her arms away and walked over to the stone table and kicked it.

"Stop that. You don't know your own strength yet. You'll break it."

35

His toes hurt and he squatted down to rub them. They were very dirty. He scraped the worst of the black filth out from between his toes with his fingers, resentful now that they had not even cleaned up the body carefully before delivering it to him. As he scraped, he began to calm down.

"What kind of a hero?" There was a hint of curiosity in his voice and Tanee smiled.

"A millitary hero, of course. We only have those kind here or we did have them here and now we don't have them here." She was not explaining well and knew it. She started all over again.

"You are to become an outstanding general, a brave warrior, and a sort of military genius all rolled into one." Her voice became little girl-like and her beige face turned pinkish. He had been coolly staring at her.

"Now why should they, whoever they are, expect all this from me?"

"Now don't get angry again, Kengee, please don't. I was ordered to find that kind of person in an alien world and bring his mind back to Ta to do a little job for us. The Director of Ta and the Committee of Five believe you were a great conqueror on your own planet, a real terror like Attila or Hitler or Geronimo." She giggled nervously.

"And they can never prove that you were not such a conqueror," she said smugly. "Trust me to take care of that."

"Why didn't you try the Pentagon?"

"I looked over a few generals and rejected them. I felt they would not be happy on Ta with our primitive weapons and methods of warfare. And basically, I didn't like them. When Aka once went to Earth centuries ago, she came back with some brave Italians."

"Brave Italians?"

"Yes, Renaissance men. You know the type. Good with words, poisons, and swords, and with a sound knowledge of science and the arts. But you just don't have that type of man around anymore."

"So you picked me."

"You were the very best, Kengee, and besides I didn't

have much time. Now let's don't argue anymore. We have a lot of work to do and only a few days in which to complete your orientation program before they come and take you away. Now to begin with the brain of the body you occupy is dead. You have nothing to fear from it and everything to learn from it. Just relax, sit back, and read it like a book. You'll quickly absorb the former life of the brain and learn about Ta in the process. Once that's done, push it in the background for occasional reference only. We want you to be yourself on Ta. That's why we brought you here." She smiled encouragingly, and Kengee shrugged his new massive shoulders.

After breakfast, Kengee flipped through the pages of the life of a man named Tano—the former occupant of this body. Tano was the dumbest son of a poor but honorable swordholder who existed on a living scratched out of the ground by his tenant farmers along the bleak northern frontier where long cold winters froze eyelids shut and the short hot summers kept the inhabitants glistening and dripping in sweat. It became apparent quickly to Kengee that Tano was retarded. He barely knew how to read and write. He got passing grades in the provincial school because the schoolmasters were afraid of him even at an early age. He was the school champion in fencing, however. Good swordsmanship earned much praise but no profits in modern Ta. Big landholders, the owners of big factories, and sharp traders were the ones who raked in what was really important on Ta now—money.

Tano lived a wild life in his teens since he could not indulge in the normal mental activities of his peers—adding and subtracting, memorizing technical manuals on manufacturing of Takusite products, and so forth. He spent too much of his father's money in the rural pillow houses, even though prices were cut-rate in the provinces compared to the bills of the luxurious pillow houses in the capital. There were damages to pay also. Tano brawled in the streets, occasionally maiming some equally poor swordholder's son or crippling a tenant farmer, who, if he was young and healthy, might be worth more in absolute money value than a swordholder. By custom, compensation had to be paid for permanent injuries inflicted on others by Tano's fists and feet.

Sometimes after too much tabo wine, Tano would lop off the heads of street torches with his sword. Once this kind of playfulness started a fire that consumed a small factory—melting the machinery and asphyxiating half the tenant workers and their families. In desperation, his father sent him to the capital with a scroll of introduction to a third secretary of one of the Committee of Five. The secretary obtained a commission for Tano in the escort service for traders and sent him to Cagu, the swordmaster of Ta, for basic training. Cagu was impressed by the boy's ferocity in mock duels and Tano was truly happy for the first time in his life. His limited talents at last were fully appreciated, and he willingly submitted to the discipline of the service, the only standing army on Ta.

To please Cagu, he worked hard to become a good escort soldier. But in an excess of zeal and youthful spirits, he one day accidentally killed another recruit in a practice duel. It was an extraordinary feat since they were battling with practice swords that had no cutting edge or sharpened prongs. It was an embarrassment to the camp and irksome for Cagu, who had to go through the ritual of apologizing to the dead recruit's family, a procedure which required a week of calls with and without Tano.

Tano's father was required to pay compensation after the value of the dead recruit had been carefully determined in lengthy negotiations between Cagu and the victim's family. Eventually it was settled, and since the recruit also came from a poor family and had poor prospects, the amount was low and Tano's father was able to cover the cost by selling two of his farm girls to a second-rate pillow house in the south. Tano resumed his training, only this time he was issued a very dull and soft practice sword. His unlucky dueling partners henceforth suffered only bruises.

"You would make a great leader of swordholders if you only had brains," Cagu told him once. Tano only grinned. He had no ambition to be a leader of men. He was happy to swing his real sword with its needle-sharp prongs and slicing edge at the practice block, and dream of the day when he would have the opportunity to split a barbarian in half, vertically. Cagu understood his desire and smiled tolerantly as he watched Tano hack through the thick block. When Cagu had been a boy, he too had hoped to someday split a barbarian in half. But there really were no good opportunities these days of fulfilling this age-old dream of warriors. There were no wars in the first place. And even when there had been wars, swordholders seldom got the chance to choose the stroke which would accomplish such bloody surgery. The barbarians always preferred to fight the men from upper Ta at spear-throwing distance, closing only when victory was sure.

Cagu knew that the only action Tano would see in the service would be against thieves stealing from the traders. But Cagu could at least enjoy perfecting this killing machine, powerful and deadly and too stupid to know fear. Never in his long career as a swordholder and a swordmaster had he had such a student. To his instructors, Cagu referred to Tano as "my beautiful beast." When Tano learned of this, he swelled with pride.

The recruits like all swordholders spent most of their free evenings and money in the pillow houses. These houses interested Kengee. The one Tano most frequently visited was located along a twisting narrow street in a town near the camp. Outside hung lanterns shaped like swollen female bellies that cast a green light on the street below. The lookout, a girl of about six, scuttled inside shouting the news of the arrival of Tano and his friends. The laughing proprietress accompanied by three laughing girls shouted their welcome as Tano and his three friends stomped through the doorway, their sword scabbards clanking against the wall. Each pinched the heavy bottom of the aging proprietress. She shrieked four times in mock pleasure and each time called her assailant a pervert for preferring old women to young ones. They replied that they had all come to service her, and she answered that the four of them together would never even tickle up an interest. They all laughed.

39

Crap, thought Kengee, but the memory continued to unfold.

One of the girls boldly reached under Tano's robe and grabbed hold. She led him yelping and laughing into the pillow room, and the others followed holding their groins to prevent similar capture. The floor was springy, made from foam Takusite plastic, and scattered around the room were pillows of many colors and obscene shapes. The recruits dropped hard on the pillows and bellowed their demands for drink. This had been anticipated and girls rushed into the room with bowls of tabo wine. The men cocked back their heads and the girls poured the liquor down their throats. "More, more . . . I'm a big bottle," shouted Tano and there was much laughter. A real clown, thought Kengee.

The bowls kept coming and the recruits kept drinking. They began pouring the wine into the mouths of the pillow house girls, but these women were crafty and let most of the wine spill into their robes, over their breasts and down their bellies. It was safer to stay sober. Next, the recruits began throwing the pillows at each other and then at the girls and the girls threw them back. Tano sent one pillow house girl crashing against the wall after he cannon-balled a pillow into her stomach. But she quickly staggered to her feet smiling. A pillow house girl was used to rough play.

The pillow fight went on for a half-hour and was the highlight of any evening spent in a pillow house. After the guests tired of the game, they began the traditional stripping of the girls. The girls begged, protested, fought off their attackers and screamed, but one by one the robes were jerked off and tossed into the air. In mock fright, the girls cowered on the floor arousing the desire of the recruits. Kengee studied the girls in Tano's memory. They were pretty, but he noticed that their breasts were only tiny peaks and their asses were small too. They had almost identical measurements. Less deviation from the standard was permitted for women than men on Ta.

Pillow house girls came from the farms and factories, and the prettier ones brought good prices. It was a sideline business for swordholders who selected the salable girls from the homes of their tenant farmers and workers. It was not the worst that could happen to a girl from a family who had never touched the sword and most were content enough. They quickly became hardened veterans of the nightly frolics with young and old swordholders who reenacted the violence and rape of the One Thousand Year War in their pillow house games.

Tano had drawn his sword and was playfully threatening one of the cringing girls with its two sharp points. She was terrified, truly terrified. Tano had in the past drawn blood with his toying jabs. But Tano suddenly sheathed his sword and began to caress the girl's neck. She was a beauty—the best of the lot, Kengee thought, and both he and the girl were relieved that Tano had become more gentle.

The other recruits were attacking their girls with teasing slaps and slobbering, wet kisses. And the girls' calculated resistance was weakening. Tano seemed no longer interested in this kind of sport. He was raking the girl's long black hair with his fingers while looking at her with warm, moist eyes. The girl became even more frightened by this strange behavior. When his friends and the girls began squirming and thrashing and gasping and moaning on the floor and the pillows, Tano grasped the girl's hand and lifted her to her feet. He pulled her toward him and kissed her lightly on the cheek and trembling she returned an equally modest kiss.

Tano led her from the room into the hallway where the proprietress had been observing the pillow room through a tiny hole in the door, ready to intervene tactfully if it appeared that one of the girls was about to be badly maimed. She pointed toward the polished stone stairs, and Tano and the girl went up arm in arm to a second-floor room. Even in a pillow house, there was privacy for the few who desired it. Once inside the room, Tano fell heavily to his knees and said over and over again: "My feelings are strong." The girl now feared for her life. Never before had this huge man displayed such emotions, and she doubted her ability to control his frightening passion. One wrong word or gesture could bring his huge fists down in fury on her head.

41

The girl was an experienced pillow house entertainer. She knew how to dodge heavy blows and roll with a hard slap and how to resist to the point when a guest would be willing to accept her surrender. She had a few scars and had suffered her share of swollen faces and black eyes. All this she could cope with. But girls in pillow houses were occasionally beaten to death—not often certainly since compensation money to the proprietress was high. But the killers were never turned away afterward, providing they had made the correct apologies and paid up. The girl had always thought that any pillow house girl who let herself be killed was inept at her trade. A fool. She had thought she could handle any swordholder, but now she knew she could not manage this one.

While Tano confessed his love for her at her knees, the girl was thinking fast. Finally, she pushed back her fear and pressed his head into her firm stomach and confessed her love for him. He believed her. For the first time in his life, Tano was enjoying the ecstasy of love. When the girl smiled, her eyes sparkled and her nose crinkled up. This he interpreted as a true sign of love. No one had ever loved him before, not even his long-dead mother, although she had cuddled him as a child before he grew strong enough to repel her hugs with pounding tiny fists.

When the recruits called to him from below, he ignored them and they left. He could not bear to be separated from this girl. When he touched her body, she shivered but kept smiling. He pulled her toward him and she closed her eyes and responded like a well-programmed machine. Only when dawn came did their long embrace end. He departed for the training camp, after whispering his love for her and promising to return that night. He had also promised during the long night to buy her from the proprietress. The girl had heard promises like this before and knew very well Tano did not have even a small fraction of the money to buy such an accomplished pillow house girl.

Kengee felt that Tano could have had the girl for nothing. In Tano's memory, he saw the terror in the face of

42

the proprietress who only wanted this monster to stop visiting her house. She probably had heard how he had killed another recruit at the training camp and feared his great strength and unpredictable violence. The girl was reserved exclusively for Tano in the upstairs room where he came and went nightly. The girl hoped his love would cool slowly but instead it grew even more intense. The girl strained harder and harder to please and to act the part of a devoted lover. Tano sensed no deceit.

A military exercise in the desert kept Tano away from the pillow house for three nights. The exercise was designed to test the stamina of the recruits under the harshest conditions, but it was a pointless drill since it in no way prepared the escort officers for the wet marshes and damp heat of the south where their duties would take them. Tano marched vigorously while the others limped and staggered in the hot sun and pleaded for water. On the last day, he carried one recruit on his back for four hours.

After returning to the camp, the other recruits fell into their hammocks too tired to even eat. Tano gulped down six bowls of water, buckled on his sword, and headed for the pillow house. It was obvious that he was not expected. The eyes of the proprietress widened and her mouth began to twitch nervously when she saw him, well tanned and happy at the door. He pinched her ass good-naturedly.

"She is out," the proprietress said trying to control her voice. "But please go up and wait. I'll send a girl to bring her to you."

Male laughter came from the pillow room and a girl giggled. Tano recognized the giggle. He kicked down the flimsy door and entered with his sword in hand. Three men and three girls were entwined amidst the pillows. They quickly broke their embraces. Tano's swordsmanship was superb. He executed his downward slashes and backhand slashes with amazing speed and beautiful grace. Three male heads rolled among the pillows. His naked love and her two companions dove through the window. He heard the slap of bare feet on the paved road outside. There was no other sound. The customers had died with a minimum of noise. Tano hacked away at their quivering torsos until his rage was spent and then he wiped the blade on a pillow and sheathed it. There was no point in looking for the girl, so he walked miserably back to camp, weeping for his unfaithful love.

The next morning Cagu sadly locked Tano in a small windowless cell where he remained confined for months. His father did not have the means to pay the compensation because the victims were all wealthy factory owners and their families placed an extremely high value on their lives. Cagu informed Tano that he must be beheaded to pay for his crimes, but in consideration of his swordholder rank, he would be allowed to behead himself if he chose.

Tano was allowed to test the machine that would end his life. When he pulled a lever, his own sword dropped fifty feet along the greased grooves of the machine. After a couple of tries, Cagu was convinced that the sword would never slice through all of Tano's thick-muscled neck and begged him to allow an executioner to behead him by chopping through the throat. But Tano was stubborn and Cagu decided to at least let the boy try.

The execution date was set, but Tano never got the chance to test the effectiveness of the machine. Cagu rushed into his cell on the night before the appointed date to tell the young man that the Director of Ta and the Committee of Five had agreed to pay the compensation money to the families out of their own funds— something never before done in the history of Ta. Tano was elated and began making plans for a reunion with his pillow house girl. But three nights later, his food was salted with a powerful drug and he was removed secretly from the camp and taken to Tanee's cave by Hoso's agents.

"Dumb, really dumb," Kengee said aloud.

"Is it dumb to fall in love? Is it such a foolish thing?"

"It is if it destroys you."

"It was the only decent thing that Tano ever did."

"Where's the girl?"

"Do you want her now?" He shook his head.

"The girl and all the girls of that pillow house have been banished by Mako to the far north. It would be bad for your reputation if there were people near the capital talking about your youthful tantrum. Heroes don't fall in love with pillow house girls, and they don't behead respectable, rich swordholders. It was a disgraceful episode, but Mako is shutting up the whole affair."

"Tano was very good with a sword. I suppose that was why you gave his body to my mind."

"Mako made the selection. He does most things well."

"Since Mako can do a little mind-snooping, isn't he likely to find out I'm not a world conqueror?"

"He can't get into your mind. I've erected mental barriers against that kind of spying. But how did you know about Mako's talents?"

"It was the crash course in Ta politics you gave me right after the transplant. I think you let some information slip out inadvertently. I also learned that you're pretty smart."

"Yes, I am."

"But what I can't understand is, if you're so smart, why do you live in this hot cave?"

"It's cool at night and I live here because I have abnormalities. I don't measure up to my brother's standards."

"What kind of abnormalities?" Kengee was interested.

"Don't ask. It is time for you to read the history of the One Thousand Year War. As you know, Tano never read anything. The history won't help you much but you had better keep it in mind."

"Why don't you give me a crash course in history, too?"

"You have to do something on your own." Tanee handed him the historical scrolls and he bent over them and began to read. Tano had learned to read but badly, and Kengee stumbled through the histories slowly.

The long war was fought for real estate. The men of Ta came out of their ice caves with spears made from bones and horns of animals and fought the tribes who lived in the plains, away from the cold. Once the men from the north seized a few valleys, they were determined never to return to their ice caves again. This was the beginning of Ta, and the men from the north called themselves the men of Ta, excluding from the human race the men who eventually would be known as barbarians. As the men of Ta multiplied, they grabbed more and more land, moving always southward.

The barbarians fell back but the retreat to the swamps took one thousand years and during those years there were battles every spring and autumn when the weather was at its best. Midway through the war, one man of Ta went to sleep one night an ordinary warrior and woke up a genius at warfare and many other things as well. He invented metallurgy and the sword. And this was as far as arms development had ever gone on Ta. Sometime later, another hero fainted one day and when he revived hours later, he announced that plants could be tamed. He taught the men of Ta how to plant, cultivate, and harvest crops. Those who farmed gave up fighting and those who fought became swordholders with all the privileges men bearing weapons usually have. The main privilege was that they no longer had to work. There was a footnote which said that in the past men foolishly believed a possessor named Aka had brought all the great knowledge from the stars.

The swordholders soon felt themselves above the other men and began to think up ways to make their military profession even more exclusive. They thought up complicated and at times senseless rules of conduct and behavior which no practical man—a farmer, for instance— would ever consider adopting.

Swordholders initially were ranked according to age groups—the age at which boys were first allowed to touch the sword. At first the age was ten and later twelve. They gained status within the age group through feats of valor or good thinking. Every swordholder had dozens of superiors and dozens of inferiors and each had to be treated with measured degrees of deference or contempt. In the confusion of battle, it was difficult for a swordholder to remember who had the right to command him, so swordholders tended to fight as individuals or in disorganized mobs. Kengee felt that this had prolonged the One Thousand Year War by at least four hundred years.

Those who died in battle were esteemed and honored, and there were abundant opportunities for this kind of exit from Ta. However, some warriors managed to grow old and when their time came to die of disease or the infirmities of age, they impaled themselves on their swords. If they lacked the strength to do this, then relatives lifted them up and sat them down hard on the sword points. Those who never touched the sword, the farmers and servants in the early days, were permitted peaceful deaths in bed. Nothing honorable was expected of them or allowed them, and Kengee suspected that they had snickered in their huts at the pretensions of the swordholders and may even have believed that after all they had got the best of the bargain in the division of labor.

Heroes and those not quite so heroic fought and died in battle or committed suicide in old age as the warfare progressed deeper into the fertile flatlands. The war ended when the men of Ta had what they thought then was the only valuable land on Ta. With peace, swordholders became farm owners, factory managers, and traders. Those who had never touched the sword did the hard work with few complaints. There was no mention in the text of a peasant uprising and no hint of discontent among the workers in Ta's industrial age. Kengee yawned and rolled up the last scroll. It was dull history.

He watched Tanee light the torches and drop tabo and purplish vegetables into a pot for dinner. He was amazed how calm he had become. He no longer hated her since he realized she had snatched his mind to save her own life and this to him seemed a very reasonable thing to do. And he was becoming curious about Ta and aware that there were possibilities of picking up some change if he kept his head.

"You don't think much of Ta's history."

"Only heroes, or so the scrolls say, and not one bitching soldier in a thousand years. That's unbelievable."

"Swordholders never complain. They are taught not to from the day they take their first steps as infants and fall. They are taught never to protest against fate and they are taught to obey their superiors and to seek an honorable death."

"A very simple philosophy and religion."

"Oh we pray also. We pray to those who have become for eternity a part of the soil of Ta. At least, we pray to those ancestors who were honorable."

"Who decides which ancestor was honorable and which was not?"

"The family head. He decides whether a name is to be entered into the family scroll. If your name is not written into the scroll, you are forgotten."

"Mistakes could be made."

"There have been mistakes and cases are often reviewed even many years later. In my own family, a name was forgotten because it was reported that one of my ancestors dropped his sword and fled in battle. Actually, many years later it was learned from the testimony of another swordholder that my ancestor's arm had been severed by the enemy, so naturally he dropped his sword. And since the barbarians also lopped off both his legs with their long knives, he could not possibly have run from the fight. His name is now remembered as a brave swordholder."

"Brave! He was cut to pieces."

"You make heroes out of lesser people where you come from."

"Not in my war."

"You never fought in that war."

"I was around and learned plenty about war. I had to learn what the sound of an incoming rocket was like and the sound of a mortar popping out of a tube so that I could dive into a bunker. And I also learned heroes are forgotten quicker than your dishonorable ancestors, and there is no profit in being a hero. But here on Ta, swordholders no longer use their swords, and they make profits in trading and manufacturing. So don't expect me to forfeit my arms and legs, and don't expect me to sit on a sword if I fail." Tanee laughed. "I'm funny somehow?"

"No, not really. You're just perfect. But I would not say such things in front of Mako and the others. They may not practice the old codes but they believe in them."

"Haven't you betrayed Mako and the rest by passing me off as a military hero?"

"I am giving them a man who'll do the job for them. They will have no complaints at least about that. I chose you after all with some care."

"Ex-chaplain's assistant, ex-thief, ex-dancer, ex-gambler, ex-actor. Sure all these many and varied careers and talents prepare me for a hero's role, I think you have a great sense of humor."

"You forgot to mention ex-pimp and ex-gigolo. Now eat your food." He did, in silence.

THREE

Rural Ta was a flat, healthy green on both sides of the canal that ran straight and wide toward the capital. They passed farm houses made of dirty yellow Takusite with roofs that swelled into domes and then twisted themselves into coiled points. They rose from amid the tabo fields—squares of regimented green plants that poked through the muddy water. On the dikes, purple flowers bloomed in a bad shade. Occasionally, they steamed past the homes of swordholders. These were much larger than the farmers' houses and constructed of Takusite in brighter and more attractive colors. The design, however, was basically the same. Kangee took little interest in the passing rustic dullness. He had never liked the country and now was eager only to reach the capital where there was less vegetation and more people.

Seven nights after his arrival on Ta, Hoso had come for him. He shouted a greeting to his sister at the cave entrance and she responded sulkily. Kengee had gone out to meet Hoso, but Tanee had not followed, and Hoso quickly hurried him away from the cave in the desert. They had boarded the boat just before dawn. When there was enough light, the boat shuddered as its steam engine started. The paddle wheels on both sides propelled them over the water.

Throughout the morning, Hoso asked Kengee questions in an awkward attempt at interrogation. Kengee replied politely but disclosed nothing about his past. Hoso, he knew, was the chief spy on Ta, and he was determined not to make his job easy. Hoso finally gave up and sat sullenly on the deck, glaring at the tabo fields. Kengee tried to ignore him and his three agents who lounged on the lower deck caressing the handles of their knives that protruded from their boots and staring blankly into the sky.

When the sun was overhead, two women crew members served lunch. They dropped to their knees before each guest offering bowls of boiled tabo peppered with finely chopped vegetables and chunks of tasteless canal fish. Hoso and the agents ate quickly and hungrily with spoons while Kengee consumed the meal with indifference.

"You do not like Ta's food?" Hoso asked.

"It fills the stomach." Although showing nothing, Kengee's remark had enraged Hoso. The alien had insulted the food of Ta. No outsider should insult anything about Ta. In Hoso's mind, Ta's food, Ta's manufactured goods, Ta's civilization, and the code of the swordholders were above criticism. It was all right to enjoy black grass wine or jewels from the east, but these were only luxuries after all. The basic things of life in Ta were sacred and only a barbarian with the crude tastes of a barbarian could think otherwise.

He had never agreed with Mako's scheme to import a hero, and this man's contempt for Ta's food convinced him even more strongly that he had been right. If Mako and the Committee of Five were not aware of the danger, he was. He would watch every move this Kengee made. He would protect Ta from this man—a freak in the body of a swordholder. He had long felt that the regulations of the Institute for Human Perfection should be expanded to cover malformed or radically different minds as well as malformed bodies. Some day, Kengee's behavior might justify the rewriting of the law.

Hoso sulked and Kengee watched him sulk, knowing of his disapproval and sensing his hatred. Tanee had told him who her brother was and what he did on Ta. The Director of Ta and the Committee of Five were powerful. They made the decisions and they controlled in one way or another most of the wealth. But outside these six men, Hoso and his army of agents were the next most important organization on Ta. Kengee deliberately stared at the agents who had never looked directly at him but who were aware of his every movement. They looked like cops anywhere with most of their human feelings numbed by years of police work. As a former thief, Kengee felt uneasy around them. It was sad to learn that there were no worlds without cops.

He would feel safer and more comfortable among the escort officers—soldiers were simple and not so dangerous. In fact, unknowingly he shared Mako's opinions on military men. But before he took up his life as a commander of troops, he would be carefully examined by Mako, and Hoso had informed him that his first meeting with the Director of Ta would take place that evening. Mako obviously was in a hurry. If Mako ever suspected that Tanee had imported a fraud, Hoso would have his way with him and Tanee too. It was the time for good acting.

Toward late afternoon, the boat moved slower and slower as the canal became congested with boats and barges on the outskirts of the capital. They bumped into other boats frequently, backed off and started on their way again. He saw factories—long buildings shaped like bisected tubes and again constructed of Takusite. Low-pitched gongs clanged dully and the work gangs began leaving the buildings. Both male and female workers wore short robes and their hair was cut above the shoulder. Only swordholders, their women, and the women of the pillow houses were permitted to wear their hair long.

The workers from each factory were dressed identically in distinctive colors and designs, and he could see that the colors clung together even in the mingling of workers on the narrow roads. Those from one factory did not mix with those from another. It was not forbidden but it was a custom. Workers were expected to prove their loyalty by devoting their entire lives to the factory that employed them. There were company apartments in the colors of the factory which rose twelve floors above the ground. A staircase spiraled around these vertical apartment tubes. Those with the least seniority climbed the highest level to their drab homes.

The two women crew members were now banging the boat's gong incessantly, trying to clear the way. Theirs was an official boat with an official Director of Ta pennant flying from a pole and should have been given the right of way. But the canal was too clogged with traffic and there were longer and longer delays.

Once the boat began to penetrate the capital, Kengee saw the homes of the rich merchants and factory owners. The roofs were similar in design to those of the dwellings in the countryside but were far more ornate than those on the homes of country swordholders. Brilliant stones from the east and the desert glistened from the roofs, and high black walls of polished stonelike plastic surrounded each house. The gates were of wood, rare now in Ta and a mark of real wealth.

In the heart of the capital, the warehouses of the famous trading families lined the canal. Barges piled with sealed containers were docked before their open doors. Laborers were rushing to finish the unloading for the day. They worked in silence, unlike the swearing, shouting stevedores whom Kengee had known in the past. The boat's flat prow bumped lightly against the official dock, reserved for the Director and the Committee of Five. Dockmen secured the boat with ropes and the engine hissed as it expelled its unused steam. They disembarked, stiff-legged, and were greeted by an escort of young swordholders in Mako's service. One of these young men bent down and whispered into Hoso's ear. Hoso then dismissed his agents reluctantly, and he and Kengee fell in behind the escort.

Kengee expected to be taken to the office of the Director of Ta, but the escort turned into a lane which Tano's memory held no record of. Night came first to the narrow streets of the capital and torches were being lit by the torchlighters employed by the Committee of Five. On both sides of the lane were stand-up wine bars, restaurants, and pillow houses. The residents of the capital plunged early into their nightly pleasures and already men were shouting, singing, staggering along the lane, and bending over to vomit into the gutter. Kengee heard a woman laugh and later he heard a woman scream.

The escort led them into a court where blocks of ice had been carved earlier in the day into the shapes of mountains, giant northern ice caterpillars, and nude women with their icy legs spread far apart. The display was supposed to cool one's mind, to refresh it. After the appropriate words of admiration were voiced by all, one of the young swordholders stepped forward to rap on the door. It slid open before his knuckles tapped the Takusite boards. Women in short colorful robes beckoned them without speaking, and Kengee and Hoso entered, leaving their escort behind among the ice sculptures.

The women patted the dirt and sweat off their faces with perfumed yellow sponges. With quick finger movements, dirt was twisted out of Kengee's ears and nose. His robe was brushed and then his boots were removed and his feet washed. He realized that this was a high-class pillow house.

The girls, who had remained silent while grooming the guests, led them by the hand into a large room where cushioned stools and tables were arranged on platforms of varying heights. They stood waiting. One of the Committee of Five entered wearing the distinctive gray robe of his office, and Hoso and Kengee covered their eyes with their hands briefly in respectful greeting. The committeeman only half lifted his own hands in acknowledgment and then sat down on a stool on a platform higher than all, except for one in the center of the room. He began squinting at a scroll, occasionally peering over it at Kengee with astonishment apparent on his face. Kengee avoided his probing eyes and studied the room arrangements.

The height of each platform obviously determined the rank of the guest. The Committee of Five member

53

knew exactly where to sit down. His platform was only slightly lower than the one in the center of the room, which most certainly was reserved for the Director. However, the other guests who began to crowd into the room did not know where to sit, since they did not know the status of the stranger Kengee in Ta society. The guests eyed him as if they were trying to judge his social weight and then looked nervously elsewhere. To cover their embarrassment, they burst into loud conversation all at once, praising each other's robes and describing their adventures in pillow houses on the previous night.

Suddenly the noisy mouths all stopped and there was silence as the Director of Ta entered the room. The hands of the guests fluttered before their eyes, and Mako casually returned these salutes and chatted to two lower officials for a moment. He then turned toward Kengee.

"Welcome. Please sit here." He pointed to a stool on a platform only slightly lower than the one occupied by the committeeman. Hoso sucked in air and his face turned a blotchy red. It appeared that Kengee now outranked even the chief of the Institute for Human Perfection. Mako enjoyed Hoso's discomfort for a few moments and then allowed him to retrieve his lost honor.

"Hoso, you must join me on my platform for at least one drink before your duties take you into the night," Mako said. Hoso looked relieved. He would not be humiliated after all.

Kengee and the other guests sat down, now able to determine their platforms, and the girls rushed in with bowls of wine and food. Mako suddenly stood up and then slammed the heel of his boot down three times on the platform. The drinking began. The first bowl was slurped down hurriedly and the empty bowl was slammed down hard on the surface of the Takusite table. It was an old Ta custom.

"I hope your journey was not too tiring?" Mako smiled down at Kengee. Kengee did not know whether Mako meant the boat trip or the much longer voyage, so he quickly thought of a reply that would cover both.

"A soldier expects long marches in his life." Kengee

had decided to become a simple soldier before Mako, voicing a simple soldier's third-rate maxims. Mako beamed, stroking his double chins below his round smooth face. They toasted each other Ta style—spitting the first mouthful on the floor and drinking the next. This custom was supposed to show that although swordholders loved their wine, they valued friendship even more. Mako stood up again and slammed his stool down once and the serving girls swarmed into the room with more bowls of wine. The ritual of the first drink was over and now hard drinking and entertainment could begin.

Ten giggling girls pushed the two-thousand-string Ta harp into the room. Then eight of the girls scurried back and forth plucking the strings which twanged out a cheerful tune and the men began keeping time by tapping the tables with wine bowls, empty or full. One of the serving girls skidded on spilt wine and fell. She hit her head hard on the floor and lay there groaning and ignored for a long time. Finally, she was dragged feet first from the room by four girls as the music became even more lively.

The girls began whirling in a dance between the platforms—their loose robes flying higher and higher, first above their knees and then almost above their thighs. The applause was loud. Next the dancers leaped onto the tables and began gyrating. Their long hair whipped through the wine-saturated air. And then they stood on their heads and the guests cheered in a deafening roar. It was the custom on Ta not to wear underwear.

Mako watched with a tolerant smile, while Kengee twisted his head this way and that in an attempt to see all of the girls. He was beginning to enjoy Ta for the first time. When the girls flipped back to their feet on the platforms, Mako rose. The dancing ended abruptly, but he signaled the dancers to start again. He motioned to Kengee to follow him, and they departed through the rear door of the room. They went to a quiet room down the hall where they sat face to face on stools while a woman served them a thick, sweet tea made from a desert plant which only grows on the eastern edge of the great desert.

"I imagine our entertainments are very different from what you are used to."

"Camp followers and medical corpsmen are unfortunately necessary to any army," Kengee said and Mako looked puzzled.

"Yes, of course," he finally said, "and I suppose to any bureaucracy." Mako then slurped the desert tea with obvious delight. To Kengee, it tasted like a mixture of coffee and salt.

"This is the rarest and most expensive of all our teas. To gather the ingredients for a single cup requires the labor of ten men-for ten days. For this reason, it is highly appreciated on Ta." He jiggled the cup while speaking, spilling most of this highly appreciated tea on the floor. "It is so rare that perhaps only one hundred persons now alive have ever tasted it."

"I feel very honored." Kengee drained his cup.

"Your sash is blank." Mako was looking directly at Kengee's stomach with disapproval. He gave the door a kick, and when the woman stuck her head in, he ordered her to bring a pen and ink. They were delivered a second later. A Ta pen has a big ball on its end which is soaked in ink and then pressed on scrolls to make the dots and smears of Ta writing. Mako asked Kengee for his sash and then drew his family crest on the blank band—a jagged ice mountain and a broken tooth. Kengee could not decide if the tooth was from a man or an animal. He supposed it made little difference.

"It is our custom," Mako explained. "I draw my family crest on your sash and you draw yours on mine when we become acquainted formally. The more prestigious the crests which you have on your sash, the more prestige you have on Ta. Of course, you have no family crest yet. I must wait awhile for you to return the honor." Kengee briefly covered his eyes in expected gratitude.

"You have learned the courtesies and customs of Ta from Tano's poor weak brain cells, but you could learn little of our culture from him. I must apologize for giving you such a poor brain for reference, but although Tano was a very stupid man, he was a skilled swordsman with amazing bodily stamina. I knew you would appre-

56

ciate these qualities more than intellect." Mako looked embarrassed for a brief moment and then went on to another subject.

"Tanee, the outcast, informed us that you conducted numerous military campaigns in your own world. How did you win your greatest fame as a commander of troops?"

"In desert warfare," Kengee blurted out and then wished he had said something else.

"Our enemies, of course, live in swamps."

"Tactics with modifications are transferable to any terrain," Kengee lectured. "What counts in warfare is the massing of forces and using that force at the right moment. Bold but carefully planned strokes that shatter the enemy's formations and spirit are the tactics that win battles."

"But in Ta, the enemy never form up and fight as they should. They prefer to enter battle only when the conditions are favorable to them and they have the maddening habit of striking quickly and vanishing into the mists. Cowards, I admit, but nevertheless clever fighters. Don't you agree?"

"In my experience, native irregulars can be defeated by building up a superior ratio of forces and then employing those forces to destroy their villages, crops, sanctuaries, and lines of communication. I foresee little trouble. Now in my first desert campaign . . ."

"Yes but there is another problem," Mako interrupted. "Our swordholders do not adapt well to the marshes, mist, water, and heat of the south. We have frankly never managed to move a force deeply enough into enemy territory to cause much damage. In all truth, our past campaigns have been disasters, so disastrous in fact that we abandoned all thought of military conquest years ago. But as you must know by now, war is being pressed upon us. It is a case of fight or go broke. We have brought you to Ta to give us a smashing, total victory."

"I accept the command," Kengee said simply and directly.

"Excellent. There were a few in the Committee of Five who feared that you would be less cooperative in

57

resentment against the rather unusual way we recruited you. But I can see you are a real soldier, prepared to do your duty anywhere. Good. But first we must provide you with the necessary social status so that you will be able to command with authority on Ta. Later, we will introduce you, or reintroduce you, to Cagu, the swordmaster. He'll be surprised to see how much you've learned in such a short time. But Cagu is a simple military man and will accept you as you are without questions."

A loud female scream came down the hall from the playroom and then another and then yet another. There were howls of male laughter and Mako smiled.

"I don't want to take Denzo from the girl baiting. He enjoys it so much. You'll have to wait patiently for a few more minutes before becoming his son."

"I don't really need a father," Kengee said.

"You most certainly do. On Ta anyone with any social status must have a father, and an important one, too. Denzo is descended from swordholders who were great warriors for a thousand years. He is wealthy. He is one of the Committee of Five which means in one way or another he controls through his companies and allied companies almost a fifth of the wealth on Ta. Fortunately for you, he has no male heir. Only a daughter. You will become his heir and reside with him while you are in the capital between wars. And someday, if everything goes right, you will inherit all that is his, except the portion which reverts to the Director upon a committeeman's death. Denzo consented to adopt you in appreciation of the services you will soon render Ta. The adoption scroll is drawn up and Denzo has read it and I personally will witness the signing with my own crest this very night."

A half hour later, Kengee's father-to-be staggered into the room supported by two women with torn robes. His own robe was open and his eyes still held the excitement of the girl baiting in the main banquet hall. Mako guided his hand as he stamped his family crest on the document—a figure of a headless man with both hands still gripping a battle sword. Then in an outburst

58

of emotion, Denzo embraced Kengee. They walked down the hall arm in arm.

To their right along the passageway a door was open and they paused for a few minutes to watch the guests and the pillow house girls frolicking in the wine pool. It was a circular tub about three feet deep and occupied most of the room. The men sucked in wine and spewed it out at each other. Two men held a girl's head below the surface until in the frenzy of near drowning she swallowed wine. They then tossed her out of the pool and she lay on the floor coughing. One fat swordholder dog-paddled about, grinning at everyone. "No time for a dip, son?"

"It's too late father."

Two of Denzo's husky servants were waiting outside, shivering in the ice garden. They automatically caught Denzo under his arms and began propelling him into the street. Denzo sang: "A swordholder has two swords —both are for thrusting but only one is trusting." The song died suddenly and his head flopped down with his long gray hair falling over his face. The servants tightened their grip without breaking their stride. In respect for Denzo's rank, drunken swordholders pressed against the wall of the narrow lane to give him free passage. Kengee strode behind the servants and Denzo, thinking about the wealth his new father possessed. He wondered how long it would take for the boozing to finish him off. But he remembered that there were a lot of old drunks on Earth and assumed they lived just as long on Ta. This did not discourage him. Denzo was a long-term investment. All he had to do was wait, and waiting came easy. It cost nothing. But then it struck him that the life expectancy of a commander of swordholders in the war he was soon to wage was probably much less than Denzo's.

A drunk lurched out of a narrow byway, and Kengee's hand instinctively went for his sword, but he had none. He would have to mention this to Denzo, but Denzo already was sound asleep between the two servants with the toes of his boots dragging on the paved road. At Denzo's mansion, four more servants came rushing forward and carried their master off to bed. Kengee was led to an apartment prepared for him. He climbed into his hammock and immediately fell into a sound sleep.

In the morning, a serving girl child awakened him by tugging at his big toe. The girl child covered her eyes as he swung out of the hammock, and then she pulled back the curtains of tightly woven Takusite. The tall purple-green blades of Ta grass which rose three stories from the garden below quivered in the morning breeze. The girl left and Kengee began to eat his breakfast—small grayish eggs boiled in a sweet brown sauce, peppery white roots, and hot tea that tasted like salty machinery oil. There were also tabo cakes smeared with green honey produced by sluglike creatures that lived in large communities underground. He watched the small birds with spread talons descend like helicopters on their prey—furry ten-legged creatures which made noises like little girls belching.

Kengee turned away from the murder going on outside and began to explore his apartment. The rooms at first appeared disappointingly bare, but careful inspection revealed that the simplicity was an intentional deception. Everything in the rooms was expensive. The floor, for example, was of polished wood and not Takusite plastic. Good wood was now very rare in Ta because in the early days, before Takusa was discovered, the forests were demolished to feed the infant industries. On the wall was an ancient shield with the house crest —the headless man. The walls, also of wood, were decorated here and there with embedded desert jewels placed at discreet distances from each other so that the sparkle of one jewel did not compete with the sparkle of another. He opened a closet where a dozen robes hung over three pairs of new boots made of shiny Takusite. There was a tapping at the door and a man entered carrying a long slender box in his hands. He put the box reverently on the floor at Kengee's feet and then covered his eyes.

"I am Gijo. I am to serve you." Since this man wore a sword, Kengee knew he was more important than an ordinary servant. Gijo pointed to the box, and Kengee knelt and lifted the lid. Inside was a typical two-pronged sword with a very untypical hilt inlaid with smoky gray gems. Kengee's hands surprised him as they grasped the weapon eagerly. His thumb flicked over the sharp blade and the points of its two prongs. When his right hand gripped the hilt, Kengee felt a tingling sensation race through his body and down to his groin. The sensation disgusted him. Something of Tano remained in his person.

"It pleases you." Gijo's eyes twinkled beneath his gray eyebrows.

"It does." But Kengee thought he would be more pleased with an M-16 rifle and a box of grenades. These would have made his job of becoming a hero on Ta easy. There were no advanced weapons in this world and the commercial-minded swordholders were unlikely to ever develop such products which most certainly would not retail well. Gijo found a sword belt in the closet, and then they both went down into the garden. Straw practice dummies had been set up by Gijo, and when he saw them, Kengee felt that uncomfortable surge of pleasure in his body again. He began dismembering the dummies with slashing strokes. Gijo looked on approvingly and only once gave Kengee advice. He felt his backhand slashes were a little slow.

"Well done," Gijo said after the last dummy had been cut and scattered on the ground. "Swordholders with your skill are too rare these days. There's hope for Ta yet." Gijo began to wipe the sweat off Kengee's face and neck with a towel. He then rubbed oil carefully onto the blade of the sword.

"This sword was a hungry blood-drinker in the old days. You are giving it an appetite again." Gijo's joke made Kengee's stomach heave. What was left of Tano in him might be excited by a sword, but Kengee did not like swords at all. He had, of course, been born in an age and place where swords were in museums without value or meaning to man, even to a soldier. He recalled that he had seen them used in ridiculous pirate movies. Kengee felt if he had to kill someone, he would rather do it at a distance. He was of his times.

In the old days, swordholders carried their swords always in their hands on Ta. Now the swords were carried in scabbards. Kengee sarcastically decided that swordholders nowadays needed both hands free to make money. And he did not consider that really a bad thing.

"Good morning, brother."

He turned and saw a girl sitting on a bench from where she obviously had been watching him for some time. Her eyes were dark, inquisitive, and unfriendly.

"I'm your new sister, Macha." The voice was haughty, icy, and a little threatening. He nodded. No woman rated any other greeting on Ta, even if she came from the womb of a swordholder's legal wife. Kengee walked toward her.

"I am delighted to have such a beauty for a sister." He beamed down on her and she glared back.

"My father has lost all judgment. How could he choose a killer and a lover of a pillow house girl for a son? I'm too ashamed to meet my friends. A brute and a fool for a brother. Society on Ta has begun its downward slide."

Gijo had backed hurriedly out of the garden, and Kengee was now alone with Macha. He took a quick step toward her and slapped her hard across the face. She rolled into a bush but was on her feet almost instantly, ready to spring, and Kengee somehow knew she was dangerous and armed. His sword was three paces away, and she caught him searching for it and smiled.

"It may be a man's right to do that, but no man has ever done that to me before," she said angrily.

"I'll do it again if it needs to be done again."

"I hate you."

Kengee raised his hand, hoping to God the girl would not accept the challenge. Her hand had slipped into her sleeve but came out empty. She dropped her arms to her side.

"Only fools speak their hate," Kengee said. He had discovered long ago that a hard slap improved the relationship between man and woman and required less energy than a long argument. But he decided that slapping Macha was something like slapping a Doberman pinscher. The girl had fangs. He turned to leave.

"Wait," she said. "There is no point in having bad feelings in the family. I'll show you the house." Her sudden meekness made him even more suspicious but he followed her through the door and for an hour trailed her as she took him on a tour of Denzo's mansion.

Macha had learned one thing about him: he was by reputation stupid but he was not stupid. She would have to find out why. She watched him carefully and listened to everything he said as they moved from room to room. She was relieved when he did not become overly curious when she explained that they could not enter her mother's apartment. Her mother had secluded herself in these rooms ten years ago, and saw no one except a few trusted servants and friends and Macha.

Denzo was nowhere in the house. Macha told him that he had gone off early to visit one of his factories and at midday was to attend a Committee of Five meeting. He was not expected home until very late and had asked Macha to entertain Kengee. As the minutes slipped by, Macha slowly transformed herself into a charming hostess, but Kengee was on guard against her easily shifting moods. The slap had forced her to reveal the dangerous side of her nature.

Macha suddenly grabbed his hand and led him into her own apartment. She sat down and gestured for him to sit on a stool beside her. He took a sudden interest in a large wall picture made of twisted, colorful Takusite cords which portrayed a headless warrior slashing his way through terrified barbarians.

"Our ancestor," she said without irony. "They say he fought for an hour after being decapitated."

"Do you believe that?"

"Why not?"

Five girls entered with tiny dishes of gray moss, which is scraped from the side of canals in the late fall and is considered a delicacy on Ta. They also brought in a type of tea, new to Kengee, that had the steamy aroma of damp earth. Two of the five girls wore veils over their faces and three did not. These were not ordinary servants but the daughters of poor but respected swordholders who came to Denzo's home to be trained in the culture of Ta women. They paid for their education by waiting upon Macha. Kengee asked why two of the girls covered their faces with veils.

"It is both a courtesy and an insult. They believe they are more beautiful than I, and they do not wish to offend their patron by showing their beauty. They are pretty but not that pretty. I allow them this vanity."

"You are very kind," he said. She laughed.

One of the girls without a veil performed the art of making tabo ball cakes. It was a long, tedious process but done with graceful finger motions and spiritual concentration. The grain was pounded into a powder and mixed with twenty seasonings and water, and then the dough was rolled in the palm of the girl's hand until small round pellets were formed. These were skewered on a long needle and then dipped into the milk of the michu —a ratlike creature which was domesticated, kept in cages on farms, and milked. Finally the ball cakes were roasted over a tiny flame and served ceremoniously by the girl who covered her eyes while thrusting the ball cakes on the end of a hot needle toward Kengee. He removed the cake and ate it. It tasted like sweat, and this was no doubt due to the michu milk. The cakes were small enough to swallow without tasting them, and this he did with the others.

"It requires five years of practice under the instruction of a tabo ball cake master to become accomplished in the making of tabo ball cakes," Macha explained. "I'm afraid I've never had the patience to become skilled in this art."

"It was beautifully done," Kengee said. The girl blushed and withdrew to a corner of the room. Next two girls sang an old Ta love ballad. Once long ago, so the ballad went, a girl loved a young swordholder and was made pregnant by him, and then he went off to war unaware of her condition. Because of his strong love for her, he performed badly in battle and was disgraced. He therefore sat on his sword while holding a wilted flower she had given him. When the news reached the girl, she wept for three days and three nights, and then set fire to her father's house where she perished with twenty-five faithful, weeping servants, two small brothers, and an invalid mother. When the father returned from the war, he shed tears over the ashes of his home and family. It was a sad song and tears fell from the eyes of the singers.

The young women performed other entertainments through the long afternoon, pleased that for the first time they had a male audience. Fathers spent much money to train their daughters in Ta culture so they would be more marriageable. Once they were married, however, their husbands never wanted to be entertained by their accomplished wives, preferring the cruder entertainments of the pillow houses. But no swordholder would consider marrying a girl who lacked cultural training.

The tall blades of grass brushing against the window were turning a deep purple in the waning light when the final performance came to an end. For a half-hour, two girls had pounded a row of tiny drums with their small fists, producing an unpleasant cadence that lingered on in his ears long after they had packed their drums in cases and left the apartment. Kengee felt stiff from sitting for so long and from pretending to enjoy the best of Ta culture. He suspected that the entertainments were at least part of Macha's revenge for the slap earlier in the day.

"Poor warrior, you've been defeated in your first encounter with culture." Macha's voice had taken on a deliberate huskiness. "In the north you lived a much simpler life, I know. Come rest in the hammock." He obediently climbed in and she began to rock him gently. She then began to massage his neck with the tips of her fingers. Occasionally, her sharp nails dug deep with a promise of violent passion.

"You are so strong," she whispered. Her hands began to slip inside his robe and work their way down. Her own robe had fallen partly open revealing all of her very small and very peaked breasts. They all had tiny tits on Ta, he thought, but reached for them eagerly. There was no coy retreat. Macha gracefully swung into the hammock. He violently forced her beneath him but he had been too violent. The hammock flipped them both to the floor. Macha was choking with laughter.

"It takes practice, Kengee." She laughed again.

Tano's body was conditioned only to pillow house floors or tabo dikes. Lovemaking in hammocks was a refined sexual exercise practiced and perfected by married couples from the upper classes of swordholders and by ladies and their swordholder lovers. Lovemaking in a hammock required a great deal of balance and restraint on the part of both participants, and Kengee doubted whether Tano's clumsy body would ever be able to adapt to this Ta custom. Down below, he heard the slapping of dozens of slippers on the polished wood floor and commands voiced in whispers.

"My father has returned early," she said, pulling the robe around her and brushing back her hair.

He then was sure that she had known exactly what time Denzo intended to return. The mishap in the hammock had been fortunate. His clumsiness had gotten him out of a trap. If he had been caught in the hammock with his new sister, he would have been condemned for incest and given the choice of sitting on his sword or allowing himself to be trussed with cords, shoved into a sack, and dropped into the nearest canal. It was only the man who was punished, and once the debt was paid, the girl's honor was fully restored. But in fairness, only women were punished for adultery. For this crime, they were driven naked into the desert and forgotten. Adultery and incest were crimes only the swordholder class could commit. No one worried about the morals of the farmers and factory workers, except themselves.

Denzo entered the room. His face already was flushed with the first wine of the evening. He unbuckled his sword and let it fall with a clang to the floor and then sat down on a stool across from his son and daughter. A male servant served two bowls of wine to the men only. The women of Ta did their drinking secretly and among themselves. Denzo lapped up the liquor like an Earth dog and wiped his beardless face with the back of his hand. Kengee was amused when he saw that Macha was embarrassed by her father's rough manners and deliberately mimicked him. He made even more noise slurping the wine and ostentatiously wiped the back of his hand across his lips several times. This pleased Denzo but Macha glared menacingly at him.

"The ways of true warriors offend my daughter."

"I see that you chose a son in your own image."

"If you do not sweeten your tongue, I will choose a husband for you in my own image, too. Macha has been alone too long. She needs a swing in a hammock with a partner of skill. But enough. Macha leave the room. Kengee and I have matters to discuss of importance." She left, pink in the face and refusing to look at Kengee. Denzo caught Kengee's eyes following the girl and he peered into his face with a flicker of drunken understanding.

"Macha is much like her mother when she was young," Denzo said. "I paid a high price for my wife. I got a woman with more hammock experience than I had expected and a woman with a bad temper and a woman with too much intelligence. We coupled until we produced Macha and then my interest in my wife evaporated. She has been nursing her hatred of me for ten years behind closed doors. For me, it is a very satisfactory arrangement. But this is family talk and we have something more important to converse about." Two more bowls of wine were set before them.

"Events are chasing us faster than we wish to run. Lornz again has reduced the Takusa milk supply. Not by much, but by enough so that I and others must cut back on production in the factories. We've again tried to start negotiations with the barbarians. We offered them better barter prices. But they say nothing and give us nothing." He was silent for a moment.

"They treat us with sullen contempt, and this we cannot tolerate from base men," Denzo suddenly shouted.

"What have Mako and the Committee of Five decided?"

"I like the directness of a soldier's mind. Mako remains cautious, too cautious. He is of the opinion that the barbarians will cut off all our supplies if we irritate them only and not punish them severely. The Committee of Five feel the opposite. We believe the barbarians must be shown that the swordholders who drove them into the swamps can still defeat them. They must be taught to fear us again. At the meeting today, we compromised. Mako agreed to a limited experiment in terror, providing the action taken against the barbarians seems accidental, resulting from the inflamed passions of a single commander."

"I am to perform this experiment in terror?" He knew the answer before it was given. But Kengee was puzzled why Mako should have gone to the trouble to import a hero and then advise caution to the Committee of Five. Was Mako vacillating or was he being clever?

"We want you to accompany a trading mission to the south and provoke an incident. You have a reputation for being hotheaded and a fool, although you seem to be neither. The barbarians have spies in the capital and already they know of you and your reputation and may accept what you do as the act of an individual.

"You will select twenty swordholders from the escort service. This will be enough to start trouble but not too much trouble. Your old friend Cagu will help you choose these men. You will leave in the morning to prepare for your great adventure."

Denzo thumped the heel of his boot on the floor and more bowls of wine were rushed to their tiny tables. This time Denzo downed the bowl before the servant left and he was ordered to bring another.

"I would like to go with you, Kengee. There were great swordholders in my family in the past. I would like to go with you and hack those stinking barbarians to pieces." Tears splattered on his robe and he staggered to his feet with his sword clutched in his hands. The sword sang in the air as Denzo slashed at the stinking phantom barbarians in his drunken imagination. Kengee once was forced to dive to the floor to escape the singing blade. But soon Denzo began to pant and then he sank to the floor next to Kengee. Kengee offered him a bowl of wine and he lapped it up greedily. He burst into tears again.

"I would like to go with you, Kengee," he kept muttering until his head dropped and he fell into a drunken sleep with the hilt of his sword in his hands. Kengee gently removed the weapon, sheathed it, and then went to his own apartment.

FOUR

Generations of boots had pounded the surface of the drill ground into a fine powder which was lifted into the air by a gentle wind and shrouded the exercising recruits in an eerie mist. The dull sounds of Takusite practice swords slapping against each other brought back pleasant memories to the Tano in Kengee's mind. The escort service recruits screamed threats and grunted with each swing of their swords. Kengee's sword arm began to tingle again but then other memories took over. He searched in vain for the EM club with its end-of-the-day smell of beer and soldiers in green combat uniforms, spotted black under the arms with sweat.

Kengee was brought back to the present when a drill leader struck a gong. The mock duels ceased abruptly, and the recruits lowered their swords and then fell into a rough formation. Cagu bellowed an order and the recruits raced toward the barracks. Cagu then came toward Kengee, stopping a few paces away. He rocked on his feet, eyeing the crest of Denzo's family on Kengee's blue robe and then covered his eyes in salute while smiling broadly.

"By the prongs of my sword, the Director of Ta has shown good sense at last. These are not days to waste a good swordsman over the killing of worthless factory owners."

"It's good to be a free man on the old drill ground again," Kengee replied, handing Cagu a scroll with Mako's crest on it.

Cagu stared at the scroll in his big hand for a few moments and then bit through the seal with his teeth. He mouthed the words as he read and then reread the orders again.

"About time," he snorted. "And now we must try to find men who can do the job from these pillow house warriors. It won't be easy. Escort recruits are not what they used to be. Mako should have ordered me and some of the veterans to go with you. You and I, Tano, could hack a hundred of them to pieces in an afternoon. Sorry, your name is now Kengee, but you don't change a man by changing his name. I promise I'll select the very best men, but don't expect too much. It will be you and your sword who will have to do most of the fighting."

They spent the rest of the day carefully observing the recruits. Kengee took Cagu's advice on what men would form his company without question, since he doubted his own judgment in picking a good soldier. He suspected that instinctively he would choose those who would shirk their duty and try to profit from whatever war they started—men like himself. Upon Cagu's urging, he fought mock duels with several of the selected recruits. Cagu commented that he was technically still excellent but, "Where's the old killer in you?" Kengee avoided Cagu's questioning eyes.

Late in the afternoon, Kengee lined up the twenty recruits and briefed them on their mission. When he told them that their swords might soon be cutting into real flesh, they all looked frightened. He could offer them nothing but blood, and he knew they did not want that. There was really little he could say to them. They had no choice but to come with him. They were all from the families of poor swordholders with no future except in the escort service. He decided to say no more because there was no possible way to motivate these soldiers. He looked at them a moment with what he hoped were hard, confident eyes, and then turned on his heel and walked off the drill ground. Cagu promised to whip them into shape over the next few days and deliver them under guard to the capital to prevent any last minute desertions.

Kengee was depressed. He was depressed all the way back to the capital and depressed as he lay in his hammock with his eyes tightly closed and his fists between his knees. He was supposed to win a victory with the most reluctant soldiers he had ever seen and with, he admitted honestly, the most reluctant commander. He resented having to do something stupid and dangerous and made up his mind then to try his utmost to avoid bloody combat, although no one must ever guess that he feared battle.

Upon his arrival home, he had intentionally rushed to his apartment and locked his door. He did not want to talk to Macha, and he left the next morning early with Gijo before she was up. Gijo guided him to the wide, main commercial canal where the godowns of the richest trading families were located. They entered the godown of Gosho, son of the trader Ojo who now was semiretired from the business.

Mako had ordered him to accompany Gosho on a trading expedition to the south in search of Takusa milk. Mako believed the expedition was doomed to failure from the start and therefore felt little would be lost if Kengee and his warriors caused trouble with the barbarians on one of the southern islands.

Kengee and Gijo weaved their way between huge crates and bales on the godown floor and then climbed the narrow stairs to Gosho's offices. Inside men and women employees sat at a long table with their heads hidden behind piles of brown, aging scrolls stacked everywhere in great disorder. No one looked up. Occasionally Kengee heard a seal thump on paper above the continuous light, muffled tapping of the scribes' pens. Gosho sat alone on a stool in front of an empty table by a dusty window. He was staring dreamily down on the canal below and pretending not to notice them. Gosho was fashionably dressed in a yellow robe with the black crest of his family on each sleeve—a severed foot dripping blood. Gosho wore his sword even in the office. His boots glistened from a recent, vigorous polish.

71

An old man at the head of the worktable finally peered at the visitors over the piles of scrolls and then rose slowly. He crept toward Gosho who swiveled his head when he heard the old man's slippers scratching along the floor. He ignored the man and lazily inspected the visitors and then slowly stood up to greet Kengee. Gijo slipped out of the office and was gone.

"You must be Kengee, commander of the escort service recruits who are to protect me on my journey." The tone of his voice was not sarcastic. It was plain nasty, but Kengee forced a smile.

"You must understand that I resent your presence on this journey. I do not need protection and I certainly do not need twenty-one swordsmen. Your warriors will make the barbarians suspicious and even more reluctant to trade. And I fear there will be trouble and no trader wants trouble. But I have my orders from the Director of Ta to take you and your men with me into lower Ta. I am afraid now there will be little profit in this venture. But I have my orders and I suppose you have your orders, too. We will not make the happiest of traveling companions."

"I have my orders, of course."

"You also have a reputation for violence. It is very strange that Mako should have given you command of the escort guards on this trading mission. We long ago gave up fighting the barbarians for a very good reason. You know nothing about them, but I warn you that they will not fall on their knees so that you and your men can easily behead them."

"I don't expect them to."

"Then what do you expect them to do?"

"I expect them not to die foolishly."

"And you?"

"I'm not a fool either." Gosho laughed. "We may after all become good companions."

Kengee looked down on the long line of barges in the canal as Gosho rattled off the contents of the bales and boxes being loaded aboard the fleet of stubby barges and squat steamboats. They were taking with them for trade to lower Ta waterproof boots, bright colored clothing, insect nets, pots and pans, and small family-size steam-boats. All the products were made of Takusite.

"The barbarians used to come racing to the beaches when our trading fleet arrived," Gosho said. "They would point to the vats we had provided and these always were full to the brim with Takusa milk. The trading then was easy, but now we must go from island to island, bartering for small quantities of Takusa milk if there is any at all. They no longer seem interested in our manu-factured products, and this is puzzling because they have found no substitutes. They seem content to live with less and less, and this is very unnatural for human be-ings. They do not go hungry in the swamps but why should even barbarians desire less of what makes life more enjoyable and easier when all they have to do is milk the Takusa plant? It is a mystery."

"Isn't Lornz to blame?"

"We really know nothing about Lornz. Maybe the supply of Takusa milk is being reduced on his orders and maybe he has nothing to do with it. All we know is that the barbarians either will not or cannot explain why Takusa milk is withheld."

"They must know why."

"You do not understand these people. And if you or Mako think you can force them to give us more Takusa milk with swords, you will be making a mistake, a mis-take you will not be permitted to make twice."

"Mako is concerned only about the dwindling trade."

"He should be, but he is no more worried than I and my father and every trader and factory owner. Our wealth is based on Takusa milk. Without it, we are noth-ing and Ta is nothing. I would support any reasonable plan to convince them to supply us with more Takusa milk, but losing another war, even a small one, is not a reasonable plan."

"Do you really expect me to wage a war in lower Ta with twenty inexperienced recruits?"

"No. But I believe you and Mako have some mischief in mind."

"I'm only going along to learn about lower Ta and the barbarians."

"Reconnoitering in force."

"Something like that."

"I will stop trying to wheedle your secret from you, but remember, I know you have one. Will your men be ready in three days? I would not like to delay my departure. If we go south too late, we will miss the good weather in lower Ta. In the good weather, you are only slowly boiled in the heavy mists, but in the bad weather, your brains are roasted as fast as a tabo ball cake on a needle."

They went to the dock and inspected the loading of the barges and then toured the godown as Gosho discussed the trading business and the expedition. Kengee was warned to be prepared for anything in lower Ta, most of it bad and frightening. Gosho told him that at a minimum they would lose 10 percent of the boatmen and junior traders from the fevers and other dangers, known and unknown. As a general practice, traders kept to the fringe of lower Ta, stopping only at islands which had been trading posts for years. They did not venture deep into the terrifying mists.

The barbarians spoke of terrible perils in the deep south, but Gosho did not know if they created these frights to keep the men of Ta from traveling too far into their homeland or if the horrors described really existed. There were supposed to be monsters capable of demolishing boats and barges by bombarding them with iron-hard mucus balls spat out of their mouths with great velocity. Other monsters with the taste of gourmets plucked with their claws the plumpest and youngest boatmen off the decks and swallowed them with grunts of deep satisfaction before submerging into the swamps. There were monsters with breaths so foul and poisonous that they only had to exhale to asphyxiate an entire fleet, leaving the men choking, gasping, and dying. And there were humanlike creatures with flat heads who paddled from island to island on rafts made of swamp weeds and who, when angered, threw swamp shells or any other available object, including their own babies, at intruders.

"Do you believe these tales?" Kengee asked nervously.

"The flatheads exist," Gosho said. "I've seen them. But

I don't believe in the other monsters because I have not seen them yet." He laughed.

The torches were being lit in their wall sockets when Kengee and Gosho left the office. The scribes, straining their eyes in the flickering light, continued to write furiously, paying no attention to their departure.

"When do they stop work?"

"After our chief scribe leaves, and he never leaves until long after I have left. And even after he departs, some work on late into the night. They become too tired to accomplish much but it is their way of showing loyalty to me and the firm. Over the years, a few have died from exhaustion and were discovered the next morning with their hands rigidly gripping their pens. Once no one noticed that an old scribe had died. He sat hunched over the table for two days in the winter cold, appearing to be deep in thought on some accounting problem. My father and I seldom return late at night to see them at work, but once or twice a year we do and the late workers feel rewarded. I personally don't even know half their names, but my father somehow manages to remember them. But only the chief scribe comes from a family of swordholders, and the rest really don't count."

"Why is so much writing necessary?"

"They must keep the records of the firm. Our family's company is more than two hundred years old, and we have stored in a godown up the canal thousands of scrolls, rolled up and tightly bound with ribbons. Every transaction the company ever has carried out in its long history is preserved, every decision is recorded. It is all very important. Occasionally we need to restudy a business transaction of the past, and then three scribes and six girl assistants are sent to the godown. It usually takes them a week to locate the desired scroll and then restack the disturbed scrolls in proper chronological order. Records must be kept. Every enterprise must have a recorded history or it is nothing. Without records, our company would have no more substance than a boot mender's business."

Gosho pointed his two fingers in the Ta way toward a boot mender squatted at the edge of a narrow lane with

75

his tools laid out neatly before him. The boot mender's eyes never rose above boot level. He surveyed their soles and heels, thoughtfully pronouncing them in sound health to himself. But he shouted after Gosho: "Come back in a month or that right boot will be a dead loss."

They wheeled left at the next narrow road so abruptly that their swords slapped hard against their legs. The flames of street torches wavered in the night wind and the lanterns before the restaurants, wine shops, and pillow houses swayed back and forth, creating the impression that the entire street was on fire. At intervals the main road was bisected by narrow lanes barely the width of a man's shoulders. Young street children lounged in these square doors of darkness, studying the passersby. The children were formed into bands of thieves and preyed on lone drunks. A swordholder had the right—in fact the duty—to lop off their stealing hands if they were caught practicing their trade. But there were few so maimed—a proof of their agility and skill. It was too early to start stealing. The children were only marking likely victims for later, and it was apparent to them that Gosho and Kengee were too dangerous to rob.

One child, a girl of about twelve, watched the two swordholders intently and then shot past them, vanishing around a curve in the road. A few minutes later, they halted in front of a pillow house with two green lanterns molded into the shape of female buttocks hanging heavily outside. "My favorite pillow house," announced Gosho and shoved Kengee toward the door which immediately slid open.

"A change in management," Gosho said looking at the attractive middle-aged woman who greeted them.

"Not so Gosho," she said. "The proprietress is away visiting her sister. I occupy her place only temporarily, but I offer you everything she would offer you."

Gosho lifted her high off the ground and let her slip slowly back to the ground again. Her robe bunched in his arms and her body was exposed from the waist down. Kengee thought it was a very youthful body with trim, muscular legs.

"There are young girls inside eager to play with you

and your friend," the woman gasped. Gosho released his grip and laughed.

"My friend is Kengee, a skilled warrior."

"Welcome, Kengee, but our girls do the swordholding here." She chuckled at this very old joke. Ta humor had never impressed Kengee but he forced a laugh. Gosho exploded with laughter and then three girls came out the door laughing. They pulled both of them into the pillow house, over the slippery polished Takusite floor, and into the pillow room. There were no other guests in the establishment, they were informed.

"Business is on the decline everywhere," Gosho said to the proprietress who brought in the first bowls of tabo wine.

"True. Last night no one came at all."

Five young girls crowded around them, pouring more wine and pressing their bodies against Gosho and Kengee. With delight, Kengee hugged one in each arm. He had been deprived of women so far on Ta and was anxious to experience lovemaking Ta style. There was a hard rapping at the front door and the proprietress rushed out of the room. They heard rough male voices raised first in protest and then in anger.

"If business is so bad, why does she turn away customers?" Gosho asked.

"Those are poor swordholders who never pay their bills," the girl whom Kengee was now grappling with said. "We like only rich swordholders." Gosho laughed loudly and more wine was gulped down. Gosho offered a girl his bowl of wine. She sipped too little to please the trader. He jerked her head back by pulling her long black hair, pried open her mouth with his fingers, and demanded that Kengee pour wine down her throat. Kengee did not like doing it but after all Gosho was paying the bill. The girl choked and laughed and choked some more as the wine went down.

Gosho finally let go of the girl and threw himself back on the floor and began trying to juggle pillows in the air with his feet. The girls cheered and then began hurling pillows at Gosho, but he ignored the challenge to Kengee's relief. He was in no mood for a pillow fight.

Gosho with indecent impatience reached out and began jerking off the robe of the pillow house girl nearest him. She giggled, but it was a practiced giggle and Kengee noticed that she was coolly studying her playful rapist. One of the other girls was dancing in front of Kengee. Her robe fell open and she began making love to her body in time to the tune she was humming.

As Kengee reached out with groping hands, she launched her attack. Her robe dropped to the floor and she shoved him backward and then fell on top of him. She squirmed over his body. Her fingernails clawed at his now bare chest. She was strong and he had to use his knee as a fulcrum to roll her over. Vaguely Kengee was aware that the unoccupied girls were quickly slipping out of the room and also that Gosho and his pillow house partner were breathing hard and bumping across the floor from pillow to pillow. Kengee's girl began to kiss him roughly with mock passion and he responded with more honest lust.

"Fool!"

The word was shouted inside his head and then he felt Tanee taking over. She commanded and his body obeyed. He rolled over holding the girl in a tight grip, and as he did so, Tanee jerked his head back a little too sharply. He was looking straight up at the ceiling where a panel had been removed. He saw a heavy dart fly from a hand out of the darkness above. It thudded into the back of the girl who gasped but no scream came before the quick-acting poison sent her into the final gyrations of death.

Kengee's voice shouted a warning to Gosho and then he flung the girl's body aside and reached for his sword. As he did so, the three pillow house girls who had earlier left the room rushed through the door with daggers held low. Their Takusite tips dripped an oily black fluid. Kengee met their attack on one knee with his sword cutting an arc in the air. One girl skillfully leaped clear, but the blade severed the head of another. Kengee felt sick, but Tanee slapped him from within his mind and he pulled himself together quickly.

"Poisoned daggers," screamed Gosho who was now

78

battling for his life with the girl he had only seconds before been making love to.

The girl who had dodged Kengee's blade slashed at him with her dagger. The point of the blade caught in his sleeve. He slapped her wrist with his free hand and the dagger fell to the floor. He then thrust out his foot, catching the girl on her delicate jaw, and she slammed against the wall and slid to the floor unconscious. Another badly aimed dart quivered in the floor next to his foot. Kengee seized it and with an underhand pitch sent it flying back into the dark opening of the ceiling. A second later, the proprietress tumbled out and fell hard on the pillows, dead almost before she reached the floor. The other girl, who had been circling Kengee waiting for an opening, dashed out the door and escaped.

Gosho struggled to his feet. He had turned the dagger against the girl. There was a slash along the side of her throat and she also was dead. Gosho went to the girl whom Kengee had kicked and bound her arms and legs with two robe sashes.

"I'll question her later," he said.

Kengee did not hear him. He heard only the voice shout "fool" inside his head, and then Tanee was gone. Kengee shuddered as Gosho walked around the room nudging the bodies with his bare toes and muttering to himself. If Tanee had not possessed him a few minutes ago, he would have been dead. She was gone now, but she had left her feelings of disgust and contempt behind as punishment. He needed none. The killing his arms had done horrified him.

"Let's find out who your enemies are," Gosho said moving toward the bound girl whose alert eyes stared back at him with hatred.

"Who sent you?" Gosho demanded, pressing the points of his sword against the girl's throat. She hissed her defiance and then hurled herself against the sharp prongs. She fell sideways with her throat slashed and a grin on her face. Kengee looked away.

"I have heard that they always do that," Gosho said. "Kill themselves if captured. I should have been more cautious." He wiped the blade of his sword on a yellow pillow while shaking his head in regret.

"Who were they?"

"This one and the rest are all flowers of the Zabo." He turned one of the bodies over with his foot and studied the blackened face.

"Some poison," Gosho muttered.

"Flowers of the Zabo?" Kengee repeated in a quiet voice.

"What else but the Zabo could produce such women. The Zabo is an ancient society of assassins and spies. It is a secret society and few even know of its existence. They say they start training them as children in the arts of murder and espionage. The Zabo is for hire and someone hired them to kill you, and me too, but only because I was with you. You were their target. The darts were aimed at you and the three poisoned daggers went against you. But there is no one left to tell us who sent them."

"Does the Zabo always use women?"

"Only if it suits their plans. Women are the flowers and men the singing birds. The male assassins, they say, whistle a tune at the moment of killing. The girls only breathe hard. No one knows where they stay or how they are recruited or who rules the Zabo. There are secret ways to contact the Zabo. My father knows how. Every trader does. There are times in business when spies or assassins are needed."

With their swords in their hands, they searched the house. They found the real proprietress and two of her girls bound and fluttering their eyes as they slowly awoke from a durgged sleep. Gosho untied them and began patting the older woman's face gently.

"They don't kill unless they're paid to. Innocent by-standers are usually spared. But these won't talk when they become fully awake. They'll be too frightened to talk." The woman's eyes came into focus and she looked surprised to see him.

"Your pillow room is very untidy, old woman," he said grinning.

When they went down the stairs and looked again

into the pillow room, they both gasped. The bodies were gone. Only the blood-smeared pillows remained.

"We should have waited," Gosho said. "But then they were watching us and knew when to come to remove the Zabo dead."

"Let's leave," Kengee said. He was happy the bodies were gone but he still was frightened and his stomach still was shaky. These were the first people he had ever killed. He knew it had been necessary to kill them and he knew also that Tanee really had done the killing with his strength and sword. But nevertheless the blood of these women now stained his robe.

"We'll leave the back way and cautiously with our swords in our hands," Gosho said. "They're still out there somewhere." They went out and walked together along the strangely deserted road.

"For all we know, this attack was only a diversion for the real attack. The Zabo works in strange ways. And Zabo assassins seldom fail. There really was no good reason why they did fail. How did you happen to see the dart in time?"

"The girl was looking at the ceiling in a strange way and I got suspicious," Kengee lied. "So I flipped her over and wham, the dart hit her instead of me. After that, I let my sword do the work."

"You just might survive in the south after all, Kengee." Gosho was looking at him oddly in the light from a street torch. There were no further encounters with the Zabo that night. Once Kengee reached Denzo's house, he went directly to his apartment and tossed his bloody robe to Gijo who examined the stains with delight.

"You've given the great sword a snack," Gijo chuckled.

"A poor meal, Gijo. A very poor meal." And then Kengee began to feel sick again.

When Gijo left the apartment with his robe, Kengee bolted the door, locked the windows, and climbed into his hammock. He rocked himself back and forth with his trembling hands between his knees until he felt calm enough to think.

Who was trying to kill him? Why would anyone have a reason to kill him since he had been on Ta for only a short time and had done nothing but accept command of twenty warriors for a mission that very likely would fail. Tanee must know. She had rescued him. He would have liked to talk to her again, but Mako and Hoso would never permit any further relations with the possessor. He wondered if Hoso was behind the assassination plot. But this did not make sense. Hoso hated him enough to have him killed, but he had his own agents to do such work and would not need help from the Zabo. And Hoso was a clever, cautious man who had the patience to wait for him to blunder badly first before destroying him.

There seemed to be no one to turn to for advice or information. Denzo would be useless. He had long ago concluded that Denzo was the most unaware man in all of Ta. In this, only Tanee seemed to be his friend and ally and he felt warm gratitude toward her for a moment. "But the fucking desert witch got me into this by stealing my mind and she got me into this for her own goddamned reasons." He felt Tanee would protect him only as long as he served her purpose; whatever that purpose was. He slept badly, jerking awake at every sound the house made as it shifted with the night wind and groaned in response to its own internal stresses.

Macha burst into his room the next morning right behind the serving child. Her black hair was brushed to a shimmering brilliance and her eyes were glowing with excitement. She would have been beautiful if her mouth was not locked in an unpleasant smile. She perched on a stool across from Kengee with her tiny hands clasped in her lap.

"You are the only man I know who believes pillow houses are for war-making."

"Who told you?"

"A pillow house girl told a torchlighter and he told a vegetable merchant and he told a house servant and that house servant told another house servant. The news of your exploit was here with the first rays of the sun and the gardener. But I should congratulate you on your escape. Just how did you manage that? The Zabo does not fail often."

82

"It did this time," he mumbled deliberately cramming a spoonful of sticky tabo into his mouth.

"Aren't you going to tell me about your heroic battle —your victory with your sword over four women has brought new glory to our family."

"They were assassins, and anyway Gosho helped."

"Gosho! That little trader. No, brother, the victory belongs to you."

"I do not intend to boast of such killings."

"But why not? Those women were more skilled in the arts of killing than anyone you are likely to encounter, unless of course you looked into a mirror."

"You hate me, don't you?"

"Oh not any more. Someone apparently hates you much more than I did. I have retired as a hater of the great Kengee. I'll let your other enemy have all the hate without competition from me."

"So now you love me."

She laughed. "Do you want to try it in the hammock again?" she whispered maliciously. "I feel it my sisterly duty to educate you out of your crude northern ways. But if that's too much, I'll have some pillows brought in."

"I must be off early, dear sister. But I thank you for your new tender interest in me."

"Caution in the morning and none at night. A very typical man."

"I've never claimed to be anything else."

"Some believe you to be a very extraordinary man. And you did defeat the Zabo. Please tell me how you did that."

"I saw the danger and reacted quickly. That's all."

"You saw the danger and reacted quickly." She mocked his words. "You're such a modest hero and such a reticent one."

"It really was nothing at all."

"I suspect you had more help than Gosho could provide."

Kengee shrugged but did not respond. He was suspicious of her probing. If she thought he was incapable of escaping a Zabo trap on his own, she was right. But he would never admit that to her or anyone else. He would never tell anyone that Tanee had saved him. He could not tell if he wanted to. Tanee had left a censor behind that gave him a sharp pain between the eyes every time he even thought about mentioning her name aloud.

Macha sat there touching her hair with the tips of her fingers and smiling that unpleasant smile. He ate hurriedly but well. He had learned that Tano's huge body required vast quantities of food. After a while, Macha's hands dropped to her lap again. That smile was still fixed, maybe for the whole damned day.

"I must go."

"It would seem that imprisonment changed you," she said. "I've talked with people who knew you before and they describe you as a blundering, stupid fool, skilled only with the sword. And now you cleverly kill Zabo assassins and then sit here and cleverly duel with words. An amazing transformation, don't you think?"

"No one really ever understood me. Inside every fool, there is a wise man struggling to get out. The Director of Ta was kind enough to pay compensation to the victims of my sword. His kindness touched me so deeply that I changed. I wish now only to serve him and Ta with the few skills which I possess."

"You also have become a great liar, and that is the only compliment you get from me this morning."

"We are truly brother and sister at last."

Her smile widened and she left the room slowly, her body moving in deliberate rhythms beneath her robe. Kengee watched her departure with interest. He almost called her back but "fool" echoed faintly in his head. Macha was a dangerous bitch, he knew, but a well built one.

He had an appointment with Mako. He strapped on his sword, called Gijo, and together they headed toward the heart of the capital. It was midmorning and most of the men walking leisurely on the roads and in the lanes wore swords. Swordholders rose late and walked slowly. Even if they had someplace to go, they wished to appear as if they did not. Only servants and the poor got

84

up early and rushed through the streets to known destinations.

A swordholder brushed by him and Kengee tensed. He realized how vulnerable he was in the streets. Anyone could have a poisoned dagger concealed in his or her robe. He abandoned the dignified slow shuffle of his class and began to hurry.

The street children were beginning to creep out of the narrow alleys, rubbing their sleepy eyes. They yawned and winked at the poor swordholders who hired themselves out as guards. These men stood with bored faces in front of shops and commercial houses with their right hands resting menacingly on the hilts of their swords. A thief who came in range of their sword arms would be hacked to pieces on the spot with no mercy shown for age or sex. They did not prevent crime but they did make criminals wary. Kengee was happy that he was not a burglar on Ta.

At the Director's offices, he gave his name to a swordholder at the door. It was an old building. The windows had not been washed in years and the peaked roof was stained orange from the droppings of generations of Ta birds. He was led up steps that were littered with wadded up scrolls tossed out of the offices for the sweepers to dispose of. But the sweepers were aged men and women, and by the time they were able to work their way down to the bottom of the stairs dragging their sacks behind them, the stairs were littered again. On the third floor, the swordholder tapped on a door and then entered without waiting for permission.

A young woman bounced up from her stool at a table where scrolls made of the highest grade Takusite and ribbons were scattered in disorder. She hurriedly covered her eyes before Kengee and then scuttled across the grimy floor and knocked on another door. A grunt came from deep within the room and Kengee was motioned in.

Mako sat before a completely bare table, thinking. He stared with fogged eyes at a blank wall, ignoring his visitor for several minutes. Finally the fog lifted and he pointed to a stool across from him. The girl reappeared with a tray containing two cups of desert tea, the least expensive grade sold in Ta. They sipped it without interest or comment.

"Your great adventure is about to begin," Mako said cheerfully.

"We leave in two days."

"And how do you find Gosho? I find him far too clever. Do you think he will cause trouble? He will not overtly, but he will try to obstruct your mission. Has he told you that he fears your presence will be bad for business? I know he thinks that. Is he aware that you, as a representative of the Director of Ta, have the authority to take command of the convoy? I am sure he is, but we shall make doubly sure he realizes his subordinate position." Mako straightened up, seeming to grow larger before Kengee. He glowered at a point in space above Kengee's head and then his face slowly softened and finally a smile appeared.

"Gosho believes that force will fail in lower Ta," Kengee said.

"Gosho knows nothing. He is a trader and not an administrator. We have considered everything very carefully and therefore there can be no failure. The violence you commit must appear to result from your own emotional instability; that will relieve us of responsibility. But it will be an example of what swordholders can still do and also a test of their response to attack. We will send apologies for your bad behavior and reprimand you publicly on your return. We will even pay compensation to the tribes of your victims. By our scale, the life of a barbarian is worth very little anyway. But above all else, you must demonstrate to the barbarians that we are still capable of waging warfare and winning." Mako broke off abruptly and began to caress his chins with his thumb.

"How are your swordsmen?"

"They'll do."

"No doubt our present generation of swordholders do not compare well with the warriors you are used to commanding. But remember we are a race of great soldiers. In the One Thousand Year War, our ancestors were heroes. The good blood is still there. Stimulate it. Excite it. Inspire it. You shall see what the men of Ta are really like."

"And they shall see what a real soldier is like," Kengee said a little too loudly.

"Yanzoo!" Mako shouted the great Ta war yell and Kengee yelled it back even louder, and then they were both on their feet waving their swords and shouting together: "Yanzoo, Yanzoo, Yanzoo." When their voices fell silent, Mako sat down.

"I will depend on your military genius and your personal bravery. You will choose the time and the place and the method of attack. To silence Gosho, if need be, I will provide you with written orders giving you command over the entire trading expedition. But use these orders only if you must. There is no point in making an enemy of a rich trading family without cause. And reveal nothing to Gosho. Traders don't like to suffer losses and financially this expedition is likely to be a total loss. We will sacrifice it for greater gains in the future."

The instant he stopped speaking, the girl again entered the room at a trot, covering her eyes three times as she progressed rapidly across the floor. She unrolled a scroll and held it between her hands as Mako quickly sketched his family crest on the document. She rolled it up, tied it with a ribbon, and handed it to Kengee. Mako began biting his knuckles, a nervous habit that sometimes drew blood.

"I want you to know, Kengee, that we had nothing to do with the attack by the Zabo against you last night." His voice was a little shaky. "I can assure you that neither I nor any member of the Committee of Five was involved in any way."

"I never for an instant thought you were," Kengee said.

"Well, we thought you might have thought it was some kind of a test of your skills or something like that."

"If it was a test, I almost failed."

"But you did not. Congratulations. Our confidence in you is greater than ever. You have convinced even our

87

greatest skeptic on the Committee of Five that you are the only man who can save Ta."

"Director Mako, do you know who might have hired the Zabo?"

"Your enemies, of course."

"But I have no enemies. I have not been in Ta long enough to have enemies."

"Ta must be a very different world from the one you came from. You cannot breathe in Ta without creating enemies. After all, whatever is given to you is taken from someone else. Your success means someone else's failure. Your profit someone else's loss. Even when you were only an idea of mine on Ta, you already had enemies. And now that you are here and acting—and acting well—your enemies are multiplying. Let's hope that after your mission is completed, your enemies will be too numerous to count. Let's hope that you are so successful someday that every swordholder on Ta will be your envious enemy."

"It's something to work for," Kengee said.

"Indeed it is. It would mean you had achieved all that we expect from you and that you then will be a hero on Ta as you were on . . . sorry, I always forget the name of the world you came from."

"It doesn't matter anymore."

"Very true. You are now a swordholder of Ta and that is the greatest honor that can be bestowed on anyone, anywhere in the universe. But I am talking too much and a man of action like yourself must detest talk." Mako laughed but without warmth. He rose, brushing back his gray hair. He was shorter than Kengee and at that moment his eyes were boring into Kengee's throat.

"Well goodbye, good killing, and may your ancestors stay on your right hand."

It was the formal way to say farewell to a swordholder departing for battle. Ancestors on your right hand were supposed to aid your sword arm in combat. Kengee did not know what they would do if they bunched up on the left but assumed they then would be of no more use than sidewalk spectators at a fire—doing nothing and getting in the way. Anyway Kengee had a hunch there were no great warriors on any branch of his family tree. He suspected that all his ancestors had either dodged all the conscriptions in history, or, if this had failed, had somehow managed to get assigned to all the various quartermasters' corps in history. He was not going to count on them and therefore did not care where they stood.

The wadded-up, twisted scrolls on the stairway had risen to ankle depth during his talk with Mako. The Director's office staff was warming up for the day. A shower of scrolls hit him on the head as he went down the stairs, and an office scribe shouted an apology before turning and rushing back to his work. The ancient gatherers of mistakes were inching slowly down the stairs shoving the scrolls into their bags. He brushed by them and strode out into the street where Gijo was patiently waiting.

It was lunch hour, and men and women were pouring out of the godowns and offices. They rushed for the scarce tables in eating shops, and Kengee and Gijo stepped back to avoid the running, hungry scribes. Despite the noisy crowds, Kengee felt very much alone.

FIVE

The steamboats with their engines throbbing and their paddle wheels slapping the water departed from the capital as the first shy light of dawn began to poke into the dark narrow streets—empty of people but littered with fruit skins and spat-out seeds and broken wine bowls and stained here and there by wine vomit. Gosho wished to avoid the morning traffic on the main canal leading south, and his convoy of steamboats trailing their barges was now cutting through the soft dampness of fog hovering over the dark water. Kengee lay on the stern deck staring up into the smoky whiteness and shivering. Despite the cold, he was reluctant to go below to his small, cramped cabin.

Before their departure, Kengee had lined up his twenty warriors on the dock and sent them aboard their barge one by one. He waited until seconds before the lines were cast off to leap aboard the lead steamboat to make sure there were no last minute desertions. His troops were silent, resentful and scared even before the great mission had really begun. Kengee did not blame them but he thought fear was impractical until danger was unmistakably present. With luck it was possible to side-step danger and with more luck to coax the danger onto someone else.

He had spent the last two days thinking about this voyage. He did not know much about where he was going or about the people there, but he did not think people who lived in swamps could have too much pride. He might possibly bribe them to throw a fight—to stage a battle and then run. This would make everyone happy, including Gosho who had become increasingly uneasy about Kengee after catching a glimpse of Mako's official scroll which had dropped accidently from his sleeve the night before. He had asked no questions then, and Kengee had looked quickly away.

Gosho was now coming toward him along the deck. He tripped over some misplaced cargo and growled at a deck hand. But when he reached Kengee, he was smiling broadly, relaxed and happy now that the expedition was underway.

"How are your intrepid warriors?"

"Scared."

"Good. Maybe they'll behave themselves. And how are you?"

"Cold and miserable."

"At least all your swordholders reported for duty. Two of my cooks suddenly became ill, and I had to take on two untried men only a day before departure. We may have bad food on this trip, although they claim they can cook anything that grows, flies, wiggles, or swims."

"When does the fog lift?"

"Here in an hour or so. Farther south, sometimes never. But as long as we can see both sides of the canal, we keep going."

"Three weeks on this canal," Kengee moaned.

"A little less. Earlier I was making calculations with the boatmaster. Big Sister Moon and Little Brother Moon will be with us most nights, so we won't have to tie up for more than an hour or so on the whole trip."

Kengee liked Ta's moons. They were two of the nicest things in this new world. When both moons were in the night sky at the same time, Ta was like a lit up football stadium. But at that moment, he was not thinking about Big Sister Moon or Little Brother Moon. He was dreaming about coffee. This he missed most. He smelled low-grade desert tea brewing somewhere below deck. When one of the new cooks brought tea to him later, he shook his head. The man looked disappointed. Gosho drank his straight down and then stretched his arms into the thinning fog.

The sun burned away the fog long before midmorning, and Kengee could then see the farm workers knee-deep in the tabo fields. It was the same dreary pastoral scene which he had seen on his trip to the capital from Tanee's desert cave, and he turned away from it with a yawn.

Tanee had not visited him in her disturbing way since the encounter with the women assassins in the pillow house. It angered him that she had the power to pop into his brain and take over, but he was beginning to miss her a little just then. He suspected that this occasional longing for her might very well have been implanted in his mind during her last quick visit. How could he possibly be truly fond of the desert witch?

He looked back at the barge where his twenty warriors were sprawled on the cargo crates chatting quietly among themselves. They no longer appeared frightened. They seemed sulky. Too many days on the barge would make them irritable and then there could be trouble. He hoped not, because he doubted if he could become an effective disciplinarian. He personally had never had much use for discipline. Gosho was up front with the boatmaster carefully observing the line of steamboats and barges behind them. Occasionally, he would frantically wave a flag, signaling one or another of the boatmasters to speed up or slow down. On these voyages, boats of a convoy were supposed to stay close together.

When the sun was almost overhead, Gosho rejoined him. Minutes later, one of the cooks arrived with food and tea which he placed between them on the deck. Kengee had just lifted the tea bowl when the boat shuddered and came to a near stop.

"That fool farmer got his boat in front of the convoy," Gosho said angrily. "We ought to ram and sink him."

Kengee hardly heard him. He was staring down at where his tea had spilled on the deck. The tea was eating into the Takusite planks at a furious rate, staining it an ugly black.

"Strong tea," Kengee said.

Gosho made no comment but rose quickly, signaling Kengee to remain seated. The two cooks already were racing toward the railing of the boat, but Gosho was too fast. His sword flamed beautifully in the bright noonday sun and one of the cooks screamed. The other cook dove over the side. Kengee watched the water for several minutes but the man did not surface.

"Drowned."

"Not likely. The Zabo have ways of staying underwater."

"The Zabo again?"

"Who else concocts such potent poisons? But we're rid of them now. One dead and the other playing at being a fish. We won't be bothered again on this trip. I'll order a fresh cup of tea."

Kengee shook his head and pitched the bowls of tea and food over the side.

"Someone does not wish you to go south," Gosho said.

"He and I agree. I don't want to go either. Maybe we could make a deal."

During the rest of the trip, Kengee got into the habit of spilling a little of his tea on the deck before drinking it and sniffing suspiciously at his food. Gosho smiled when he did this and explained each time that it was a pointless test since the Zabo knew dozens of poisons, each with a different odor and reaction time.

Sometimes, when Gosho was in a very good mood, he

would pantomime the death of a poisoned man. He would flop around on the deck, twitching and clutching his throat. These performances ended with howling laughter from Gosho and snickers from the junior traders and crew. Kengee was not amused.

Days later, as they grew nearer to lower Ta, farms were fewer and much of the acreage along the canal was left entirely uncultivated. Grass grew at flagpole heights, and occasionally Kengee caught sight of Ta stabbers—water animals with bony armor and claws like knives. They seemed always to give Kengee a wicked stare just before their eyes sank below the surface. They were unpleasant but very small—two feet in length at the most. He was told that these creatures were almost lovable compared to the animals deeper in the south.

The canal ended abruptly at what appeared to be a wide, steaming lake. They tied up for the night but the heat of the day stubbornly clung to the water. They slept beneath strong mesh netting to keep out insects as large as a man's finger which dove like a whistling bullet and tore small bits of flesh from exposed faces, arms, and hands. Gosho said these insects were too delicate to even survive farther south in lower Ta.

The convoy started off the next morning, picking its way carefully through a channel which cut deep through the floating weeds on either side. The boatmaster knew the channel but proceeded cautiously because its course changed frequently with time and the seasons. The steam engines startled birds nesting on the small islands. They screamed like a woman burning her fingers in the kitchen and rose into the air where they hovered menacingly over the boats and barges. Their coloring was pink, similar to the marsh vegetation which flourished on all the islands, and they were large. Kengee calculated they were a third the weight of a man. Gosho tossed the contents of his breakfast bowl into the water and the birds screamed even more shrilly as they dove to snap up the floating chunks of cooked tabo. He assured Kengee that these birds were only dangerous if you approached too closely to their nests.

The route which they were taking south was a well-known one, explored first more than two hundred years before and used regularly since that time by the traders of Ta. By midday the damp heat became almost unbearable, and Kengee rested languidly on the deck, watching the water and islands slide by in a shimmering blur. Several times he saw the largest of all of Ta's water snakes, with bodies that stretched the length of the longest barge. Gosho assured him that these too were harmless creatures and that you could swim alongside them without fear since they subsisted entirely on swamp vegetation. You could swim alongside them unmolested, he was told, providing they were not in the mood for a mate and could not find one. In this state of frustration, they sublimated by attacking anything in sight worthy of attacking. If sex was not available, their desires could only be satisfied by biting into flesh—the flesh of swamp animals or reptiles or men if they were about. One of these creatures rubbed its tubular body along the side of the boat to scratch its hide and set off a disturbing vibration throughout the vessel.

The swamps also had their clowns. The jumpers were comically strange with parasite weeds and small creatures attached in messy disorder to their large bodies. The jumpers leaped from the water and while in the air slapped their webbed hands together to applaud this feat. Their mouths were twisted into a perpetual grin. Kengee laughed at them. But Gosho warned him that these creatures were truly dangerous at all times. The crew hurriedly tossed food to them, which they caught with their webbed hands and pushed into their mouths as they dropped back into the water with a splash. Without this bribing, they might leap at the men on the deck and nip off an arm or a leg, howling with their strange laughter before vanishing into the water with the bloody stumps between their teeth. But soon the convoy left the habitat of the jumpers and water snakes and steered toward a large island.

When they were close to the island, the boatmen lowered the small boat powered by a miniature steam engine, and Gosho, Kengee, and three crewmen went aboard. They skimmed quickly over the shallow water to the muddy beach. Back from the shore was a cluster of huts made of Takusite with bowl-shaped roofs. They were all deserted.

"This is one of our main trading islands," Gosho explained. Once on the beach, he examined the mud and pointed to fresh footprints and marks left by swamp boats being pushed into the water. Gosho and Kengee walked to the recently vacated village and looked into the empty vats where Takusa milk was normally stored for trade.

"Maybe another trader got here first."

"No. The vats have not held Takusa milk for more than a year." Gosho rubbed his finger along the brown crust on the rim of a vat.

"It's happened before. When they have nothing to trade, they sometimes flee upon our arrival. I believe it embarrasses them to have nothing in their hands when we come with hands full. A native custom."

They wandered inland along a well-worn path between the heavy vegetation, most of it light pink in color. It reminded Kengee of a baby's flesh but it smelled like the dampness and urine of a pedestrian underpass in any large city. Gosho pointed to a huge green plant amid all the pink ones.

"That's it. That's a Takusa plant."

It was really big. Its spiked green leaves spread out on the ground for fifty feet in every direction and in its center a large yellow ball shook on its stem in the breeze. On the underside of the leaves, Kengee saw rows of swollen, nipplelike protuberances.

"She's ready for milking," Gosho said. "But the barbarians won't milk her."

Kengee approached the plant and reached out his hand to touch one of the strange nipples. The whole leaf began to shake and then the leaf slapped at his hand which he withdrew just in time. He tried again, and this time the plant managed to strike his hand. It stung painfully for a few seconds.

"Takusa doesn't like you very much." Gosho chuckled. "In the past traders tried to milk them but the Takusa plants always struggled and resisted and withheld their

95

milk. It's not worth the effort. Only the barbarians seem to have a way with the Takusa and they only can extract the milk. But now for their own mysterious reasons, they do not milk these ugly green plants."

At that moment, a row of nipples hardened and Gosho threw Kengee to the ground just as the plant sprayed its milk. The milk shot over their heads and struck a pink plant which immediately began to wither.

"It isn't pleasant to get sprayed in the face. If it gets into your eyes, you'll be blinded for a day or two and in great pain. We'd better leave our Takusa plant in peace. It's getting very angry."

"Do you mean it's capable of feeling anger?"

"Only in a manner of speaking, but when it feels threatened, it begins to thrash around and to spray a very potent milk. If it can't drive off its tormentors, it will commit suicide—just cease living, and in a few hours the plant is nothing but a dried husk. And if that should happen, the barbarians would hate us and then they most certainly would not trade with us."

"They won't anyway. But why do the barbarians alone have this special relationship with the Takusa?"

"I don't know but I have seen their children lying comfortably among its leaves with Takusa rocking them gently. And, of course, the barbarians milk Takusa regularly and no man from upper Ta can do that. The barbarians say the plant is like a human and can feel happiness, pain, and sorrow. I don't believe all of that, but surely Takusa is a very extraordinary plant."

Kengee looked back and saw that Takusa had stopped quivering in fear or rage and was lying still again like the less talented pink plants around it.

"Its roots spread out for long distances. They probably extend throughout this island. It is almost as if Takusa wished to claim all the land where it grows and permit other plants and men to exist in its domain on sufferance. Almost certainly this is the only Takusa plant on the island, but if the barbarians cooperated, it could fill all of our barges with milk.

"But even when the trading was good, the barbarians only milked small amounts. Whenever we pressed them for more, they would say that this was all that Takusa would allow us to take north. This was nonsense. The barbarians were just too lazy to milk and carry the milk to the vats, and now they will not milk at all, at least not on this island."

As Gosho talked, they retraced their steps to the beach. Standing ankle-deep in the muck at the edge of the water was a barbarian who was waving his arms and beating his chest. His boat, they noticed, had been pulled up on the beach. The three boatmen stood quietly watching him. When Kengee got closer, he saw that the savage was crying.

"He came in his boat while you were inland," one of the boatmen reported.

"What troubles you?" Gosho beamed his most friendly, commercial smile on the unhappy barbarian.

"You disturbed the Takusa and she is angry and we cannot return home while her anger lasts."

"We are truly sorry. We meant Takusa no insult nor harm."

"Did you tell her that? Did you apologize?"

"We did not. Unlike you, we do not know what pleases and what displeases Takusa."

"Please apologize to her. It may do no good now, but please try or we shall have to find a new island until her anger cools."

"We certainly will. Kengee, since you insulted Takusa by grabbing one of her teats, it is you who must tell her how sorry you are." Gosho winked with a trace of a smile.

Kengee set off at once back along the path on his fool's errand to appease a weeping native. He sniffed with distaste as he passed the pinkish plants. When he again approached Takusa, its leaves began twitching nervously. The movement reminded him of the way some women fluff their hair when upset.

"I'm sorry, honey, but I couldn't control myself. Those green boobs of yours really turned me on." He spoke in English.

The plant stopped twitching and began to pulsate in heartlike beats. The nipples began to harden, and then

Takusa milk began oozing out. Kengee approached one of the leaves and stroked it gently. The milk began to drip faster.

"You can trust me, baby," he said. The plant warmed under his touch and the heartbeats, or whatever they were, quickened. Bemused, he continued to fondle the plant.

"There's all kinds of women in this world, but you're something really special. Kid, you've got class. You're a real lady, and a sexy lady, too." The words tumbled out automatically and he began to feel silly.

"How many others have you told that to?"

It was a simpering female voice using words he had heard too many times before. He spun around, but saw no one but the pinkish plants. The voice, he then realized, came from the Takusa and he began to back rapidly away from it.

"See you again soon, love," the plant said.

He bolted down the path and slowed only when the beach was in sight again. "God almighty. The damned plant talked to me." And Takusa was very much a woman or a female or at least feminine. She definitely was on the make and on the make for him, or so he felt with growing terror. But even more shocking was the fact that Takusa had spoken in *English*. Shaken, he walked on, returning Gosho's wave limply.

"Did you apologize to Takusa?" Gosho asked in mock sternness.

"Most sincerely," Kengee said and forced a wink.

The native was wiping the tears away and smiling. Then he cocked his head as if listening to a distant voice. He wheeled and raced to his boat, pushing it quickly into the water.

"He's gone and there will be no business done here. The barbarian, the island's headman, said he had come to apologize himself to us because there was no Takusa milk. He said Takusa had been sulky for a year and in no mood to give milk. He wished us luck on the other islands, but I'm sure he felt we would have none. I'm sorry I had to send you on such a silly mission, but the

98

barbarians are very touchy about Takusa and there is no point in making enemies of potential suppliers."

Kengee decided to say nothing about his too intimate encounter with the giant green plant. He was still too stunned and he also doubted if Gosho would believe him. But he could not help thinking about Takusa as they headed back to the steamboat and he thought of Takusa definitely as a "her." He did not understand this plant but he did know something about women and he had been subjected to feminine possessiveness in the past. This kind of woman always made him very nervous. Even when he was back on the deck, he had the uncomfortable sensation that something somehow was hugging him around the knees. Yes, he knew the type well; overly demanding and overly generous—the big smothering mother. And Takusa he knew would be generous. Hadn't she gushed milk all over the place in response to a few kind words and a couple of quick feels?

He did not feel free from Takusa until the island disappeared into the mist. He was certain that the damned green bitch must be terribly frustrated. She probably had been brooding alone for too long on that small island. Illogically, he thought that if there were female Takusa plants, maybe there must also be male Takusa plants. He wondered if he could hit it off with a male—make a deal. He would offer to transplant the male Takusa to the island where the female Takusa dwelled. The charge for this pleasurable mating would be Takusa milk from the female. "Hi friend, looking for a good time. I know a hot little Takusa plant just itching to get plowed, or is that the word? Anyway, she'll do anything, absolutely anything. Sorry, no short time. It would be difficult under the circumstances but how would you like her all year?" He squirmed mentally. "Shit. A pimp for plants." And then he remembered that plants didn't screw and reproduce like humans, at least normal plants didn't.

Gosho began to island-hop. He would go ashore, discover the barbarians were gone and the milk vats empty, and then push on to the next island. Kengee stayed on board most of the time. Within a few weeks, they had visited all of the company's trading outposts with nothing to show for it except a sharp increase in the number of swamp fever cases. Two of Kengee's warriors died from fevers. They burned their bodies on an island and packed their ashes in Takusite boxes to bring back to upper Ta. Others also died. Those who were not sword-holders were pitched overboard and forgotten.

Gosho became more and more irritable, and he and Kengee spoke less and less to each other. The heat was unrelenting. The decks were slimy with the warm moisture. For Kengee, it was a dull, miserable cruise. He was only thankful that they had not encountered barbarians in sufficient numbers to stage an incident.

One morning, Gosho came up to him looking grim and determined. "Kengee, we're going into new territory," he announced. "We're going into the deep south."

"Lornz may not like that," Kengee said. "There may be trouble."

"If we find trouble, I know I can count on you and your swordsmen. It would be better to die in the swamps than to face the humiliation of returning to the capital without profits. We traders have our pride. I and my family shall not be disgraced. We go south."

Kengee shrugged and Gosho slapped him on the back. He then shouted an order to the boatmaster and two or three boatmen cheered weakly. Pretending to be as enthusiastic as Gosho, Kengee shouted an order to his swordholders to sharpen their weapons. They looked at him at first with surprise and then surly contempt. With little else to do, they had been sharpening their swords for weeks just to kill time. But they dutifully picked up their whetstones and went to work.

As they steamed proudly into the unknown south, the mists became even thicker and damper. In the hot afternoons, the black waters appeared ready to boil into a thick and tasteless soup. Convoluted gray vegetation looking like the brains of giants floated in the water. Occasionally, this gray mass clogged the paddle wheels, and frightened boatmen went over the side and pulled the spongy matter from the machinery, watched by schools of fish with red, hateful eyes. Progress was

100

slow since they searched every island for people and Takusa plants. They found neither.

But they did encounter the flatheads, creatures made in the likeness of men but far too hairy and pale to really resemble either the barbarians or the men from upper Ta. And they were all less than three feet tall. They swarmed over one island, clawing into the shallow water for shellfish and fucking animal-fashion on the beaches. These activities stopped abruptly when they noticed the convoy. They all rushed to the shoreline and began throwing shells and rocks, hooting hideously whenever one of their missiles clunked onto a deck. Gosho signaled the convoy to swing away from the island but in carrying out this maneuver, one of the rear barges slammed into the muddy bottom at high speed, hurling a boatman overboard.

The flatheads waded into the water and dragged the man ashore, where males, females, and their children tore his flesh from his living body with their strong sharp teeth. Five loud screams and the man was devoured. There was no point in intervening so they steamed on. With cheerful innocence, the flatheads waved at the departing convoy. Kengee even saw what resembled smiles on their pale, hairy faces. No doubt they considered the boatman a gift and were expressing their gratitude. They threw no more rocks or shells.

Gosho told him that the barbarians treated the flatheads brutally, hunting them for sport and food, and spearing even the infants which, of course, had the most succulent meat. Gosho said that this illustrated just how barbaric the barbarians really were. Kengee could work up little sympathy for the flatheads, even though Gosho pointed out that they had not after all eaten a swordholder.

"Then you would not mind eating a flathead," Gosho said. "They're not half bad if roasted with the proper seasonings. In the good days, the barbarians served us feasts which always included roasted flathead meat. They taste a little like a fishy egg. But the meat is tender. Of course, I was repulsed by the idea at first, but I could not risk offending a supplier by insulting his cuisine."

The next day, they sighted an island inhabited by barbarians and steered toward it, fearing that at any moment the barbarians would rush to their boats and disappear into the mists. But they did not. They gathered solemnly on the beach to watch the approach of the convoy. It was the first time that Kengee had seen any number of barbarians gathered in one place. Some resembled the men of upper Ta. But others were fairer and their hair ranged from blue black to brownish red in color. Their eyes were rounder and their noses bigger. The men on the average were taller and more slender than the men from upper Ta, and the women appeared to be fuller breasted and wider hipped. However, it was difficult to be sure because the women, like the men, wore colorful, loose-fitting tunics and baggy pants tucked into Takusite swamp boots. Kengee was sure that Hoso would have been horrified to see such variations in body structure and hair color. It proved what could happen to a race if indiscriminate breeding was permitted. And Kengee had been in upper Ta long enough to feel superior to these creatures.

As they drew near, Kengee saw that the barbarians were neither overly friendly nor hostile. They just stood there watching them. They did however seem a little sad. Kengee jumped into the small boat with Gosho and the boatmen.

"We come for peaceful trade," Gosho shouted to the barbarians from the boat. They all nodded at once and waded out into the water to help drag the boat onto the beach. Then they pointed to a man who stood apart from the others, and Gosho went toward him smiling and slipping on the slick mud.

"We come for peaceful trade," he repeated. The man just kept staring out across the water. Finally, he jerked his boots free from the slime and turned to face them.

"You have traveled far," he said.

"We did so because our honor demanded it. We seek only Takusa milk. We came not to cause trouble but to exchange our products for the milk. We respect you and your tribe and your Lornz. Please tell him we have come as peaceful traders."

"Lornz is neither alarmed nor offended that you have come this far south. He sent word to us to expect such a visit and to do you no harm. He understands your problems."

"Our greetings to Lornz. Someday we would like to be honored by being allowed to meet him."

"Lornz sees no one from the north."

"We then will respect his wish for solitude."

"Lornz is a very sociable man. He does not wish solitude."

"Then we shall respect his sociability and not approach him."

"That is wise. Lornz sent word that you would always say things and do things to please us."

"That has always been my policy. But now we find there is no more Takusa milk for us, although we bring trading goods to your people—goods your people have always desired before."

"We still desire your manufactured things."

"Then you have Takusa milk to exchange for these things."

"It will be a disappointment to you after your long and difficult journey to learn that we have none."

"Do you have none or do you withhold it?"

"It is Takusa who withholds. It is her decision and it is final. From time to time, we try to milk her but she gently dissuades us with squirts of stinging milk."

"Strange," Gosho said coolly.

"It is indeed strange and only Takusa and Lornz know the reason for the withholding. We are simple island people and are not taken into their confidence."

"I would like to camp on your island for a few days to give my men a rest. Is this allowed?"

"You are welcome. We shall prepare a feast."

Gosho winked at Kengee who grimaced. He was no trader with a trader's honor and would be damned before he ate a flathead, even one roasted to perfection in the best seasonings. While the crewmen and the warriors disembarked, Gosho whispered to him.

"He lies. This nonsense about Takusa withholding is only an excuse. The barbarians cut off our supplies and

103

then pretend it's beyond their control. No doubt we will someday learn that it is Lornz's plot to raise the price of Takusa milk, and that price could be anything, even land in the north. But I have seen that many of their swamp boats are patched and repatched, as are their boots. We may convince these islanders to do a little illegal trading. Keep your warriors in tight check."

Traders, boatmen, and warriors stretched their legs on the beach and began mingling amicably with the barbarian men. The barbarian women stayed apart from the visitors, never once looking directly at the men from upper Ta. Gosho explained that the women were very different at night. Then, he said, they came with bold demands, having secretly divided the newcomers among themselves. The barbarian men did not object. They were content with a show of virtue in the daytime and cared little about what happened in the darkness when they could not see what their women—both young and old—did. And since it was dark, visitors could never be sure which women they had laid. In the morning, virtue returned with the sun. Kengee felt a growing excitement as he watched these women. Even in their heavy boots, they walked like women. The traders and the boatmen also watched and waited for the fun-filled night ahead.

Both the men and women helped prepare the feast, which after all did not include flatheads. There was a type of water snake, chopped up and wrapped in swamp weeds and eaten raw, and there was an assortment of fish and strangely shaped waterfowl. Bowls of potent red juice made from berries that fell off island bushes and were crushed and fermented were passed around. As the hours went by, Kengee becamee worried because all of his warriors were getting drunk. But then so were the barbarians. They staggered off now and again to collapse on the mud and sleep. Later, they returned refreshed and ready for more of the berry wine. Kengee relaxed and began drinking heavily himself from a bowl and then passed it to the headman who drank and in turn passed it to Gosho.

"Do you have a Takusa plant on this island?" asked Gosho.

"We have a Takusa plant, but she does not wish to be disturbed. I do not know why. And she won't allow us to milk her."

"It is sometimes necessary to try harder."

"You do not understand because you are from upper Ta and there are no Takusa plants there. Takusa can be very stubborn."

"Man is more stubborn than any plant."

"Man is a fool and Takusa is not."

"Takusa can be neither foolish nor wise. It is only a plant and therefore only exists, albeit with a few interesting peculiarities."

Gosho went on badgering the headman in this fashion, and the headman continued to reply with patience and courtesy. The headman explained again and again that Gosho could know nothing about the Takusa because he was from upper Ta. Kengee became bored and irritated and finally decided to take a walk to get away from this absurd debate.

He headed inland staggering a little and feeling very hot. A dozen barbarians began to follow him, and then five of his own warriors got shakily to their feet and out of some sense of duty began to trail behind the barbarians. But the barbarians seemed friendly and appeared to be going with him as though they thought a walk in the hot afternoon a fine idea.

Kengee ignored the parade behind him. He was hoping to climb high enough to be able to get his head above the damp mist which had settled on the beach. He kept climbing with his drunken, grunting entourage behind him past the pale pink plants with their sickening stink. His foot came down heavily on one of these plants. It seemed to squirm and then it popped soiling his boot with its thick pink life's fluid.

Near the top of the hill, he saw a Takusa plant with its distinctive green spiked leaves and stopped. The barbarians began to gather behind him nervously and his drunken warriors groped for their sword hilts with their trembling hands. Kengee suddenly felt very dizzy from the native drink and glared at the plant as if it were to blame.

"I've met stubborn bitches before," he suddenly shouted. "It's just an act. You all give in eventually." The plant began quivering, seemingly in fright, and this spurred him into greater aggressiveness.

"You're nothing special," he said thickly. "In fact, you're overweight and damned lazy." He was speaking in English with his heavy Ta accent, and this bewildered the barbarians.

"Trouble with you is, you've never met a real man before. You've had nothing but little boys." The green leaves turned a bright red for an instant.

"You're nothing special." He repeated this again and again as he stumbled among the leaves which began flapping wildly. "You need a kick in the ass," he snarled. "But I don't know where your ass is." Kengee kicked the plant anyway. He felt rather than heard a whimper and then the leaves began rubbing against his legs.

The barbarians gasped. They gaped, now shocked and frightened. Then shouting, they tried to drag Kengee away from the Takusa. He shook them off, vaguely now realizing the trouble he had gotten himself into. His warriors drew their swords and one slashed at a barbarian. He missed and plunged into the pale pink undergrowth. Another man had a little better luck and knicked a barbarian in the ear with the point of his sword. The barbarian yelped and ran.

The barbarians who were unarmed dashed into the undergrowth and quickly reappeared with clubs and rocks. The battle began. Two of the warriors were knocked down and the other two retired down the path, waving their swords and shouting to Kengee to follow. The one who had fallen into the undergrowth was moaning in pain. When the barbarians began to close in, Kengee searched frantically for a way to escape, but he was surrounded. He drew his sword trembling and waited for the first blow of a club.

Then he heard a noise like a shower running full blast and three barbarians began screaming and rubbing their eyes. Takusa had squirted them with her stinging milk. Those who were not blinded fell back, dropping their rocks and clubs. They gaped at Kengee who stood among the protective leaves of the Takusa.

"See what happens when you try to break up a lovers' quarrel," he snarled in English. The mysterious words spat out harshly were felt to be an incantation by the barbarians, who began trembling. Kengee looked down upon the submissive Takusa.

"She will give milk now," he said firmly in Ta. "Get the rest of the tribe and start milking her." The barbarians ran toward the beach and Kengee stroked the plant.

"Good girl." The Takusa leaves were shaking with emotion. As he headed back to the beach, he heard a long, sexy sigh behind him and shuddered. It sobered him up immediately.

Before he reached the beach, the barbarians began rushing past him with pots in their hands and their eyes averted. His bewildered warriors were standing in a circle with their swords drawn, except for three who were dead drunk and lying nearby in the mud. The swordholder who had pitched himself into the pink vegetation was trailing behind him. Gosho was among the armed men and opened his mouth to question Kengee, but Kengee ignored him and went directly up to the warrior who had slit the barbarian's ear with his sword. He embraced the man and praised him for his courage.

"Swordholders of Ta, my brave comrades," Kengee began. "You have proved that the blood of heroes still courses through the bodies of the men of Ta. Your bravery today will be remembered for generations. We have won a great victory. Sheathe your swords. The defeated barbarians will bring Takusa milk in tribute." The swordholders cheered the myth all upper Ta would soon believe.

"What has happened?" Gosho asked.

"The barbarians are milking Takusa. We should be loaded and away in a few days."

"This was done with swords?"

"Certainly. It is the only way to deal with stubborn

natives. You've been a trader too long." Kengee jutted out his jaw and his warriors cheered again.

The barbarians with the first pots full of Takusa milk began arriving on the beach. They poured the contents into the vats and immediately went back for more. Kengee stood with his legs apart and glowered at them. They kept their eyes on the mud of the beach. Kengee held this pose for a half-hour and then went back to Gosho and sat down. They both watched silently as the barbarians trekked up the hill to the Takusa plant and then came down again. When night came, the children guided the laborers with torches. There could be no stopping when Takusa was giving.

In the morning, the line of barbarians was still moving. By midday, some dropped exhausted and slept for an hour and then were prodded awake by the children to start the long climb again. They did not complain. In fact, they were too tired to talk. Kengee was sure they would work until they died or until the Takusa stopped giving milk. But the vats were filling up and already Gosho had ordered the junior traders and boatmen to start loading the barges. On the following morning, Kengee approached the headman and told him to tell his people to take a rest.

"We cannot," he said in a very tired voice. "Takusa gives and we must take. We must do as she wishes."

Often during the day, Gosho took quick paces along the beach whirling and retracing his steps in a kind of upper Ta profit dance. He joked with the boatmen and junior traders as they filled the barges with Takusa milk. He was very happy.

"The fools are going to kill themselves," Kengee said.

"Look at the Takusa milk. Look at it. They're bringing in a day what we used to get in weeks of trading. Look at that sweet Takusa milk."

On the morning of the fifth day, the barges were full. The junior traders and the boatmen cheered. The barbarians grunted but kept climbing the hill with their pots. Kengee had purposely stayed away from Takusa. Its responses to him, although useful, were disturbing and a little frightening. But he knew he had to stop her. Once up the hill, he watched the barbarians set their pots on the ground and stroke the nipples of the plant which promptly squirted the milk neatly into the containers. Takusa appeared to be still swollen with milk.

Kengee wondered if her supply was endless. After the last barbarian in the group filled her pot and painfully began descending the hill, Kengee approached the plant. He fingered a nozzle out of which the fluid immediately gushed. Slowly the plant changed color. It became sky blue, Kengee's favorite color. He felt the leaves of the plant gently embrace his legs and then the leaves tightened their grip.

"Cut it out." The plant let go and turned green again. The green, however, was a little too intense.

"No more damned milk," he ordered. "We have enough. We're all filled up and ready to go. No more milk. Don't you have any fucking sense?"

"Whatever you say, love." The voice was distinct and came from somewhere, although he could see no possible mouth. He felt the plant grinning mischievously at him, but, of course, there was no grin to be seen.

"Christ. I need a double martini."

"Try this." One of the nipples erected and shot Takusa milk into his mouth. It tasted like a dry martini but there was no olive and the liquid was chalky white and warm.

"It doesn't look like a martini," he complained.

The entire plant seemed to shake with girlish giggles and Kengee started backing away. The giggling subsided and there were a few seconds of uncomfortable silence and then he thought he heard a choking sob.

"I got to go, baby." He tried to be gentle. "I really do. But I'll look you up again the next time I'm down south." From past experience, he had learned that a few kind words and a little lying sentiment go a long way toward quieting a crying female. If this didn't work, he usually stormed out of the apartment, slamming the door. Shock treatment. He did not like crying females. He had no real sympathy for them. To hell with them.

But he felt Takusa smile a little, and he knew this was the best time to depart before any more invisible tears were shed. He waved to Takusa once and the plant fluttered her leaves in response.

When he reached the beach, the exhausted barbarians already were crawling into their huts to sleep. The word had come from the Takusa. Gosho and his men were piling the trade goods on the mud, but only the headman was there to receive the products of upper Ta, and he obviously was forcing back his desperate need for sleep in order to be polite. He stared long and hard at Kengee.

Gosho and Kengee were the last to board the steamboat. Once they were on the deck, the engine began its noisy revolutions and the boat with the convoy behind it got underway, swinging in a wide half circle until it was pointed north. Kengee sat quietly, looking back at the island.

"Have you ever known a woman who wanted to give you everything she had, who was determined to smother you with herself until you could smell nothing but her, taste nothing but her, feel nothing but her? Have you? Probably not."

"A daughter of a swordholder once opened her robe during the first hour of our acquaintanceship. I've had that kind of giving."

"That's quick giving and quick taking with no obligations," Kengee said. "And I don't mean just small swordthrusting."

"What do you mean?"

"There are some women who want to be your lover, your teacher, your mother, your sole companion, your everything. They demand you totally. They wrap themselves around you and give, give, give. But they also take everything from you, by making life just too easy."

"It sounds like you got involved with one of those barbarian women."

"Something like that."

"Forget her. Barbarians are barbarians because they make love when they feel like it without restraint or

110

even teasing a little. They don't know how to control themselves and that's why they are barbarians. Forget her. We will soon be back among civilized women, and you'll have the pick of them."

SIX

Macha strode head high through the streets crowded with late afternoon shoppers, pulling her robe close to her body in disgust whenever there was a chance of brushing against a person who had never touched the sword. Her special training since childhood had taught her never to make a distinction between the two classes but to despise them both. However, she really never could forget that she was the daughter of Denzo—a female born into an illustrious family of heroes and women of worth. She was of the swordholder class, and it required strong mental discipline to disassociate herself from it to do the work she must.

Without hesitation she turned into a narrow byway reeking of damp filth and the rotting corpses of tiny city mammals with black fur which roamed the dark alleys in such numbers that they were often crushed underfoot. Women of her class never ventured into these dangerous capital byways, and with good reason. But Macha had no fear. Three street devilkins pressed respectfully against the damp wall of a building to allow her to pass. She smiled coldly at these stealing, murderous children whose sharpened street instincts warned them that she was a woman to avoid. They were right. If they had threatened her, she would have killed them instantly. She went everywhere fully armed with an arsenal of small deadly weapons.

Macha stopped before a blue door set back in a keyhole-shaped recess. She lifted the latch and pushed the creaking door open. In the pale light, she saw a stairway and went up. The stairs ended abruptly at an open door. She paused a few seconds to adjust her eyes to the dim light and then entered. A large man was sitting on a table in the center of the room with his feet dangling and with his hands clasped in his lap to show they held no weapon.

"Kengee returns to the capital tomorrow, a hero," the man said without enthusiasm. "Mako's plans went well. And worse for you, Gosho brings back barges full of Takusa milk. Your lucrative business in selling secret supplies is ruined for the time being. But this is your worry and not ours."

"How did they get it?"

"Why did you fail to kill him? We warned you he was a threat to both our enterprises."

"The first time we tried, he had unexpected help. He was warned at the last moment and there was no one there who could have warned him. We are convinced that only the possessor Tanee could have intervened to save his life. We have learned that Kengee spent many days in her cave and left that cave with Hoso. It may become necessary to kill Tanee, but killing a possessor is not an easy thing to do."

"And the second time? I suppose you have excuses for that failure, too."

Macha was flustered and worried by the man's harsh questioning. She surreptitiously loosened her sleeves so that the poison darts could fall easily into her hands if needed.

"That was due to bad luck. A boat bumped into Kengee's barge, spilling the poisoned tea onto the deck where it betrayed itself. One of our assassins escaped by diving off the boat and staying submerged until the entire convoy passed. He reported the failure and now is dead."

"How do you people stay alive underwater?"

"That is our secret, Shoomud. We have many secrets, most of them deadly."

"They do not interest me much nor do your threats. I had thought the Zabo was more efficient than it has shown itself to be in trying to kill this Kengee. We are providing you with Takusa milk so that you can make

112

great profits. We are living up to our part of the bargain but you have not rid Ta of our principal enemy."

"Why do you fear him so?"

"We were told to fear him, and when such a warning comes from the source it did, we heeded the warning."

"Why are Gosho's barges full? You say you are living up to your side of the bargain, but you permitted him to obtain great quantities of Takusa milk in lower Ta."

"We do not know why but we do know that so long as Kengee lives, our plans are in jeopardy."

"As you have seen, Kengee is not easy to kill, and therefore the price grows higher."

"The price will be paid if the job is done."

"Good. We have a plan but it is one that Lornz himself personally must approve. And we must know his answer quickly because much work must be done quietly and carefully. Our price is a complete monopoly over the supply of all Takusa milk forever."

"Your master is ambitious. It would appear that he plots to seize power in upper Ta. I do not believe my beloved leader would approve of such a political upheaval here now."

"My master anticipated his objections. Nothing will change on the surface and no company will go without Takusa milk. We want only control over the supply, so that my master can influence decisions in upper Ta."

"I can only submit your proposal to Lornz. You will have an answer by early evening."

"How is that possible? The distance is far."

"We barbarians have our secrets too."

"We work well together."

Shoomud said nothing but looked into her eyes. They were innocent and candid eyes. But Shoomud knew Macha was aware that the alliance was temporary and that both intended betrayal some day. Macha handed him the scroll on which was written the plan to be sent to Lornz and left without another word.

Shoomud waited until dark before leaving the building. Although he was disguised in upper Ta dress, he was a little too large to be acceptable by the standards of the Institute for Human Perfection. He had read the plan and approved it. In a chink in the wall of the building, he left Lornz's reply. It amused him that the Zabo would be impressed by the speed with which he pretended to communicate with Lornz. Later that night, Shoomud left the capital in a steamboat for the south where he would inform Lornz of his decision.

Once back home, Macha first made sure her father was absent and then ordered the servants and female companions to leave her in solitude for two hours. When they were gone, she pushed the wall in several places and a panel swung out revealing a secret passageway that led to the sequestered apartment of her mother, Sheebu.

The next morning, Gosho's convoy steamed into the capital triumphantly with gongs clanging. The good news had traveled up the canal in advance of their arrival, and the traders and factory owners of the capital were on the docks to cheer their trader hero. Pennants with the crests of all the famous houses flapped in the breeze, flowers were strewn on the dock, and pillow house girls, roused early from their sleep, were performing erotic dances as the boats and barges docked.

When Gosho and Kengee leaped ashore, "Yanzoo"—the ancient battle cry—was shouted by the swordholders over and over again. The two heroes saluted the crowd by covering their eyes and then by stretching their arms up like two bank robbers surrendering. More and louder battle cries sent flocks of birds soaring into the sky. As they started up the road to the Director of Ta's offices, the traders and factory owners raced to the edge of the docks to see the Takusa milk in the sealed vats on the decks of the barges. Kengee looked back and watched as the warriors disembarked. First one and then another was lifted onto the shoulders of the young traders, and then they were all carried to a pillow house which had opened early to accommodate the desires of the heroes. Kengee regretted that he was not with his men.

As Kengee and Gosho proceeded up the road, women from even the best swordholder families rushed forward to encircle them with their arms and to kiss their cheeks and hands. They whispered offers, times and places of meetings. The two heroes shook them off good-naturedly and tried desperately to remember all the promised rendezvous. They were looking forward to a very busy couple of weeks.

This was the first time that Kengee had ever been a hero to a large audience and he was enjoying himself. In the past, he had been a hero to several young girls with underdeveloped intelligences and overdeveloped sexual drives and to one or two small children. But this was something wonderfully different. The masses adored him. He glanced at Gosho whose teeth gleamed through a frozen, happy grin. Kengee felt superior to his friend. He was after all only a commercial success. Kengee had won acclaim with the sword, and there was something traditional and nice about doing it with a sword.

For the first time in decades, the stairs leading up to the Director of Ta's office had been swept clean of discarded scrolls. This was touching. Mako beamed his congratulations at Kengee and praised his bravery and military skill.

"They were not worthy adversaries," Kengee protested several times in a small voice when Mako pressed for details of the great bloody battle in the south. Mako was too impatient to worm the account out of this modest hero and began relating his own version of the victorious encounter which had been manufactured in the pillow houses and drinking places of the capital. By these accounts, Kengee and the Glorious Eighteen—as they were now called—had slaughtered five hundred barbarian men, women, and children and had broken off the combat only after the blood became so deep and slippery on the ground that it was impossible to get a foothold. By the time Kengee had thought up an even more gruesome story with even higher numbers of enemy casualties, Mako had lost interest and changed the subject.

"A brilliant exploit, Kengee, absolutely brilliant and certainly heroic," Mako said. "But then it was only an exploit. A battle and not a war won."

Mako was bringing him down fast. He glanced toward his friend, but Gosho was not listening to Mako. He

115

was staring out the window toward the canal where his wealth was already being unloaded. Getting rich after all was perhaps better than becoming a famous war hero.

"Gosho! Kengee and I have military matters to discuss," Mako said, and Gosho stood up, covered his eyes, and walked briskly toward the door, eager to return to the barges.

"He cannot stay away from his Takusa milk," Mako said.

"He's rich now. He has all the Takusa milk there is to sell in upper Ta."

"Almost all, but not quite all. We've learned of an illicit trade. Only a trickle now, but worrisome since we do not know how it is obtained. And a few trading expeditions have returned with small amounts. Of course, nothing compares to your highly successful venture. But even the large amount brought back in Gosho's barges will not keep our factories running for long. The problem remains. Lornz deprives us of regular supplies."

Kengee nodded unhappily. He had hoped that the Director of Ta would be satisfied for at least awhile with his supposed victory over the barbarians, but he knew that Mako already was planning a new heroic exploit for Kengee to undertake. Mako began probing in his mouth with his finger, scratching a tooth clean with his fingernail. He then flicked a bit of breakfast on the floor.

"We held a committee meeting early this morning to discuss what must be done. We concluded that you and only you can really conquer all of lower Ta. We now have absolute faith in you." Kengee stared hard at Mako who rattled off a series of nervous little laughs.

"We don't expect even Ta's greatest warrior to subdue all of the barbarians with his sword. We are reasonable men after all. We have devised a clever plan to make that unnecessary. All you have to do is kill one man and the problem is solved."

"Lornz."

"Yes, Lornz. And we have a plan that might just work."

"*Might* work."

"We have every expectation that it will be successful. We certainly would not send you on a suicide mission, and to reassure you, I will tell you in confidence that it was your own father who devised the plan and presented it to the meeting this morning."

"I hardly know my father."

"Many of us do not really know our fathers well. Now I do not want to be insulting, but in the proper clothes and with some training, you could very well pass as a barbarian. In disguise you could easily penetrate Lornz's capital, slay him, and make your escape. We shall provide you with everything you need. We would only give you the honor of killing Lornz. You have proved yourself a hero, a great soldier, and a man who gets things done."

Kengee nodded gloomily.

"Good." Mako smiled broadly. "We proudly accept your offer to carry out this most important and dangerous assignment. Needless to say, this is a very secret mission and you must discuss it with no one. We have chosen a quiet and comfortable little hideaway in the desert where your old friend Hoso will provide the experts to train you for the task ahead. But you must be tired. Take a few days rest first." Three crackling laughs and the interview with Mako was over.

Mako's swordholders escorted Kengee home to the house of Denzo. Only a few scattered cheers from lowborn women greeted the hero on the way. Like the residents of any busy and sophisticated capital, the citizens of the capital of Ta lost their enthusiasm quickly. Fresh events of the morning were stale and ignored in the heat of the afternoon. But there was a warm homecoming. Denzo drunkenly embraced him and thanked him for bringing new fame to their family.

"Father, I understand that you have proposed a plan to bestow even greater honor on our family," Kengee said with a trace of bitterness which Denzo chose to ignore.

"Quiet, that's our secret." He winked and then tugged Kengee by his sleeve into his apartment where drink and food were spread out on two tables. Macha was not there nor did she join them later.

Kengee spent the next two nights in pillow houses

but with little satisfaction. He could not take his eyes off the ceiling, and Kengee had really never liked doing it that way. Within three days the Glorious Eighteen—his warriors—proved themselves fighters at last. Five were slain in pillow house quarrels, four were arrested for beating and raping the daughters of swordholders, and the rest were banned from the capital for minor offenses. Kengee was forgotten, but Gosho was not. Often as they walked together, wealthy swordholders stopped them to congratulate Gosho and invite him to their homes. Kengee was not invited. He began to realize that he had fallen into the wrong profession on Ta.

It was a relief when the day came for him to go to the training camp in the desert. He and the instructors chosen by Hoso were housed in a large, drafty cave which had been well stocked with food and wine. No women were provided. Kengee was told that a swordholder preparing for single combat traditionally was expected to abstain from sex.

After the first day of lessons, he lost faith in most of his instructors. They knew less about lower Ta and the barbarians than he did and certainly less than Gosho. However, Hoso's two poisoners were good at their trade. They taught him how to administer various poisons with different reaction times, different appearances, and different tastes and odors. Since he could not arm himself with a sword in lower Ta, Kengee was instructed in how to use the spear and the long knife—typical barbarian weapons. A geographer from one of Ta's better schools spent hours with him going over crude maps of lower Ta and discussing possible routes to its capital. But since neither he nor Kengee knew where the capital was, these discussions were rather pointless.

By the end of the first week of classes, Kengee was beginning to feel like a murder machine. Buttons which dissolved into deadly poisons were sewn onto his rough barbarian tunic. Two hand knives were fitted into his swamp boots and strangling wire made of Takusite was coiled around his wrist. The two poisoners lectured him on the techniques of murder and then put him through rough drills. He would be made to use his weapons

118

sitting down, standing up, squatting, and lying on his stomach and back. He practiced diligently and pleased the instructors, but he seriously considered dumping the knives, poisons, and strangling wire into the water long before he reached the capital of Lornz. He felt he could never kill with such weapons. It was not in him.

One afternoon, he was lectured on the barbarians by a scholarly expert. Although education in upper Ta concentrated on bookkeeping, industrial technology, and the history of the One Thousand Year War, there was an occasional course offered on other subjects at top-level schools. The scholar Tako was a man in his late sixties who taught barbarian folk culture, the social and political structure of barbarian society, and barbarian religion at Ta's third-best school to students aspiring to be traders. No one else was interested in the barbarians.

The people of lower Ta, Tako explained, are divided into tribes, each led by a headman, and these tribes inhabit the islands that dot the swamps and waters of the south. The position of headman usually falls to the cleverest and laziest man who prefers administrative work to hunting and fishing. The headman keeps the census—the number of adult males and females and children, subtracting and adding as the births and deaths occur. In war, he plans the strategy and then sits at home fasting until the results are known. If there are disputes among members of the tribe, the headman sits on a rock or any other elevated place and observes the duel conducted with fists or spears or knives, depending on the seriousness of the argument. When one of the combatants falls dead or unconscious, he judges the other legally in the right. The headman does not hunt for fish, but is given more than the average share of the communal kill. If the hunting or fishing goes badly—and this seldom happens in the bountiful south—he is given a beating by the tribe. If anything approaching mass starvation occurs, he is stoned to death. No job is perfect. Still, most headmen live to an old age.

The headman is the tribe's diplomat. He negotiates with other tribes over fishing rights and the like and talks to the men from the north when they come to trade. The diplomatic language of lower Ta cleverly deletes the words for "yes" and "no." It is after all the diplomat's duty to please everyone.

The exceptional headman is a respected headman. To become respected, the headman must have a strong personality and above all else a lot of luck. Rarer still is a headman who has any influence outside his own little tribe, and much rarer still is the headman who has a following among a majority of the barbarians.

"Lornz is such a man," Tako told Kengee. "At times in barbarian history, a big headman has arisen and trouble always ensues. The barbarians are so used to mediocrity that a spark of genius sets their imaginations and hopes ablaze. They are overawed by anyone who thinks or pretends to think with any degree of complexity. It is an unsettling experience for them. From infancy, they learn to respect no one, and truly their mothers and fathers present bad models for respect, or love, either.

"It is the habit of their women to push the rearing of their children off on the weakest women of the tribe—the ones who cannot resist the burden with fists and kicks. And you can imagine what kind of foster mothers these women make. They care for the children grudgingly, giving food and the other necessities only to children who learn quickly to wail noisily when infants and to bully their guardians when older by kicking them or throwing small stones at them.

"The other women once relieved of their motherly duties turn to activities which lead to more unwanted babies. The barbarian male ignores female society and female battles, devoting himself to fishing and hunting. The children learn how to become adults through observation mainly and what they observe are poor examples of what men and women should be. The children watch and listen but receive only a few miserly words of advice.

"Barbarians cooperate in the hunt or in war but are prone to pursue their own selfish, personal goals outside of these essential group activities. They despise each other and are quick to see and ridicule any weakness or deformity, big or small, in others, and these are many since barbarians come in many sizes, shapes, and colors. Their lack of uniformity is disgusting.

"For these reasons, they will glorify the exceptional man. He becomes in a way the father they never knew —a soft Takusite doll for adults to hug and love. Miserable people."

"What makes Lornz so exceptional?"

"We can only speculate because no one from upper Ta has ever seen or heard Lornz." Tako was now speaking excitedly. "We do know that he is preaching some kind of religion and is promising to make the barbarians a great people again."

"If there were no Lornz, whom or what would they worship?"

"Worship is not the word. They pay respect to things, simple and obvious things like the sun which seldom appears through the mists or a big dry rock or even the Takusa plant. When they see the things they respect, they wave and shout and flatter the object with praise, but they do not pray before these objects or really consider them sacred. However, if one of them ever was so foolish as to piss on a big dry rock considered special by the tribe or on the Takusa plant, I am quite sure they would be punished to death by other members of the tribe.

"The barbarians are preoccupied with sex. It dominates their primitive art. Their favorite artistic theme in their skillfuly executed bone carvings is a chain orgy which includes all the breathing, growing things on Ta. These are pornographically magnificent. You must come see my collection sometime, but then you will soon be seeing these carvings yourself."

"How can Lornz really have power over these people?" Kengee wanted to get back to the point or more correctly the target.

"Little tricks, I suspect. I've heard he is an amateur meteorologist and can with some accuracy predict when the sun will shine through the mists. And he has a way with plants. It is said that near his residence grows the biggest and most bountiful lactating Takusa plant in lower Ta. And one thing more. Some say he copulates with the plant. This is disgusting if true." Kengee was properly disgusted and a little frightened.

"Of course, that's just hearsay," Tako said brightly.

"Who is allowed to see Lornz?"

"Why, any barbarian I am told. I understand they go in the hundreds to his capital. They squat in a clearing in a woods and wait for hours or even days for him to appear before them. Every man and woman in lower Ta now believes he must go to the father Lornz. When those who have gone to Lornz return to their tribes, others are caught by the desire to seek out Lornz. They say he promises to lead them into the dry lands of the north again. Fanatics, all of them."

"Do you really believe he can do that?"

"How can anyone say? But we can be sure that if he wishes to retain power over the barbarians, he must entertain them somehow. Perhaps, he plans a war or some other interesting amusement. But whatever he does is a menace to the true men of Ta. I hope you are successful in destroying this man to save our industry and commerce—our way of life."

"I'm going south with that in mind."

That night after the others had fallen asleep in their hammocks suspended from hooks driven into the stone wall, he slipped out into the night. He walked rapidly north, pulled by the overwhelming desire to see Tanee again. He had known that her cave was not too far distant but until that night he had never thought of visiting her. When he reached the dark shadow of the mesa, he climbed the path and entered the cave without shouting a greeting.

It was not necessary. Tanee was sitting at the stone table set for two, waiting for him.

"Dinner is ready," she said smiling. "It was time to bring the hero of Ta to my home."

"In Ta only rich traders and factory owners remain heroes for long."

"Is that so different from the ways of Earth? Have you decided that being a warrior is less gratifying than being a pimp, a burglar, or a gigolo?"

"I'm not ashamed of anything I've ever done. Most

122

have done worse things without even knowing it and at least I am aware of what I do. I've always been a professional and have conformed to the ethics of whatever profession I was momentarily practicing. Even burglars and pimps have ethical standards which they often respect more than some doctors respect their own ethical standards and certainly more than lawyers do."

"No speeches, please. You did well in lower Ta, surprisingly well. Somehow you must have a way with the barbarians, and no doubt your previous careers made it easier for you to adjust in lower Ta. I have always suspected there was a good deal of barbarian in you and something much more important than that."

"I had little to do with the barbarians."

"I can't believe you stayed away from their women."

"I'd forgotten that you cannot spy on me down there. Are you curious? And that reminds me. I have not thanked you for helping me out in the pillow house. Of course, you apparently were too busy to be around when they tried to poison me. But never mind that now. Who hates me enough to want to kill me?"

"The Zabo is trying to kill you, but the Zabo really has no likes or dislikes. It does its work for pay and someone is paying the Zabo a lot to murder you."

"You're not being too helpful. Is it your brother, Hoso? He never thought I was pure enough to exist in upper Ta, and he distrusts me."

"Hoso? No. He distrusts you but then so do Mako and the rest. You are an alien and considered a dangerous alien, even more so now that you have succeeded in the south. They do not understand my Kengee."

"Maybe Mako thinks it is time to get rid of me." He told Tanee about his mission and training and she listened without saying anything until he had finished.

"No. Mako believes you will complete this mission or at least survive it. Otherwise he would not risk your life at this time, because he truly cannot dispense with your help yet. He is now convinced that you have special powers in lower Ta, as I do, and that these powers and not this stupid training will preserve you."

Tanee rose from the stone table and came toward Kengee. She stood before him and looked into his face intently. If she had asked what his special powers were in lower Ta, he would have gladly told her. But she did not. When she touched his shoulder, his fear of the mission vanished. When he reached for her, she quickly stepped back.

"Mako is not your enemy yet," she said.

"Is it Denzo? He suggested the plan."

"Denzo is a fool, and if he proposed this plan, then someone else is using him and that person may very well be your principal enemy. We can be sure that the Zabo is aware of this plan and we should assume they will set traps, even more clever ones this time, and perhaps the plan itself is a trap."

"Can't you find out?"

"I've been snooping around but I dare not go near the Zabo. We have an agreement. I don't spy on the Zabo and the Zabo does not kill me."

"Can't you help me in the south?"

"I'm afraid to go south. There is something there which threatens to overwhelm me. When I approach too close to lower Ta, I feel a warning, a threat. I think you know very well what keeps me out of the south, but that is your secret and your power."

"I don't know and I could get killed down there." His voice was petulant and accusing.

"Be brave. When you go, you must disregard all their advice and any of the routes they suggest. You must set your own course. But if you reach your destination, will you kill Lornz to please Mako?"

"I would rather make a deal with him."

"Lornz, they say, makes no deals with the men from upper Ta, and you have nothing to offer him."

"Then better him dead than me."

"You said that like you meant it. I'm rather pleased with you. You're shaping up well. But then Mako might be content with something less than assassination."

"What?"

"How should I know?"

"And what will you be doing while I'm gone?"

"Puttering around the cave and taking a trip or two and worrying."

"About me?"

"Yes, Kengee, about you."

Kengee reached out and pulled her toward him a little too roughly. She bounced against his chest. While she was trying to catch her breath, he kissed her hard on the mouth. She broke free, still panting.

"No. I'm a freak."

"I don't care."

"Definitely no."

"Please, Tanee." He was surprised at the tone of his voice. Never before had he begged a woman, and she saw his bewilderment and smiled. Her will to resist him was gone.

"All right. But only in the dark." He whirled around the cave snatching the torches from the wall and beating them out on the floor in a dance of sparks and love. When it was dark, she called to him.

"I'm in the hammock over here."

"Please get out."

"Why?"

He mumbled an answer and she giggled. Plates and bowls tumbled from the table, smashing on the cave floor. But neither Kengee nor Tanee noticed the noise. She felt the cold stone on her back and pushed her body against his warmth. The table was quickly cleared of the remaining bowls and food. A scream burst from her mouth, and then they lay quietly side by side. He began exploring her body with his hands, looking for some deformity. He found none. She was a complete and appealing woman. Perhaps, there was a birthmark or something like that, he thought.

When he later lit a torch, Tanee was wearing her robe with the sash tightly knotted.

"We've broken a law of the Institute for Human Perfection," she said.

"No one knows that but you and me, and now I want to sleep with my crime." He beat the torch out again, and they slept quietly in one hammock. Long before dawn, she awakened him with a bowl of hot desert tea which he gulped down before hurrying toward the cave entrance.

"Was I different?" she asked in a quiet voice.

"Different and better," he shouted and was gone.

Tanee watched him move down the path in the darkness. Her eyes were good at night and she could see him walking quickly over the desert toward the training camp. It had been a dangerous thing to do but she felt no regrets. She did begin to wonder, however, if it really had been for this that she had kidnapped Kengee's brain. It was an unsettling thought. If her emotions and not her cool possessor's logic had selected this man, then all might fail and she might also lose him forever. She could not let this happen.

When the sky began to lighten, Kengee hurried. He touched a scratch on his face and his fingers disturbed the dried blood. Tanee had clawed him violently on the table. He would tell his instructors that he had scratched himself during a nightmare. But his luck was bad. One of Hoso's poisoners was sitting outside the cave on a large rock. He had been watching Kengee run along the edge of the desert.

"Out for a morning run," he said cheerfully. "Got to keep in shape. I had a bad fall. Scratched my face."

The poisoner nodded but said nothing. But the man's suspicious coplike eyes bothered Kengee. He knew he could not risk another visit to Tanee's cave, not at least until he went south and returned—if he returned. But he wanted her now, wanted her more than he had ever wanted a woman before. He would not admit to himself that he was in love with Tanee. Love in his life back on Earth was an emotion he had always faked. He told himself he liked Tanee because she was a safe lover. The laws of Ta forbade her marriage. If he survived this mission, he could enjoy her without obligation. And if he survived, he would survive as a hero and no one would worry too much about a hero breaking a few laws.

The sun that evening plunged below the horizon in seemingly cowardly haste as if chased from the sky by Ta's twin moons which were already rising in the sun's fading light. The hulking mesas of the desert blurred into indistinct shapes and then slowly turned into white, squat towers in the brilliant moonlight. His instructors, with the exception of the two poisoners, had already left after orders arrived in the afternoon from Mako. He watched the sails of the sand ships on course for eastern Ta. There was little danger in sailing across the desert even in a sandstorm. If the ship foundered, the crew either walked out of the desert or let loose a message-carrying bird and help eventually came. There were pools of water here and there in the desert sheltered from the sun by overhanging rocks or mesas. When commerce with eastern Ta began, men trekked across the desert on foot. The desert was safe but the swamps of the south were not.

He heard the poisoners come up behind him. Without a word, they walked off together toward the tabo fields and the canal where a steamboat waited. When they arrived at the canal, they saw nothing but black, empty water.

"Not here yet," grumbled one of the poisoners. "Wait. I'll go look for it." He went off along the bank whistling a signal now and again and five minutes later, Kengee heard a steam engine come to life. A short time later the boat bumped into the soft embankment and stopped. One of the poisoners leaped onto the deck and talked quietly with the boatmaster and then he leaped ashore again. Kengee was told to go aboard. The boatmaster led him to a small cabin below decks where he was told to remain until they were well past the capital.

The boat moved cautiously, stopping often to avoid collisions with other craft tied up along the canal for the night. Eventually, they swung onto the main canal which was the waterway for commerce moving north and south. The cabin door slid back and a girl came in with a tray of food and drink. The girl wore her hair short and her narrow eyes watched him openly with interest. She placed the tray on the table and began pouring wine into a bowl. He noticed that there were two wine bowls on the tray.

"I come before or after the meal." She smiled at him. Kengee assumed she was a little graduation present from Mako. It was thoughtful of the Director to provide a woman on the long trip even if it violated the code of a swordholder preparing for signal combat.

"I hope I please you. Otherwise it will be a long and lonely journey for the both of us. I was chosen to please you. The Director of Ta knows your tastes in women and in the things women do."

"You please me." He tried to remain calm but his hands were trembling eagerly. She noticed this and poured her own wine and downed it in a gulp, belching prettily afterward. The yellow wine dripped from the corner of her mouth. One drop coursed down her chin and plunked between her breasts which were partially exposed through her loosened robe.

"It will be a long but pleasant journey," she said, leaning forward to arrange the dishes and revealing more of her breasts. Damn nice of Mako, he thought. Too damn nice of him. She must be a spy, but if I'm careful I can enjoy her.

"You're not hungry for food?" She leered at him.

"I've supped."

"The hammock."

"The floor."

The girl's eyes widened and she began to shake violently.

"All right, I'll try my luck in the hammock. I don't want to upset you."

"The floor will do." The voice had changed. It was no longer soft but harsh and mocking.

"Go home, Tanee," he shouted.

"I've got to keep you faithful, Kengee." The girl's face pouted. "And this poor little creature does not like the idea of making love on the floor one bit." Tanee dropped the robe and wiggled over to a mirror on the cabin wall and began examining the girl's body.

"Not bad. A little thin in the legs, but not bad at all." Tanee turned around and looked over her shoulder. He interrupted the next comment.

"Go home, Tanee. For God's sake, go home."

"You want her back. I don't advise it. She's got a nasty little mind."

128

"I don't want her. I'm upset and I just want to be left alone."

"But you were so eager just a few minutes ago."

"Tanee, this invasion of my privacy has got to stop. I won't take that from any woman."

"I'll leave you but you should know that your playmate has a false pointed tooth through which she can inject a deadly poison. You would not remember her kiss for very long."

"She'd kill herself, too."

"Not if she was careful, and anyway she carries an antidote with her."

"The Zabo again."

"Yes, the Zabo again. Apparently, they've discovered that you cannot resist a trap baited with a female. But you were not to die tonight."

"Then go home."

Tanee ignored him. "You were not to die at all, providing you carried out this mission. She has orders to kill you only if you decide not to go south and assassinate Lornz. Now that's very interesting. Why would the Zabo and Mako want the same thing?"

"I don't know. I know nothing about the Zabo, except that its people keep trying to kill me."

Tanee swung gracefully into the hammock. "Quite an athlete, this girl. She knows nothing else. She was given her orders but not told the reason. I've interrogated her brain. A blank. But oh she has an awful mind. She can murder in a hundred ways and she's proud of each of these skills. And the poor girl doesn't enjoy sex at all. It's just an unpleasant job to her. Some fun you would have had."

"Now what happens? If you leave her, she'll know you possessed her and she'll know I am aware that she has a poison tooth and that the Zabo for its own reasons wants me to complete the mission."

"I've been thinking about that. I could make her jump into the water and drown, after unlearning her very skillful swimming abilities, or I could make her bite her tongue with that poison fang. The Zabo might believe she did it by mistake in the heat of passion. But if I killed her with quick-acting poison, I would have to exit very fast and that could be dangerous."

"Do you have to kill her?"

"Are you still so fond of her? This murderous little girl?"

"No, but . . ."

"My soft-hearted warrior. No, I don't have to kill her. I'll make her mind unaware that I possessed it. That takes a lot of extra work, of course. But first I think I'd better remove the poison from the tooth."

She swung out of the hammock and went to the table and picked up a piece of round tabo bread. She bit into it, working up pressure by puffing out her cheeks, and then quickly rinsed out her mouth, spitting the water on the floor. A gray vapor rose from the bread where the poison had been injected.

"There now. Your little playmate is safe."

"She's a bomb defused but still a bomb."

"Then don't ignite her, Kengee. And we don't have bombs on Ta anyway. We use explosives rarely and then only for excavating canals and the like. No one ever thought of using explosives in war. Ta's men love their swords too much."

"And poisons?"

"Only the Zabo and my brother's agents use poisons. And these people have never touched the sword. Only lowborn people would murder anyone in such a despicable way."

"And that makes the swordholder moral." He was angry now to realize that Hoso considered him from a class which could kill with poisons.

"In a way it does. And you're using Earth standards to judge Ta—standards which are very questionable anyway. And if I remember correctly, your behavior on Earth was hardly moral by even the standards of Earth nor would it be considered moral on any inhabited planet I have ever visited."

"Why do you keep bringing up my past?"

"Most women do. You should have tried marriage, Kengee. You would have learned some things about women that you never suspected."

130

"Forget marriage. I'll try it in the hammock to please you."

"No. I don't really think I would enjoy it anymore with someone else's body. But you can have her when I'm gone. I'm not all that possessive." She chuckled over her bad joke.

"No, I'd keep thinking of her as a rattlesnake."

"What's a rattlesnake?"

"A snake that injects poison from its fangs when it bites you."

"What terrible monsters you have on Earth. But I can assure you Hibee, that is her name, is no longer able to do you any harm, with her tooth at least."

"Why don't you stay with me, at least until we reach the edge of lower Ta?"

"I can't do that now. I can't explain but I feel something has gone terribly wrong. I must return to myself quickly."

"What will she do when you leave?" He was looking nervously at the naked girl standing before him. The naked girl looked coolly back.

"She'll remember nothing of this. I'll see to that and I'll fix her so she won't bother you again. Be careful, Kengee, and come back to me, the real me."

Hibee pressed her hands to her eyes and moaned.

"What's the matter?"

"I've got an awful headache. I don't understand. I am sorry but it will have to be another night." She snatched up her robe and the tray of cold food and fled from the cabin.

Alone again, Kengee thought about Tanee. She meant well, he realized, but still her ability to spy on him was upsetting. Marriage to such a woman would be impossible, even living with her would be risky. She was a nice kid but too dangerous. The engine came to a full stop and there was shouting on the deck above, and then the boat started moving again, southward.

The two poisoners stood at attention with their faces registering a trained blank indifference as Hoso entered the farmer's hut. The farmer, his wife, and four children

131

had been ordered outside where they huddled together for warmth by a field dike. Hoso looked around at the sparsely furnished room. A fire was blazing in the fire hole. The two poisoners had broken up a table and two stools for fuel after the farmer's meager supply of Takusa oil had been consumed.

"Where is she?"

One of the poisoners pulled back a ragged, dirty curtain that concealed a nook and the hut's only bed. Tanee was lying unconscious on the rags and the tabo straw. Her arms and legs were bound.

"No response?"

"She's not here. An empty mind."

"She's traveling but she'll be back," Hoso said. "She has no choice but to return to herself. Has she been drugged?"

"Yes, Hoso. When she does come back, she'll be trapped. The drug will imprison her in herself and there will be no escape then. But the drug must be administered once a day."

"Your report," Hoso snapped.

"The day Kengee went south, he returned to the training camp just before dawn. I noticed a scratch on his face. After we put him aboard the boat, we both visited the possessor's cave and found her this way. We examined the hammock, the floor, the table, and all over. We have proof that she and this man made love, and violent love at that, in violation of the laws of the Institute for Human Perfection. We found broken bowls. We found boot marks on the table. We found pubic hair. And the possessor is no longer a virgin."

"You did well. We shall wait for Tanee to come back." Hoso despised these overzealous agents but smiled warmly at them. Did they not realize that what they had done was an embarrassment to him? His own sister, a freak and now something worse. She had deliberately broken the law and the rules of her exile. If he was as foolish as these two, he would order the boat stopped and Kengee arrested. But he was not that foolish. Mako would not appreciate having his plans spoiled. The whole matter must be shut up for the time being, and that would mean getting rid of Tanee. This could be done when the possessor repossessed her mind and body. He knew she would flit from mind to mind for a time but eventually her overpowering love of self would force her to return. They could wait. When she had reoccupied her body, the poisoners could administer a poison. After they had performed this duty, he would have them both killed. No one would know of this added disgrace, no one except Mako when the time came to accuse and destroy Kengee.

Tanee hovered over the farmer's hut, feeling the painful pull toward herself and yet knowing the danger. When one of the poisoners came out into the dark, opened his robe, and began pissing, she captured his mind. When she entered the hut in his body, she had to fight hard for the first few minutes not to repossess herself. She fought back this desire but the desire was strong, very strong.

Hoso and the poisoners waited through the next day. Hoso noticed that one of his agents was growing more and more irritable, and he could almost sympathize with him. The farmer's hut was a miserable place and long ago they had burned everything combustible including the bed. Tanee now rested on the floor. In the evening, he decided that Tanee was putting up more resistance than he had anticipated and ordered them to carry her drugged, empty body to the boat. He would wait for the return of Tanee in the comfort of the Institute for Human Perfection in the capital.

After reaching the Institute, Tanee's body was placed in an underground cell. He saw that the body was weakening and ordered it force fed through a Takusite hose inserted into her mouth and then into her stomach. If the body died, Tanee could not return for punishment. Hoso restricted the two poisoners to their rooms, assuring them that this was only a temporary necessity because of the sensitive nature of the case. They were ordered to talk to no one about the woman who was sleeping in the cell below upon threat of death.

SEVEN

When the steamboat was tied up for the night a day's journey away from the swamps of lower Ta, Kengee lowered his small boat over the side and drifted away in the darkness. He had no good reason for doing this, except he felt he should do the unexpected. If he was being led into a trap, it might help to leave the steamboat unseen and ahead of schedule. Since the first night, he had not been bothered by Hibee. She brought his food to the cabin door, made excuses, and left hurriedly. But several times when he went on deck, he caught her watching him and her eyes were very cold. The current carried him down the canal for several hours and at dawn he started up his miniature steam engine and the small paddle wheels pushed him rapidly southward.

In the morning, the boatmaster, who had been bribed by the Zabo, reported his disappearance to Hibee. She felt guilty. She had been able to offer him food and drink but not herself. She had not coaxed him into the hammock. She could not bring herself to do this and she did not know why. She had disobeyed orders. She had been a bad spy. And now he was gone. He had, she thought, abandoned the mission and she had not killed him. As the big boat swung around and headed north, Hibee went down to her cabin.

Once the door was slid shut and locked, she removed the dagger strapped to her outer thigh and slit open the hem of her robe. A tiny scroll fell into her hand. With her fingernail, she scraped away the protective coating of wax and then spread the tiny paper out on a table and squinted to make out the tiny letters. The message read: "In case of failure, take poison." The Zabo

134

did not waste words. Every Zabo was prepared to receive such a directive and every Zabo was ready to obey such an order. Hibee's face showed no emotion, but she breathed in deeply once.

She began her preparations. First she swallowed the message, washing it down with water. Then she undressed and sponged her body clean using the water in a bucket. She combed and brushed her short hair, until it shown in black radiance in the sunlight beginning to filter into the cabin. Hibee redressed in a clean robe and got into the hammock, tying herself securely with a sash so that in her death throes, she would not pitch herself onto the floor and die in an unsightly posture.

She was thankful at least that she had the time to make all the proper and comforting preparations. Often a Zabo had to die a quick, ugly death. Since she did not come from a family of swordholders, she was not obliged to ask her ancestors' permission to join them. Those who had never touched the sword could die simply with a minimum of ritual. She reviewed her life with distaste. Twelve years of misery as a farm child until her parents died and the Zabo purchased her. And then ten years as a Zabo. She was a little proud of her grades in the rigorous Zabo training school and the few successful assassinations she had carried out with distinction and praise. But in reality, it had been a short, barren life. There had been no love in it and now it was over.

She pressed the sharp point of her false tooth into her lip and bit hard. "I and Ta are now one," she said softly and waited to die.

A minute went by. Too bad it was such a slow poison, she thought. It was always best to go quickly. She had neglected to ask the reaction time. In these moments of waiting for death, she became more aware of herself than ever before. "This is I who am about to die. It is I and I alone." And yet someone else was there too. How could that be? She recalled suddenly the night when she had first gone to Kengee's cabin and offered herself. There was something very strange about that night. She had offered herself and the next thing she remembered

135

was a terrible headache. What had happened in between? She recalled touching the food when leaving the cabin and it was cold. A half an hour or more had been taken from her life which was now about to end. She then realized that the missing time was very important. With desperate fury, she concentrated as they had taught her to do. Her heartbeat slowed and she went into a trance. She clawed at the secret, the missing time. Nothing was clear at first and then she felt the presence of another woman.

The woman had touched the center of her being and had learned all. The woman had been gentle, forgiving, understanding. The woman gave more warmth than she had ever felt before. The woman had a name. What was the name? Tanee! What had the woman wanted? She remembered now. Tanee had wanted to know how she intended to kill Kengee and when. She had disclosed this and all of the Zabo secrets in a great, free rush of thoughts and there had been sympathetic acceptance. She had wanted to tell Tanee much more—all of her secrets, even those secrets which even the Zabo did not know. She had wanted to and still did. Where was Tanee now? Sleeping and yet not sleeping. Far away. In a room. No a cell. In the capital. Hibee saw the place, saw Tanee drugged and weak, and was pulled toward her.

She quickly untied the sash and rolled out of the hammock, knowing now the tooth had been drained of its poison days before by Tanee. She had removed all the weapons from her clothing and body in preparation for suicide and now she picked up the slender needle-sharp dagger. She knew she was supposed to kill herself, even if the poison failed, but now she felt free from the Zabo. It was as if she had died and had been reborn without obligations and duty to the Zabo. She only wanted to find Tanee again, the woman who had possessed her mind. She desired only to melt into her mind and she sensed the urgency of reaching the capital quickly.

Hibee rearmed herself. The dagger and the knife were strapped to her thighs again. The darts with poisoned tips were tucked into her sleeves. The strangling wire was coiled into her hair. The acid pellets for hurling into the faces of victims or attackers were returned to a pocket in her robe. The deadly chain and ball with sharp ejectable points was rewrapped around her waist. And the other gadgets of the Zabo were returned to their hiding places in her clothing. She was again fully armed—a dangerous Zabo, but now without a master.

Hibee went on deck and told the boatmaster to make all possible speed for the capital. He nodded. He feared this girl who stood before him and he promised to run the boat day and night. And for most of those days and nights, Hibee paced the deck restlessly.

Kengee lay back in his small boat feeling the strong, regular vibrations of the small steam engine fueled by Takusite pellets. He fingered the tiller carelessly. He had left the canal where it emptied into the swamps of lower Ta and now was navigating through the waterways that crisscrossed the floating vegetation and the islands which rose high above the low-lying mist. He had deliberately not taken the route recommended at the desert school and urged upon him by the master of the steamboat. He was traveling west, not south. After an abrupt turn into a narrow channel where the floating vegetation concealed his small boat, he looked back. The mist cleared briefly and he saw a barbarian standing on an island intently watching the main route into lower Ta, the one he was supposed to have taken. The man's back was to him, but he disappeared from sight as the smoky mist rose from the water. Kengee had no doubt that the man was waiting for him. It seemed that everyone knew where he was going. Nevertheless he decided to continue southward. It was dangerous but it would be just as dangerous to turn back now with the Zabo and Mako waiting for him. There were unknown possibilities in the south, and with any luck he would seize the right one and survive. He had always in the past managed to stay afloat. Kengee dipped his hand into the water rushing by and laughed.

In high spirits, he began zigzagging joyfully down the channel. Suddenly, the boat shuddered and stopped dead. He threw off his robe and went into the water and began pulling weeds out of the small paddle wheels.

Something, long and thick rubbed across his legs for what seemed to be a full minute. The water was too muddy to see the creature. He finished his work as fast as he could and rolled back into the boat trembling.

An hour later, the prow of the boat poked its way out of the mist and he spotted a large island to the southwest. He saw no people but he did see a battered boat pulled up on the beach. Kengee steered toward it, and when his boat slid onto the muddy bottom near the beach, he got out nervously and tied it to a large rock alive with bluish plants that lashed out at his fingers with their tiny tentacles.

There were many footprints on the beach, clear and fresh. There also was a fire still smoldering and the gnawed bones of an animal that could only have been a flathead were scattered nearby. He found a spear in the boat and a cooking pot coated inside with fleshy grease. He was sure that the inhabitants of the island would soon come back.

He decided to wait. He was confident he could pass as a barbarian. His body was a little oversized for upper Ta but very average for lower Ta. His eyes, nose, and other facial features were more typically those of a man from upper Ta, but there were barbarians who looked as he did. After a thousand years of war and rape, it was hard to find a pure barbarian.

Toward nightfall, a small fleet of boats came toward the shore. The barbarians leaped out of their craft carrying bloody carcasses of flatheads and chunks of large tubular meat. The women and children came ashore with small fish still flopping in baskets. True to their culture, the barbarians completely ignored the strange barbarian sitting on their beach and went about the tasks of rebuilding fires and cooking what they had caught or slaughtered during the day. Kengee knew he would be driven away if he approached them before they had eaten, so he built his own small fire and cooked two fish he had speared earlier.

Three hours later the barbarians were licking their fingers and belching. When they sprawled on the ground and began talking in low tones to each other, Kengee hesitantly moved toward the largest fire. If he was not wanted, he knew one of the savages would throw a bone or a shell or a burning stick over his head as a warning. No missile came his way so he walked closer. Just outside the fire's ring of warmth, Kengee lay down on his back—a nonaggressive posture and a way of saying he wanted no trouble. After a time, the headman thrust out his dirty palm, and feeling a little nauseated, Kengee licked up the bits of greasy cooked flesh in the man's hand. Once this ceremony was over, he could relax. It meant that the stranger was to be tolerated near the tribe.

Conversation among the barbarians resumed. They talked about the furry swamp worm they had killed, skinned, and eaten. The creature, before it was sliced up, had been at least thirty feet long and as round and thick as an oil drum, with bristling hair. They had come upon two of them napping in the afternoon heat. The mate of the slain beast had escaped. They discussed posting guards all night in case the female had been able to track them to the island to mourn for her love or to avenge herself. There were no volunteers.

Swamp worms, Kengee learned, could move at amazing speeds in and out of the water. In the water, they attacked their enemies by lashing them with their powerful bodies. On land, they rolled over on them or reared up and butted them to death with their heavy, bony heads. The meat of the swamp worm was succulent and spicy and almost worth the danger of hunting and killing one.

"Why do you travel alone?" The headman was staring at Kengee and the chattering of the barbarians abruptly ceased.

"No one wished to accompany me on my journey to the south."

"You go to Lornz?"

"To Lornz."

"None of us have gone to Lornz," he said with regret in his voice. "None of us have been called by Lornz. Where do you come from?"

Kengee described the island where he and Gosho had

obtained the Takusa milk. He named the headman and some of the other barbarians, but the headman of this island and the others were not interested. They did not know the island or its tribe since their migratory route did not go near those parts of lower Ta.

"I don't know exactly how to find Lornz," Kengee confessed.

"We don't either. We have not been called and therefore we have not sought the way."

The talk died down and one by one the barbarians fell asleep where they lay, their arms and legs stretched out on the soft mud. Both the men and women began trumpeting snores through their slack mouths, and the snores soon became a hideous symphony which forced Kengee to retreat to a quieter place. He was careful not to withdraw so far as to break the new intimacy with these people which had been so difficult to establish. If he slept down on the beach where it was quiet, he would be considered an outsider again in the morning.

He slept midway to the water and he slept very lightly. He woke up often as he always did in a strange bed or a strange place. Once when he awoke, he heard a loud scratching noise on the beach below him. At first he saw nothing, but then one of Ta's moons broke through the thinning mist and he saw the giant worm moving slowly toward him, sniffing the mud and then raising its head ten feet above the beach to search with its sparkling green eyes. It spotted the glowing embers of a nearly dead fire and began to pick up speed.

Kengee panicked. He leaped up and bolted to the left, hoping to get out of the way of the beast's charge toward the sleeping barbarians. But the worm saw him and veered in his direction. Kengee ran up a hill with the worm gaining fast. Kengee screamed, awakening the barbarians who reached for their spears. Kengee dashed between two rocks as the creature rammed at him with its heavy head. He could smell its thick breath—rather minty and not at all unpleasant. Kengee clung to the opposite side of the rock whimpering as the animal roared in anger and pain. It had wedged its head between the two rocks and was thrashing about violently in an effort to pry itself free. Furious, the beast arched its tubular body and lurched backward. It was free at last or at least its body was free. The beast had left her severed head still stuck between the rocks.

The barbarians from one side and Kengee from the other cautiously approached the thrashing, headless body. When her violent death throes became only a prolonged quiver, the barbarians rushed toward Kengee laughing and began rubbing and patting his stomach—the most friendly gesture known to these savages.

"You truly are one who has been called by Lornz," the headman said solemnly. "You risked your life to lead the beast away from the tribe and then brought about her death in a very clever way. Only a man called by Lornz could have been so unselfish and so smart." And then he too began to enthusiastically massage Kengee's stomach, while pushing him gently back to the fire with his free hand. Once there, the barbarians pushed and shoved each other for the brief chance to lay hands upon Kengee's belly.

In the morning, they shared with some fumbling and much embarrassment their best food with him. Except for the rare ceremonial feasts, they were not used to showing generosity to strangers or even to one another. The beast had been sliced into thin slabs of meat which were roasted on hot stones. While they ate, the barbarians told Kengee he must go farther west until he reached a great waterway which would carry him southward to Lornz. They had decided to be helpful to this heroic man who had saved them from a painful death.

He found the waterway within a few hours and without trouble and began navigating down its winding course past hundreds of circular and oblong islands decorated like cakes with the sickening pink plants that flourished in lower Ta. He did not have to use his engine since the boat drifted with the swift current in and out of the pockets of mist. There was more sunshine as he went further south and it grew hotter.

Once when he came out of the mist, he surprised three flatheads on a weed raft. They began screaming hysterically but when he drifted past them they first appeared shocked and then insulted that he had not killed them for food. The two males overcome by this humiliation threw the female into the water and then dove in themselves. The two males did not surface but he was able to shove the crude raft toward the clawing hands of the female. Without hesitation or loss of pride, she remounted the raft. As he drifted farther away from her, the female rubbed her banana-shaped breasts with one hand and between her legs with the other while giving him a simian leer. He waved back. The flathead was all woman.

When the current began to slow, he restarted the engine and putted down the waterway, lying back and working the tiller with two fingers. He smiled to himself. His luck was holding and there was no reason why it should desert him. That night, he tied up to a rock on an island, made a fire, and speared the plentiful fish swarming in the channel. He was up at the first flicker of light and on his way again.

He was driving hard toward his objective, no longer worried about the coming encounter with Lornz. It might not be so difficult to kill this barbarian chief after all. And if he did this, he would be a hero on Ta and live happily for the rest of his life with lots of money and plenty of Ta girls. The rewards were very tempting.

He began to pass tribal fishing fleets and inhabited islands, but he ignored these barbarians and they ignored him. Three days later, the traffic on the waterway increased. Men and women were crowded aboard dilapidated steamboats, exchanging smiles with him. These, he was sure, had been called by Lornz. Their beaming faces were devoid of thought, burning only with a silly ecstasy. He had seen religious fanatics in heat before. The barbarian communities on the islands became larger as Kengee and the pilgrims traveled farther south. On one island, there were a thousand Takusite huts. Downstream from this island, he went ashore for the night. Small fires burned on all the nearby islands, marking the encampments of those who had been called by Lornz.

In the morning, the pilgrim boats formed a long line

and Kengee cut in behind them to let the others lead the way. Trailing the religious convoy, he could sense the growing excitement among the pilgrims and knew the capital must be close. At noon, they reached it. In the harbor, dozens of small boats were tied up, and he could see some of those who had been called by Lornz already climbing a steep highway paved with crushed shells that wound white and sparkling among the pink plants. There were no houses to be seen anywhere.

Once his boat was secured, Kengee joined the slow-moving procession of pilgrims. No words were spoken. The only sound was the crunching noise of shells under feet. As the highway rose from the harbor, he saw hundreds of man-made caves carved into the soft, white chalk hills, and barbarians—mostly women and children—stood in the square doorways watching the procession. When a woman pilgrim fell from exhaustion, two young girls rushed from a cave with water to revive her. They got her to her feet and supported her between them for the rest of the march. It was the most kindly act Kengee had seen yet on Ta and he was impressed. Perhaps Lornz was truly a good man. If so, he would feel bad about killing him.

The road dipped and then snaked across a wide plain toward a woods which could only be the grove where Lornz preached to those he had called. The people next to him began to breathe hard and fast. Tears formed in their eyes and they clutched their chests with trembling hands. They walked on for awhile in this state and then could hold back no longer. They all broke into a wild run, shrieking the name of Lornz as they raced toward the woods. They pounded down a path leading into the grove and only stopped when they reached a clearing of flat ground rubbed into a hard smoothness by the wallowing bodies of the faithful. The newcomers tore off their clothes and rolled about on the ground, and Kengee did as they did.

This religious exercise continued until all who had been called by Lornz for the day arrived. Then a man in a pink robe emerged from the depths of the grove and clapped his delicate hands five or six times. The pilgrims rose to their knees, and fell silent. He studied their filthy bodies for a few moments before speaking.

"Lornz is pleased and Lornz will appear before you by nightfall, maybe. He bids you to rest in the shade and drink and eat."

The man then raised both arms and thundered, "Lornz is we and we are Lornz."

"Lornz is we and we are Lornz," chorused back the faithful and they began brushing the dirt off their bodies and redressing. They slipped into the coolness of the grove where jars of chilled water were waiting next to baskets of food—dried fish. The water was good but the fish were too salty and dry.

"When will Lornz come?" asked a young woman sitting next to Kengee.

"Before nightfall, maybe," he replied.

"And then Lornz will be we and we will be Lornz."

"Lornz willing," replied Kengee.

"Lornz willing," echoed the woman a little unhappily.

"He'll be willing," Kengee said to cheer her up.

"No one knows the will of Lornz."

"We shall wait and see then."

"It is the wise thing to do," she replied.

"Shall we see the great Takusa?" asked a man nearby.

"I hope not," Kengee blurted out and the man glared.

"If Lornz allows it," the woman said.

"No one knows what Lornz will allow," a voice from the grove said.

"We must wait and see," said another voice.

"It is the wise thing to do," said the woman.

This talk was getting on Kengee's nerves. He was beginning to develop a strong dislike for Lornz and decided maybe it would not be so hard to poison or stab the bastard after all.

"If Lornz is willing," the woman said again. She smiled very sweetly at Kengee.

Toward nightfall, the man in the pink robe reappeared among them and announced, "Lornz will be with you in the morning, maybe. Good night." He offered no explanation and there were no questions.

144

"Lornz is we and we are Lornz," the pilgrims chanted over and over again.

"The arrogant son of a bitch," Kengee said aloud in English. The woman looked frightened but he paid no attention to her and flopped back on the ground to sleep. After a few minutes, the woman settled down beside him and stared at his profile in the fading light.

"You frighten me," she said and shifted closer to him. Black smoke from the smudge pots set up to drive off the swarming insects enveloped both of them for a moment. She plucked a piece of flesh from a fish carcass and tried to force it into his mouth. He shook his head but she pressed her fingers with their gift into his mouth anyway. Her greasy fingertips caressed his lips on the way out.

"You speak such strange words sometimes," she said and rubbed her cheek against his.

"I become overwhelmed by the thought of Lornz and my words come tumbling out all mixed up. I am an emotional man." He touched her breast.

"Most men are," she said. "Say something nice in mixed-up words."

"I'd like to fuck you."

"That sounds so beautiful. What does it mean?"

"I love you," he translated.

"I wanted you in my nest since I first saw you on the road," she said.

"You should have been thinking about Lornz," he teased.

"I was, but my eyes were free to look."

"Close your eyes now." She did and Kengee's hand hurriedly entered her smocklike shirt.

"Lornz is we and we are Lornz," shouted a man in the darkness. Others took up the chant, waking those who already had fallen asleep, and then they joined in too.

"Shit," Kengee said.

"I love you, too," the girl said, jerking herself from his arms and body. She sat up, tilted back her head, and yelled, "Lornz is we and we are Lornz."

It was not until just before dawn that the voices grew hoarser, fainter, and fewer, and eventually there was si-

145

lence again. Everyone slept quietly in the few hours left to them, including Kengee and the girl, but they slept apart from each other.

After breakfast, they all disrobed and rolled around on the dirt in the clearing for an hour or so to work up enthusiasm for the coming of Lornz. Kengee joined the rest. They were even more dirty than yesterday and sweating heavily when the man in pink finally arrived.

"Lornz is coming," he announced in a booming voice. The rollers struggled to their feet and their eager, intense eyes turned toward the path down which Lornz would soon come. Insects sang the minutes away and tension among the pilgrims became almost unbearable. A few developed spastic twitches and others began to rock rhythmically on their feet. Kengee joined the rockers.

And then Lornz came. He wore a robe of green that brushed his bare toes. It was loose fitting and almost but not quite hid his paunch, which only a man who thinks rather than works for a living could produce in lower Ta. He had surprisingly soft features for a barbarian and he was balding. He reminded Kengee of some friendly, middle-aged supermarket clerk, but no supermarket clerk ever had eyes like his. They were big and brown and, yes, beautiful. When he gazed at one of those whom he had called, the pilgrim trembled all over. He played with his personal electricity for awhile, jolting this man and that woman. This seemed to amuse him. Standing behind Lornz was a big barbarian with a contented, cruel sneer on his face. He towered over Lornz and was armed with an axe as were the other men who guarded the great Lornz.

"Shoomud, my stool," Lornz ordered kindly. The big man raised his hand and two of the guards hurried forward with a very large stool. Lornz did not sit down on it. He mounted it and began to speak.

"I have called and you have come. Now you are I and I am you. We are one as we once were when Ta and our people, the only true humans, were young. In those long-ago days, Ta nourished us and we loved Ta in return. She offered much but we took sparingly. We

146

lived simply and honestly. We were fewer then but happier. It was a time when all plants grew free, before some were imprisoned in square plots and forced as slaves to unwillingly give themselves to the men of upper Ta. But we also sinned. We devoured plants, too. But we were forgiven because we died and they in turn ate us, and we respected their freedom. We ate no flesh in those days, neither the flesh from the water nor the land. The plants provided us with all the vitamins and proteins we needed.

"And then the men with their swords came out of the cold north. They killed not only for food but for pleasure and learned how to enslave plants in wet, square, unhealthy prisons. They pressed their two-pronged swords to the throat of Ta and forced her to obey. She was made to give more than she wished and to give without love. Our people had no choice but to rise up against this rapine, and we gave battle. We fought and retreated and fought again and retreated again. And by killing men, we learned to despise life, all life—man life, animal life, and plant life. We were corrupted and we therefore lost, and in so doing abandoned the plants in the north to the heartless men of upper Ta.

"Although we were evil, Ta forgave us and provided a refuge for us in these overheated, muggy, miserable swamps. It's a lousy place to live, but it's a home for all of us. But wherever there is land, there is rent to pay, even here. The great headman of old, Mertz, was told the price and he told the people the price. No more plant food. Eat flesh from the water and from the land and a few permissible swamp weeds and land berries. Get your nutrition this way but do not taste the forbidden plants that grow on dry land. We have obeyed. But all this meat has made us selfish and brutal. The men from upper Ta call us barbarians and they are right: we are barbarians.

"But we are very strange barbarians. We are frightened barbarians, afraid of war. In the past, we lost too many battles. But despite our cowardice, Ta protects us and provides us with a way to hold off the men from upper

Ta. Takusa gave us her milk with which we were able to appease the men from the north.

"This does not mean we are more cowardly than the men from upper Ta. We gave them too many victories. They became less interested in war with each triumph since the code of the swordholder is far more suitable to defeat than to victory. Victory means surviving and defeat means dying, and they considered dying in battle an honor. Too often, they were deprived of the chance of this honor by our poor battle performance, and this was our victory over them.

"And the Takusa milk made them traders and factory managers and businessmen who make poor warriors. They are now interested only in accumulating wealth through manufacturing and enslaving plants. They are greedy and depraved men, and the Takusa plant is weary of working for them. She has decided we can live without processed goods and products. Do not question the wisdom of the Takusa."

There were some unhappy faces in the crowd despite the reverence in which Lornz was held. He smiled down on these faces, offering a little sympathy but not much.

"The ways of the Takusa are beyond our understanding but no one can deny that the Takusa has superior intelligence and superior morality and superior cunning to any man. If we must suffer for months, years, or decades, there is a good reason for it. We should not question but in all humility accept the fate drawn for us by Takusa. And in these difficult times, we must become one people again, united in our love of Takusa and all plants. If the armies again come from the north, we must fight them. If assassins come, we must destroy them."

The last remark made Kengee feel very uneasy. He had not been impressed with all of Lornz's plant crap, but he was jarred when Lornz specifically mentioned assassins. He had also noticed that Shoomud had not been listening to Lornz but had been studying each face in the crowd including Kengee's.

"Someday, and that day may not be far off, the great Takusa plant will tell us to go north again and reclaim

148

our lost land and liberate all the plants. This sacred war, this sacred mission, we will eagerly accept.

"Since I am you and you are I, we shall remain one in everything we do. Lornz called you and Lornz will send you away but never again will we be separated. Go, but break no blade of grass without an apology. But before you go, you shall receive a sacred drink from the great Takusa, a potion that makes men and plants brothers, and women and plants sisters. It also tastes good, so good you will desire it always. But remember only Takusa can give you this potion."

Lornz then climbed off the stool, assisted by two guards. With Shoomud at his heels, he led the believers down a path that went deeper into the grove. Inside another wide, sunlit clearing, Lornz stopped and pointed to the great Takusa plant, swollen with juices and ready to start pumping. Takusa fluttered its leaves in welcome. Cups were piled high on a table and each pilgrim took one and reverently approached the great Takusa.

The believers held their cups under the nipples of the plant and a fluid gushed out. To Kengee, the fluid looked like California orange juice. He was not the first to go forward nor the last. When his turn came, the Takusa plant's green leaves brushed discreetly but deliberately against his knee. For him, Takusa squirted out not an orange-colored drink but a transparent liquid.

It tasted like a slightly warm martini. He never drank this early in the morning but it had been a bad night and he downed the sacred potion that would make him a brother to plants. As he did so, he realized that this Takusa plant was like the other he had met, knowing him and his likes and dislikes. He concluded that they chatted back and forth over some kind of plant radio network or in some other far more mysterious way. This one also knew he liked martinis but he was more disturbed by what Takusa liked. The leaf that had brushed against his knee was charged with passion.

After he had finished his drink, Kengee felt a little dizzy. He was sure that it had been a double. The others stood around bright-eyed, smacking their lips like a bunch of children. When they began drifting in twos and threes down the path again, Takusa began whispering to him.

"O.K. So I gave them California orange juice. It's good for them." The Takusa was speaking in her most sultry voice and speaking in English. Lornz swiveled his head. "We hear you, Takusa, but we do not understand your words." The plant seemed to sigh deeply and then turned itself off. Lornz after awhile began to feel a little foolish with his arms spread out waiting for some great pronouncement which after a few moments of silence was obviously not going to be uttered by Takusa. Finally, he dropped his arms and hurried off embarrassed.

"Lornz is we and we are Lornz." The pilgrims had begun their chant again but Lornz did not look back.

Kengee joined the others on the path and in shouting praises to Lornz. The man in pink led them back through the grove and pointed the way to the highway that would take them past the chalk caves and to the harbor where all their boats were moored. Kengee hung back, hoping for a chance to duck into the grove and hide. If he was ever to return to upper Ta, he knew he must kill Lornz. If he could remain concealed until night, perhaps he could find Lornz's cave and kill him quickly. He knew there was no possibility of making a deal with this fanatic.

But at that moment, the man in pink put his hand lightly on Kengee's arm. "Lornz has chosen you to talk to. It is a great honor. Follow me."

Kengee followed the man with great apprehension. He suspected that Lornz had found him out and was desperately looking for a way to run. Then the broad side of Shoomud's axe slammed against his back, knocking him flat. Shoomud glared down at him and the guards quickly bound his arms. One of them applied pressure with his fingers to Kengee's neck and he passed out.

EIGHT

Hibee had received high marks in arson at the Zabo training school. She set fire to the steamboat two miles downstream from the capital. Within minutes flames engulfed the craft and then there was a loud explosion when the Takusite fuel was ignited. For an instant, the canal was lit up for hundreds of yards in a blinding flash, and then the boat sank with a sizzling sound and the water was quiet and black again. It was a good job. There were no survivors. She had earlier knifed or poisoned the boatmaster and his crew. She doubted if anyone would bother to investigate the accident as long as the wreckage did not interfere with canal traffic, and she was certain that the steamboat had disintegrated in the blast. The Zabo knowing its own would believe that Hibee had obeyed orders and poisoned herself before the explosion or that she took this spiteful and spectacular way to commit suicide. Many of the Zabo when the time came preferred to take companions with them in death. She was certain that the Zabo would not be looking for her.

Hibee ran the two miles to the capital and then hurried at a less conspicuous speed through the dark, twisting streets that led to the Institute for Human Perfection, where she sensed Tanee was held prisoner. The feeling of dread within her told Hibee that Tanee was in extreme danger and her logic told her that the possessor was a captive in one of the Institute's underground cells.

The high wall surrounding the Institute was made of smooth, glasslike Takusite. Hoso apparently was so confident that no one could scale the wall that no towers had been erected for guards. Hibee kicked off her boots

151

and from her robe withdrew a Zabo climbing kit. With a drill, she bored the first hole into the hard surface and then inserted a spike. Pressing her body flat against the wall, she pushed herself upward with her foot and then drilled the next hole. It took her two hours to squirm to the top, but not once during the ascent had she even come close to falling. She had been practicing wall climbing since she was twelve and had gone up even more difficult walls than this under the eyes of Zabo instructors. She let her legs dangle over the top of the wall and rested, waiting patiently until her breathing returned to normal before uncoiling a strong thin cord from around her waist. This she tied firmly to two spikes and then lowered herself into the dark courtyard below.

The main Institute building with its peaked roof and rough Takusite brick exterior presented no problem. Every window and door would be easy to enter. As it turned out, the side door was open and she slipped into the main hall. She stood frozen in the darkness for a long time, listening for any human sounds. Her ears were so sensitive she could detect a heartbeat across a room or breathing at much greater distances. It was all part of the Zabo training. Soon she determined that a man was at the end of the hall. She guessed he was guarding the circular stairs which led down to the cells. She knew the building well. Several years ago one of her Zabo brothers had penetrated the Institute and assassinated a prisoner before Hoso's guards could extract by torture secrets which the Zabo did not wish disclosed. The Zabo later gave a lecture on his successful mission, and Hibee had memorized the layout of the building for future reference.

The prison cells were deep below ground and could be reached only by the circular stairwell which was always guarded. Hibee moved toward the man, taking advantage of the dark recesses in the doorways. A faint light was cast up into the hall from the stairwell and as she got closer she saw the guard was leaning against the railing, his back to the stairs. She could easily kill him but it would be best for the time being to allow him to live. Therefore, she spent more precious time quietly

152

and slowly circling behind him and then slipping down the stairs unseen and unheard.

In the long corridor below, where moisture glistened on the gray bricks, she heard men talking in loud voices in the guardroom. She darted past the open guardroom door. One of the guards was describing in detail how he had tortured a woman the night before and what devices had caused her to scream the loudest. Hibee grimaced. The doors to the cells were identical—heavy, solid Takusite, each with a peephole. She did not need to look inside the cells. Although it was very faint, she felt Tanee's presence. She picked the lock of a door by working her small finger into the large keyhole and eased the door open.

Inside the room, a torch was burning, and lying on the bed was Tanee, pale and drained of almost all life. But something was very wrong. Hibee did not feel the reunion she sought. She studied the unconscious woman, touched her, and then smelled her faint breath. Hibee realized that the spirit of Tanee was not there and had not occupied this body for some time. The body was drugged. But she was puzzled why she had been drawn here so strongly and why she still was. Tanee, she decided, must be very near, hovering perhaps hopelessly close to her real self and suffering terribly. Hibee suddenly felt Tanee's pain.

She relocked the door and retraced her route past the guardroom and up the winding steps. She roamed through the building and courtyard for a half-hour, seeing nothing, sensing nothing. And then she felt waves of fierce, almost unbearable pain coming from a low building toward the back of the compound where Hoso's agents and guards were quartered. When she reached the building, she pressed her ear against the wall, listening to the rumbling, deep sounds of male voices and laughter. Male noises of all kinds disgusted her, but she moved along the building trying to feel Tanee's pain again. She was becoming more and more desperate. At last, a voice touched her—it seemed to call to her and she listened intently.

"You're wasting away," the first poisoner said.

"I'm very tired," the second poisoner replied. "Tired of being locked up like a prisoner in the Institute."

"So am I, but my hands don't shake and I'm not losing weight. We have been ordered to wait until the possessor returns and then we can practice our trade and make her suffer for the time we have spent waiting."

"I have a headache," the second poisoner complained.

"What you need is a woman," the first poisoner said. "You haven't had a woman in weeks and that's not like you. I'll go and find one in the barracks—used already this night no doubt, but better than nothing."

"Please don't bother," said the second poisoner. "I'm not up to it. I just need rest."

Hibee quickly entered the building and went down the hall to the door where the two poisoners were talking. Her hand deftly brushed her robe back and drew the dagger from her thigh. She tapped on the door and it immediately flew open.

"I don't have to go looking," said the first poisoner. "We have a pretty one right here." He reached toward her and she came eagerly into his arms, and drove the dagger accurately and hard into the man's chest, penetrating his heart. She caught him in her arms and then lowered him quietly to the floor. Hibee grinned at the second poisoner.

"So it is Hibee of the Zabo. You remembered me after all."

"Yes, I finally remembered you. I had to come."

"And what will the Zabo say about this? You do not come on the Zabo's command, I know."

"I obeyed the Zabo's last order, but since you extracted the poison from my tooth, I did not die. No one owns me now." Her eyes were bright. "Tanee, you are beautiful."

"Your taste in men is deplorable," Tanee said. "My nose is too flat and my shoulders too thin and I have very perverted interests in women."

"I do not mean as you are now. I mean you, the real you. I saw you sleeping in a cell, drugged and very pale but still so beautiful."

"So you were there. I have never underestimated the

154

abilities of Zabo women, but still that was a remarkable feat. I know you are trying to help me, but I'm here and my body is imprisoned in a cell and drugged. I cannot rejoin myself nor can I go away."

"Tanee, I've come to take you away, all of you."

"Is that possible?"

"It is if we go within the next two hours before dawn. It will be work, but it will not be difficult work. Come."

They hurried to the main building with Hibee whispering her plan to Tanee as they went. They entered through the side door. The guard was still leaning on the railing of the circular stairway and Tanee as the poisoner strode boldly up to him. His hand grasped his sword hilt but then slipped off when he recognized the poisoner.

"Is Jore below? If so send word to him that there is something in my room worth trying." The guard smiled.

"He will not be off duty for two more hours but I'll pass the word down. If he's too tired, I'll service the something in your room." They both laughed.

"Jore cannot be that tired. He's done nothing but talk this night. There are no woman prisoners needing his attention."

The guard's reply was a surprised gasp. Hibee had slammed her foot against his spine, and Tanee at the same instant clasped her hand over his mouth to stop any further pointless talk. Hibee drove her fist into his neck, smashing his windpipe, and after a few more vicious blows he died. They then went down the stairs and past the guardroom where the voices were now only a low, tired murmur. Once inside the cell, Hibee gently lifted Tanee's body and placed it in the arms of the poisoner. "I'll need both hands free for my weapons," she explained.

But her weapons were not needed. They left the cellar and the building undetected. Hibee scaled the wall, pulling herself up by the thin cord which she had left secured to the spikes at the top. Once on top, the poisoner under Tanee's control looped the cord around her drugged body and then Hibee hauled her up and lowered her down on the other side. Another cord dropped at the poisoner's feet. The man's body was clumsy and Hibee had to exert all her strength to help him to the top of the wall.

"If you were not inside this male beast, I would have gladly let you fall." Hibee was panting hard.

"I'd like to get rid of him too. I've dwelled too long in his filthy mind. But he'll have to remain alive until the drug wears off."

The descent was much easier. Hibee came last removing the spikes as she went. She wanted no evidence left behind showing a Zabo's presence. She had used her hands to kill the guard, hoping they would believe the murders were committed by a man and not a woman.

They supported Tanee's body between them with her arms resting limply across their shoulders. They dragged her through the dark streets where most of the torches already had burned out. They were beginning to tire when a swordholder staggered out of an alley and fixed his watery eyes on them.

"Friend, you have two women and I have none. And one is in a fine wine sleep. I like them that way. As a swordholder, I demand her."

"If you carry her to my home, you can do what you wish with her," Hibee purred. "She's a nuisance and deserves a lesson. Always passing out. She is no friend of mine nor of my man here. I would enjoy watching you do painful things to her."

The swordholder took Tanee's body in his strong arms. "When I'm finished with her, she'll weep for a month. Do you object, friend?"

"She's no affair of mine," the poisoner's voice said.

When they passed under a torch which was still burning, the swordholder asked why Tanee was so pale.

"You'll put color into her again," Hibee said with a giggle. They went on for fifteen more minutes with the swordholder charging fast ahead of them, eager to begin his sport with the girl. For variety, Hibee decided to use her darts this time. She hurled one poisoned dart into the man's back, which permanently destroyed his lust. She moved fast to catch Tanee's body before it fell and was bruised. Hibee kicked the corpse after retrieving the dart. They left him dead in the middle of the road.

Hibee led the way up a narrow byway and then picked the lock of a door. She explained that this was a Zabo refuge but seldom used anymore and almost forgotten. She was sure they would not be disturbed.

Upstairs, Tanee examined herself carefully. Hoso's people had force-fed the body through tubes, but this nourishment had been sufficient only to keep the body barely alive. It would take time to regain her strength. Several days at the least. They waited beside the body late into the morning until the drug wore off. Hibee had hovered uncomfortably near the sleeping Tanee, often wiping her face with a damp cloth and holding her hand. Tanee wished the girl would leave her sleeping self alone. It was annoying.

Finally Tanee nodded, and Hibee bound the poisoner's arms and legs. When this was done, Tanee made the leap back to herself, announcing her presence in her own body with a weak voice. Hibee glared down at the bewildered poisoner. This time, she used her strangling cord. It took more effort and time, but Hibee hated this man. When it was finally over, she pushed the body down the stairs where it would wait until night when Hibee could dump it into a nearby canal. She spent the afternoon brewing and spooning thick tabo soup into Tanee's mouth and wiping her forehead frequently and clutching her hands as often as she could. Over the next few days, Tanee slept most of the time, waking only to eat. Hibee was always by her side.

Kengee woke up in a cage with bars of speckled blue coral. The bars shone like jewels in the light of the lone torch in the chalk cave wall. The walls of the cave were white, stained by tiny rivers of yellow water which trickled down from above. It was a pleasantly cool, deep cave. Kengee vaguely recalled hands searching through his robe and removing all the weapons and poisons. He knew he was defenseless, stripped of all his tools of death. He did not bother to try to sit up but lay on his back and stared up at the ceiling of the cave. He kept staring at the ceiling even when he saw out of the corner of his eye Lornz and Shoomud come down the steps, looking like two eager executioners.

"The assassin awakens," Lornz chuckled.

"It was not necessary that he wake up at all," said Shoomud. "That was your idea and a poor one."

"Silence, Shoomud. I do nothing lightly or without reason. We promised a high payment to have him delivered to us and we must get our full value out of him."

"Do you really intend to pay the Zabo?"

"No. We need the Zabo no longer."

"My faith in you is restored," Shoomud said acidly.

"Your faith always remains questionable." Lornz approached the cage and poked his finger into Kengee's stomach.

"No fat. A good, flat stomach. Sit up, Kengee. Unfortunately the cage is not high enough for you to stand up. But if it is uncomfortable, remember the discomfort you hoped to inflict upon me." Kengee sat up feeling a sharp pain where the side of the axe had slammed against his back. He looked down and saw that his knees were bloody. The bastards had dragged him to the cave.

"Mako must have searched all over upper Ta to find a swordholder with your initiative and skill. I do believe you might have succeeded if you had not been betrayed from the start." He picked up the arsenal of lethal weapons one by one from a nearby rock where they were on display.

"You do not follow orders very well, do you, Kengee? That is not like a swordholder from upper Ta. You changed your routes and arrived unobserved, causing Shoomud here all kinds of worry. Now that is interesting. Not his worrying but your behavior. Have swordholders degenerated so much in this generation that the old code of obedience can now be dismissed by any individual? And there is something else that is interesting about you. Our spies in the north say you were a stupid child and a stupider man and then suddenly you became terribly clever."

"I was always misunderstood," Kengee said.

"I am trying to understand you, Kengee, and I advise

158

you to help me in this task. First, I want to know why you accepted such a dangerous mission—a suicidal mission. You don't strike me as a courageous man."

"Better you than me."

"I can appreciate that, but did you really think you could kill Lornz and then return safely to the north?"

Actually Kengee thought he could have outsmarted the dumb barbarians, but in his situation he did not want to insult Lornz, so he hung his head as if admitting his foolishness.

"And there is another matter." Lornz was now circling the cage with his thumbs linked behind him and with a troubled face.

"There is the matter of the Takusa milk. We received rather confusing information from the island you visited, but as confusing as this information is, it establishes the fact that you had something to do with obtaining the milk. How did you manage that?"

"Ask Takusa."

"We've been treating you gently. You reside in a pretty little cage and we keep a torch burning so you can admire the chalk cave walls and we are even considering freeing you. To repay all this kindness, you could at least give me a little information."

"Let me get at him," Shoomud snarled.

"Shoomud had a very unhappy childhood and a destructive one. He was always breaking things—pulling legs off bugs and twisting the necks of small animals. He has never outgrown these infantile habits." Shoomud grinned at Kengee and Kengee managed to smile politely back.

"You do not fully realize yet where you are and what horrible things might happen to you. I will give you some time to think undisturbed in your cage."

As they departed, Shoomud, who seemed always to be in a mean mood, doused the torch in a jar of water, leaving Kengee in the dark to think about where he was and all the horrible things which very probably would happen to him. This took about a minute. Then he spent about five minutes trying to loosen the bars of the cage. Impossible. He spent the next ten minutes groaning and shedding a few tears. This made him feel very tired so he placed his arms between his knees and went to sleep.

Outside the cave, Lornz asked Shoomud what they should do about Kengee. "Roll the rock away and let the water come in and drown him," Shoomud strongly recommended.

"Why do that when we do not know enough about him yet?"

"When we do, it will be too late."

"What do you mean by that?"

"I mean that Takusa has betrayed you with this man. She has bestowed favors on a swordholder from the north after warning you about him. He is now your rival and it would be best if we kill him immediately."

"Shoomud you know nothing about Takusa, nothing at all. Only I talk with Takusa, only I alone. She has chosen me to hear her desires and to preach her word to all; to carry out her will. I was chosen from among all our people by Takusa. And if Takusa really helped this stranger, then it was because she had some plan in mind which eventually she will reveal to me. Takusa could never have any liking for a man from upper Ta where they imprison and mistreat plants. She hates them all and we need not have any concern about this Kengee."

"He thinks differently from the rest. He acted independently, chosing his own way to come to Lornz," Shoomud's voice was loud and sarcastic.

"He may have the blood of those who have never touched the sword in him, which would naturally make him different. It happens sometimes in the best families in upper Ta. Or he may be one of those Zabo murder machines. I do not trust the Zabo. I know only that he is a scoundrel and an opportunist. I'll talk to him once more and then I will allow you to roll the rock away and drown him."

Three mornings after her arrival in the Zabo safe house, Tanee woke up feeling refreshed and strong. She took her first shaky steps alone. When Hibee put her arm around her to help, she squirmed out of the girl's grasp and Hibee looked hurt.

"Hibee, I am grateful to you and all that, but I am made the way I am and there is no way I can change. I must remain myself, a woman with normal womanly desires." Hibee began to cry and Tanee patted her shoulder.

"We always will be the very closest of friends."

"That is all I want, Tanee, all that I have desired since you first possessed me."

"Possession is a very intimate act."

"Tanee, please do it again, please."

"Hibee, what are you asking?"

"I want you to enter my head, please."

"Only that? I don't suppose it would do any harm and I do feel exceptionally vigorous this morning. Maybe it would be a good idea to get back into practice again." Tanee possessed her. Their minds immediately felt an unimaginably strong rapport—a warm, overpowering, and complete relationship. Giggling silently like teen-age girls, they traded secrets and emotions—exchanging feelings and confiding hopes and desires. They also did a little gossiping. Hibee's mind was bursting with infectious high spirits which Tanee could not resist. She felt like she was running barefoot in the sunshine.

The mind-mingling went on for most of the morning. Although Tanee held much of herself back, Hibee withheld nothing. Tanee absorbed her sad, short life. She was sympathetic and tried to soothe the unhappy ex-Zabo girl. Everything poured into Tanee's mind. Tanee learned of her Zabo training that destroyed love before it could even grow. The discipline of the Zabo buried such emotions; not even friendship was permitted the Zabo. Hibee had never felt so strongly before and the sudden outpouring of her affection disturbed Tanee. With gentleness she disengaged herself from Hibee's mind and returned to the solitude of her own body.

"That was wonderful." Hibee was sobbing happily. "Can we do it again sometime?"

"Yes, but not too often. It isn't good for you too often."

"Do you love this Kengee?" Hibee asked a little too stiffly. During the mind-mingling, Hibee had tried to ferret out this secret. Tanee had walled off her feelings about Kengee, but there had been cracks in the wall.

"You fear that he will be killed, don't you?"

"I feel he needs help. He always needs help. He has no allies against the Zabo nor against Lornz. They have worked together to destroy him and somehow they employed Denzo in their plot. Mako took Denzo's advice too readily. Why? I must go south. I must. He is basically a nice boy, but he cannot do anything right alone. He's emotionally unstable and emotionally immature."

"To go south without understanding why the Zabo and Lornz are allied would be dangerous," Hibee said. "We must know their plans and the extent of their collaboration. I will go to the house of Denzo because the secret must be there." Hibee took a quick inventory of her tools and weapons and left after squeezing Tanee's hand tenderly. Tanee thought then that she should revisit Hibee's mind and try to redirect this girl's interests toward men somehow.

The wall around Denzo's garden was low and Hibee went over it without need of her climbing kit. She crouched in the dark garden when she heard the gravel on the path crunch. But it was only an old servant carrying a water jar. When she heard only the sounds of the night, she crept to the house and climbed to the second story. Balancing on a narrow ledge she worked her way to a lighted window.

Macha sat moodily with one of her veiled companions. She alone sipped tea and ate while the girl waited and watched for the moment when she must pour more tea or remove a bowl. Hibee had heard of Macha's vanity and despised her as a worthless, spoiled daughter of a rich swordholder. Finally Macha ostentatiously stretched and yawned, covering her mouth with her hand. She gave a cold command to the girl who hurriedly departed with the cups and bowls. Once the girl was gone, Macha's languor vanished in an instant. She leaped up and slid the bolts home on the door and then came to the window. Hibee hurriedly stepped away along the ledge. The curtains were drawn but not completely. Hibee moved back in time to see Macha press the wall in three places.

The wall swung outward revealing the passageway, and Macha entered. The wall swung back into place again. After carefully exploring the window, Hibee realized it was a death trap. It had been secured against entry by Zabo techniques and this puzzled her. She moved farther down the ledge until she reached another window. She saw Macha's companion inside, sitting on a stool and combing her long aristocratic black hair with her back to the open window.

Hibee uncorked a cylinder and tossed it into the room. It fell silently to the floor near the girl. Within seconds the girl slid off the stool to the floor unconscious. Hibee entered the room holding her breath and closed the container again. She breathed at the window until the room was free of fumes and then approached the girl, flipping her over with a rough kick. When she looked into the sleeping girl's face, Hibee understood why the girl thought it wise to wear a veil. She was beautiful, almost as beautiful as Tanee. She was certainly too beautiful to destroy. Hibee therefore forced a powerful drug into the girl's mouth, enough to keep her sleeping through the night. Next she removed the girl's robe and pulled it over her own and covered her face with a veil. She propped the girl's head on a pillow and went out the door. She had carefully observed the girl in Macha's room and was confident she could copy her mannerisms and walk. Unfortunately she had not heard the girl speak and so would have to avoid conversation with anyone.

Hibee walked boldly down the hall and then quickly worked the bolts free on Macha's door with a thin wire. There were no Zabo contraptions. Once inside, she pressed the wall where Macha had pressed it and the secret panel opened. She went down the passageway and hid in the shadows when she heard voices. Carefully, she edged forward. A woman with silvery white hair but with a face as smooth and youthful as Macha's reclined in a hammock. She was far too pale and occasionally exploded into prolonged coughing.

"My daughter, you have learned everything there is to know about the Zabo, and it will soon be time for you to become its mistress. You have been trained all your life for this. You are a good Zabo and a good daughter and a worthy successor to me."

"Mother, you will recover."

"No. I should have died ten years ago, but you were not ready then. To live this long, it was necessary for me to withdraw from Ta and to conserve my strength. I've stretched out my life far too long and I am tired of the struggle. Are you ready, Macha?"

"I am, Mother."

"It will be necessary for you to marry to retain the wealth and power of this house for the Zabo. I have drawn up a list of suitable husbands. All are from important trading and factory-owning families and all are well below average in intelligence and docile in nature. You will find any of them as manageable as Denzo. Your husband's only value is to hold the wealth of this house and eventually to become one of the Committee of Five. You will guide him in his career and make all of the decisions. He will be encouraged by you and our friends to spend his time in the pillow houses where he can act the part of a man, a man you will not allow him to become outside the pillow houses."

"Yes, Mother."

"When you have him well under control and advancing in his career, you will kill Denzo so that you will have all his wealth for the Zabo."

"Patricide is a punishable crime, Mother."

"Punishable, yes, but you certainly know how to murder without detection. And he is not your father anyway. I chose a better mate to conceive you and you must do the same when the time comes. You must produce a superior female to inherit the Zabo and you know how to guarantee the birth of a woman child.

"I regret that I will not live to see the emergence of an all-powerful Zabo on Ta, but I shall die with a smile, knowing of the future. We are ready and will soon control most of the trade and manufacturing through the companies we are beginning to take over secretly. When

164

your husband becomes the Director of Ta—at the appropriate time—all power will be in Zabo hands, in your hands. The Zabo will have triumphed. For centuries we have worked and waited for this chance. It will be our revenge upon the descendants of those who murdered the queen of the Zabo tribe seven centuries ago and banished her people to the ranks of those who have never touched the sword. But soon the swordholders will become our servants. Daughter, make their lives miserable."

"Yes, Mother."

"But it is critical for our plans to monopolize the milk of the Takusa. This is the only way to become dominant on Ta."

"Do you really believe the barbarians will keep their word?"

"Of course not. Lornz already is stalling. He claims there are technical difficulties to overcome before the Takusa plants gush milk for us. He lies. He has no intention of providing Takusa milk to our companies. But I anticipated this, and Kengee was only our first move in the game with Lornz."

"Where is Kengee now?" Hibee noticed a trace of anxiety in her voice which her mother did not detect.

"Delivered as promised to Lornz. He now waits in a cage to be drowned, but he is no affair of ours. A strange man this Kengee. Denzo talked in his drunkenness to his mistress, a Zabo girl, about Kengee being brought to Ta from outside of Ta by the possessor Tanee. I do not believe that deformed woman has that much power, but it may be best for all of us if Kengee drowns. He might prove difficult for our plans."

"And what are we to do about Lornz's betrayal?"

The older woman chuckled. "Betrayal is nothing that should shock a Zabo. We, however, have taught Lornz one lesson. We sent an assassin to him, warning him how and when he would come, and still the assassin almost reached the target. I had expected even better results, but Kengee was too slow to strike. As you know we have our people in the south—our best women Zabo are now completely accepted as barbarians. When the

165

time is right, we shall send them one after another against Lornz. If one succeeds, it will be easy to deal with Shoomud. But even if they all fail, Lornz may soon tire of being constantly on guard against trained killers.

"He will die or submit to our demands eventually. And we are in no hurry. It might be better if upper Ta suffered greatly from a Takusa shortage before we obtain the supplies and make them available at our price. And our price will be partnerships in the trading companies and factories. We shall gradually take them all over with our front men, men bound to us by greed or fear. And a bit of advice, Macha—if any of these men proves difficult or tries to cheat us, kill him instantly. Terror and sudden death are the Zabo's most effective weapons."

"Yes, Mother."

The older woman began coughing again, causing the hammock to heave and drop with great violence. Macha shook her mother a little too roughly, Hibee thought. But the older woman fell into a peaceful sleep, breathing steadily once more. "I'll get the medicine, Mother." And Macha did get the medicine, but she poured the contents of a small bottle into her mother's ear, which struck Hibee as very strange.

Hibee retreated back down the passageway and reentered Macha's room, well satisfied with what she had learned. She carefully closed the secret panel. It was time to get back to Tanee and report. Excited by what she had discovered, she rushed to the door and threw back a bolt. She heard a swishing sound above her and dove toward the floor but too late to escape the trap completely. Her legs were ensnared in the coils of the trap which had been installed to capture an intruder when leaving rather than when entering the room. Hibee struggled to free herself but the coils only tightened more firmly around her legs. She managed to rise to her feet but her legs were squeezed tight and only her arms remained free. There was now nothing to do but wait for Macha to return.

When the secret panel opened, Hibee hurled her poison darts, but Macha was also Zabo-trained and leaped back. Macha crouched with a dagger in her hand. There were no more darts and Hibee could not reach her own dagger now lashed against her leg by the coils of the trap. Macha saw that her opponent was unarmed but advanced cautiously. She circled behind her. No words were spoken between the two women. Macha would have liked to question the woman in the trap but knew she most certainly was a Zabo defector and far too dangerous to take chances with. Hibee waited for the dagger to pierce her body and thought about Tanee, more worried about having failed her than about her own death. Macha was alert, watching for a final trick. She stepped forward quickly and drove the dagger deep into Hibee's back.

The door burst in splinters and Denzo was suddenly there swinging his sword scabbard. He hit the side of Macha's head and she fell hard and did not rise. The dagger remained in Hibee's back and blood was forming an ever-widening circle on her robe around the blade.

"The old fool was drunk again and his body is sluggish and slow."

"It's too late, Tanee. Kengee is a prisoner of Lornz in a cave far to the south." Tanee took one look at the wound and knew it was fatal. She therefore decided to administer a radical form of first aid.

"We must work quickly. You have only seconds to live."

"It's too late."

"Be quiet and try to relax and above all cooperate. Your body is dying but Macha's is in good enough shape except for a slight concussion. I will give Macha to you, body and mind."

Tanee possessed the dying Hibee, seizing all of her, absorbing her entire mind and being in preparation for the transplant. Next she possessed the unconscious mind of Macha, grimacing at what she found. It was a shame to give Hibee such a mind but Tanee thought Hibee might be able to clean it up and make it livable in time. Macha's mind awoke to fight the intruders, but with Hibee's help Macha was subdued and then destroyed. Once she was sure Hibee was in complete command and the transplant was a success, Tanee returned to the

167

drunken, dazed body of Denzo. She looked at Macha, now Hibee, and smiled at the pained look on the woman's face.

"I have an awful headache. My mind burns like fire."

"Do you find Macha's brain bearable?"

"There are terrible memories here, and guilt too. Do you know she has just poisoned her mother because she was growing impatient to take command of the Zabo?"

"Learn what you must and bury the rest if you can. I'm sorry that we had to work so fast or I would have found you a better home and a less dangerous one. You will have to work hard to keep yourself dominant. Even if Macha now is nothing more than memories and spent emotions, these can corrode and work evil. She is her mother's child."

"I hope her mother appreciated this flattering imitation of herself as she died. She must have known poison had been poured into her ear."

"It is good that she is dead or we would have had to kill her. The mother was too shrewd a woman not to detect that her daughter had been possessed and her brain killed."

"Is it really dead? Macha's mind? It seems too alive."

"It is without regenerative powers. Her mind and self were frozen at the time you possessed her. Any mental activity henceforth is yours alone. Only the whispering ghost of Macha remains. Ignore these whispers. They will fade in time."

"A few minutes ago, I was an apostate of the Zabo and now I am its mistress. I feel the urgency to do its work. The urgency Macha felt. I understand now why the mother had to be killed. It is time for action and the old woman's grip was growing feeble. She was shrewd but left too much undone."

"The power you now hold demands decisions which only you can make and must make. I have given you a poor destiny."

"Poor, no. I have no regrets. This power I have is exciting, an emotion like love, only really stronger and more durable. As a Zabo, I always feared those above me but now no one stands above me. The fear is gone, replaced by this awful but wonderful power. There are projects half-completed, Zabo people on missions who now wait for orders. There are small schemes to set in motion and there is of course the grand plan. There is work to do. I may follow the advice of the mother up to a point. After all, I was trained as a Zabo and her reasoning is my reasoning. Did you know that Macha had one flaw, a weakness which could very well have destroyed her and the Zabo? She loved Kengee. She would have taken him as a lover if he survived, or another man of his nature, disobeying her mother's advice. I'll not make that error. There is no place for such feelings in the Zabo."

"I must go south." This was a declaration but also a way to silence Hibee. Hibee had already mutated. She no longer would wish to mingle minds with Tanee. This was both a relief and a worry. Tanee's hold over this creature was weakening fast.

"It is too dangerous." Hibee for the moment was herself again. "If you always believed it to be too dangerous then it must be so."

"It is strange but I do not now feel the old fear. And I believe there is a way. When I possessed you, I learned what you had learned. There are Zabo women living with the barbarians. Hibee, find the one closest to Lornz and the prison cave."

They opened the secret passageway and Hibee looked back for a moment at her body. "I'll have to dispose of that. Look its blood has stained the carpet." They hurried through the passageway to the apartment where the mother's body was still lying in the hammock. Tanee thought there was a surprised look on the woman's dead face. Hibee paid no attention to the body but went right to the files, pulling out one scroll from a stack without hesitation. She studied it for a few minutes before speaking.

"Oh we are efficient, we Zabo. One of our pretty little Zabo is now the mistress of Shoomud. Not his favorite mistress but a mistress nevertheless. Kasumi is her name in the north and Gerto among the barbarians. A strong girl and a clever one. A good tool for you to work with but try not to get her killed. She is valuable."

"Gerto-Kasumi, Gerto-Kasumi," Tanee repeated, concentrating very hard. "I shall take you." Tanee caught a momentary glimpse of the girl in a chalk cave but did not go to her just yet.

"Please take care of my body while I'm gone."

"I shall have you brought here by my people and kept in this room. No one shall harm you. Kill as you like in the south, but spare Lornz. I will need that man alive. Do you wish me to assassinate Hoso?"

"Let my brother live. His replacement would be no better."

"He shall live then if he cooperates. But the time has come to infiltrate and gradually take over the Institute and its agents and to destroy this power center. I will permit no organization on Ta to exist as a rival to the Zabo." She poked Denzo's protruding stomach with her finger.

"Perhaps it is also time to make father Director of Ta. Mako is too cunning. Tanee, there is much work to do. The Zabo shall soon know that they are now ruled by a harsh mistress but one who will bring about the great revenge which has been delayed for too many centuries."

Tanee listened to Hibee with a faint smile. The Zabo would not suffer from the death of Macha or her mother. The Zabo had fallen into far more capable hands. With any luck, Hibee would soon dominate Ta, smashing or absorbing all the old power centers. It would be a new and different Ta, and no one now could predict whether it would be a better or worse Ta. Tanee only felt that it was past time for change. This was what she had wanted and by chance Hibee had become the instrument of change. Tanee put Denzo into a deep sleep, concentrated again, and then she was gone.

NINE

Shoomud's cave was cheerfully primitive. Heroic murals were painted in gay, bright colors on the cave walls. Cold-eyed barbarian warriors of old ran spears through the chests of screaming men from upper Ta or sliced off their heads with the barbarian long knife. Male prisoners bound with cords cringed fearfully before their captors as they waited for painful and final retribution, while trembling female prisoners exposed their tiny breasts and not so tiny asses and awaited rape by the victors. Brilliant green grass towered over the figures, frozen in terror or ferocity. The figures curved with the inward sloping walls and appeared to be about to fall upon the human inhabitants of the cave and continue their bloody work. It was a clear day on the chalk wall. The sun sent its flaming shafts of light to warm that long-gone day on Ta. The only real light in the cave came from flickering torches which gave movement to the battle tableau. Gerto-Kasumi, now possessed by Tanee, half expected to hear war cries, screams, grunts, and gasps.

Tanee studied this primitive fantasy with distaste. She might be an outcast but nevertheless she preferred the civilized art of her own people to these badly proportioned figures. She thought a five-year-old child might paint as well. She dropped her eyes to her work again. She was running a fishbone comb through the long, dark brown hair of Feda. Shoomud watched the girls on the cave floor before him with his stool tilted back and his head against the wall. His eyes excitedly followed the strokes of the comb and they lit up with deep pleasure whenever a downstroke produced crackling sparks.

Shoomud did not move when Lornz entered the cave.

171

He showed Lornz respect only in public. In private, he had always been contemptuous of Lornz as a man and long before that as a boy. Lornz was his younger brother. Few knew that. Lornz could call men, but Shoomud knew only he could really command them. Lornz had always been physically weak and lazy and a dreamer—the stuff prophets are made of.

"And how many did Lornz call today?" Shoomud asked flatly.

"It was really a good day. Fifty-three were called and fifty-three came. They left with love in their hearts for me and a little drunk from Takusa's brew. She made it a little too strong this time."

"Have you drunk her brew?"

"No. Certainly not. I declined and she never pressed it on me."

"Good. It changes a man somehow."

"It makes a man and even a woman willing to fight," Lornz said defensively. "If I tell them to fight, they will, and you as my war chief should be grateful to Takusa."

"I know the advantages, my brother. Have you finished questioning Kengee?"

"No. I am in no hurry. One day is as good as the next, and one day is the same as the next unless you will it to be different. Unless I will it to be different. I consider each act carefully since even a small decision or move can have great consequences."

"I don't have to contemplate for days to know it is time to drown this Kengee."

"Sometimes I don't even believe you think at all, Shoomud. You should be more like the plants and less like a man or an animal."

"Please, no more. I hear too many of your sermons in the grove. In the old days, I called you and you came trotting. You did not call me then or do you call me now. Please remember that."

"I'll talk to him one last time, Shoomud."

"When?" Shoomud's eyes were filling with tears. He had never taken them off the women at his feet.

"I must meditate, meditate with Takusa."

"You really believe that plant talks to you?"

"I do, I do, I do. We talk often and she tells me many things."

"Takusa is an unusual plant. I don't deny Takusa has intelligence, but I say the talk you hear is only the echoes of your own very strange mind. You were mad as a child and you are still mad. Your madness has been profitable to both of us, but nevertheless it is madness."

"She talks to me, Shoomud. She really does." Lornz stamped his foot on the cave floor.

"Have it your way, but make sure she tells you to drown the man."

"Why, why, why? Are you, Shoomud, the great warrior, afraid of a man in a cage?"

"I fear him as you say. I feel strongly that he is very dangerous. He is like no man I have ever met on Ta upper or lower. Mako believes he is a military genius and Mako does not believe in nonsense. Now go meditate or whatever you have to do, and then go talk to him quickly so I can rid lower Ta of him."

Shoomud had taken his eyes off the women and his pleasure evaporated. "Get out," he yelled and kicked Gerto-Kasumi who dropped the comb and screamed. "Get out, out, out." Both women now screamed as his fists came down on their heads and they fled from the cave. Once they were a safe distance away from the entrance, they both burst into laughter.

They could not stop. They hugged each other and slapped each other on the back, trying to stop the laughter. But they only laughed louder. It was always like this. For an hour, they must appear serious, combing each other's hair in front of Shoomud who watched with the moist eyes of his strange perversion, and then always he got angry and kicked them out of the cave.

"It's an easy life anyway," Feda said after choking off a final burst of giggling.

"It's an easy life if all you want in your life is a man like Shoomud."

"True, Gerto, true. Sometimes I hunger for a real man. It is only natural that I do."

"It truly is only natural that you do and it is only natural that I long for the men of my island," Gerto-

173

Kasumi said. "It is a great honor to be one of Shoomud's women but so very boring. Where is the fun in life? I do believe that my only pleasure is when Shoomud kicks me, and there isn't too much fun in that either."

"Our days are all much the same. Like Lornz said, one day is like the rest unless you will it to be different."

"Feda, I wonder what the man in the cage is like."

"The guards say he is big and powerful and that he seems lonely and unhappy. A man like that could make a woman sore all over."

"He sounds interesting."

"Very interesting." They exchanged female leers.

"They say men facing death attain their greatest potency."

"Do they? It must have something to do with wanting to keep something of themselves alive after they die."

"I imagine that's it."

"I would like to see him before Shoomud drowns him. I've always been attracted to sad, unhappy men. I wonder if there might not be a way to make him a little happier through the bars of his cage. Feda do you think . . . ?"

"Oh yes."

They smiled in the dark, their teeth gleaming like those of swamp predators in the light of one of Ta's moons. And then giggling again they went off together away from Shoomud's cave. They did not go up the path to their own snug cave where warm blankets and hot broth awaited them. They went down another path.

After Lornz left his brother's cave, he descended the winding trail that led into the plain. He tripped on a rock and stumbled, sliding partway down the hill. His bruised body hurt, and he hated his brother for this pain. Shoomud could walk in the darkest night without ever tripping. Since they were children, Shoomud had scorned his weakness and clumsiness. He had bullied him then and still bullied him, even now when he was the caller of men. Someone should make him stop. When he reached the grove, he headed directly toward Takusa.

The plant was quiet. It did not even greet him in its customary way by spraying milk and hissing.

"Are you asleep?" he whispered.

"Plants don't sleep like humans," Takusa said. "I may be resting but I'm certainly not sleeping."

Lornz sat down and rubbed his cheek against a leaf which was wet and cold from the dew. "Shoomud does not believe that you talk to me. He does not believe that we talk to each other at all." Lornz was sobbing.

"Why don't you talk to Shoomud to make him believe? Why don't you make him behave? He's a bully."

"Now, now, Lornz. I have nothing to say to Shoomud. I wish only to talk to you and you alone. You among all the men of lower Ta have I chosen to talk to because I like you."

"Do you?" the sobbing stopped abruptly.

"You know I do. Forget Shoomud. Soon we'll keep him too busy to bully you."

"You promise?"

"I promise."

"Takusa."

"What is it? I know you came to ask my advice."

"I did. What should I do about the man in the cage?"

"Why do anything?"

"Shoomud insists that we drown him."

"There are humans who drown plants by watering them too much. Their intentions may be good but the results are disastrous, at least for the plants."

"You say such wise things, Takusa."

"I speak up for my own."

"But Shoomud will do it. I know he will. He does not obey me."

"You are acting like a baby again tonight. You are Lornz, the caller of men. You are a very important man and you should not behave like an infant."

"It's Shoomud."

"Forget Shoomud. Do you want to drown the man?"

"I don't really care one way or the other but I thought you did not want the man drowned, even though you warned me about his powers," Lornz said slyly.

"I have no time to worry about the individual fate of

175

a human any more than you humans worry about the individual fate of a plant."

"You are right, Takusa. We have a world to reconquer and in our schemes individuals don't count."

"Spoken with courage, Lornz."

"Someday when I call, all men will come, even the men of upper Ta, even Shoomud."

"Correct, Lornz. You keep believing that."

"Let Shoomud drown him."

"Let him try," Takusa said softly.

Feeling much better, Lornz rose and strode away through the grove. He would go to his cave and his women and he would do more than watch them comb their hair like his big brother did. He stumbled but manfully ignored his hurting, skinned knee. He was Lornz after all, the caller of men.

"Obedient fool," the plant said half aloud. "But so useful. All he needs is a little encouragement now and again and a little love, and he'll do anything I ask. Lornz and Shoomud. Two fools in one family, but not so unusual among humans I understand." The lesser plants with their lesser intelligence found humor in this remark and the grove shook with plant chuckling.

"Hush. I'm resting and thinking and dreaming, too." Takusa suddenly felt very lonely and homesick.

Gerto-Kasumi and Feda approached the cave in which Kengee was imprisoned, hand in hand, whispering to each other. The guard stepped forward with his spear leveled at the two women.

"What a charming man," said Gerto-Kasumi.

"He is so handsome, but he ought to be told that spears are for war and not for love."

"No one is allowed near the cave," the guard said in an uncertain voice.

"But you are here," Feda said mockingly.

"I am supposed to be here but you two are not."

"But I just couldn't stay away, knowing you were alone and shivering in the cool night of Ta," said Feda. "I bring you much warmth." She came closer and touched the tip of the spear with her finger.

176

"You'll prick your finger. Go away."

"I'll throw myself on the spear if you reject me."

"I didn't say I didn't want you. But another time, and somewhere else."

"It is now or never." Feda slipped past the spear and began rubbing against him. "No," he choked and then the spear crashed to the ground. Gerto-Kasumi picked it up.

"I'll hold the spear and guard the cave," she volunteered. "We'll exchange robes and no one in the dark will know the difference." He hesitated. Even in the dark tiny Gerto-Kasumi would never look like a large barbarian guard. But Feda was tugging at his robe and whispering, "Hurry, hurry, hurry." And he hurried. Feda and the guard bounded around the side of the hill. After they were gone, Gerto-Kasumi went down the stairs cut into the side of the cave wall with a torch she had picked up and lit at the entrance. Kengee watched the girl's descent with interest.

"You're the most beautiful guard I've ever seen. Put the spear away and we'll have a nice long talk."

"Be quiet, Kengee."

"You again. Do you have to follow me everywhere?"

"If you wish to remain in the cage, it is all right with me. I can exist very well without you."

"I'm sorry."

"Sorry you could not play around with a female guard?"

"I was only going to use her to get out of this cage."

Tanee ignored him. She was circling the cage, studying the coral bars fused together with what appeared to be an unbreakable cementlike substance.

"No door. It looks like they never intended that you leave."

"I know. I've looked. But Tanee you've got to get me out of here and fast. Shoomud has no patience. He wants to drown me like a rat."

Tanee smiled and Kengee glowered back through the bars. She fingered the bars, scratching at them with her fingernails and then tasting what was scraped off with her tongue. She walked to the cave wall and retrieved

177

the burning torch. She applied its flame to the bars where they were fused together. They snapped loose and fell to the cave floor with dull clunks.

"So simple." He crawled out.

"So simple," she repeated and then they both heard the water cascading down from above. Within seconds, the swirling water was up to their necks and Kengee began flailing his arms and legs in an awkward attempt to swim. Tanee already was paddling about effortlessly.

"Can't you swim?"

"I guess not." Kengee looked desperate.

She grabbed him under the chin and ordered him not to struggle. They floated upward together, higher and higher as the water rose rapidly in the cave. It was peacefully silent for a few minutes and then they heard Shoomud stomping his feet and laughing above them. He began hurling small rocks at them, but he was so excited by the sight of a man and woman floating helplessly in the water that he missed every time.

"Now what?" Kengee asked after spitting out a mouthful of water.

"We rise to meet Shoomud. What else can we do?" And so they did until the water lifted them to the entrance of the cave where Shoomud was now kneeling. He reached out and grasped Tanee's hair and then jerked her out of the water, breaking Kengee's hold with a kick. He hurled the girl behind him and then extended his spear toward Kengee. In terror of drowning, Kengee grabbed it. Shoomud allowed him to hold on for a few moments and then pulled it away, laughing.

But Shoomud had made a mistake. He thought he knew the girl whom he had dragged out of the water by her long hair. He thought she was his docile mistress who by now would be too frightened worrying over the beating he would give her to do anything but cower against the wall. He therefore was surprised and certainly hurt when she clobbered him with a large rock. He pitched forward into the water, and Tanee quickly pulled Kengee to safety. As they fled from the cave, they heard Shoomud splashing out of the water and roaring for the guards.

They dodged behind a large rock as the guards rushed by and then stumbled and slid down the hill into the plain below. Shoomud bellowed commands and a cascade of pebbles warned them that the guards were in pursuit. But they had a good start, until Kengee tripped in a hole, and turned his ankle. Both Tanee and Kengee rubbed the sprain vigorously. When the first guard came upon them, Tanee sprang at the man letting Gerto-Kasumi and her Zabo martial arts take over. The Zabo girl drove her fingers into the man's eyes and he dropped his spear. While he clutched his eyes screaming, she retrieved the spear and parried a spear thrust of another guard and then sent the point accurately and fiercely into the man's throat.

The giant Shoomud charged forward shouting a barbaric battle cry, expecting to be challenged by the great warrior from upper Ta. Instead he faced a snarling girl. Kengee limped toward her to help, but stopped when he realized how ineffective he would be without a weapon. Shoomud hurled his spear impaling the girl who flew backward, hitting the ground hard. But when he bent down to withdraw his weapon, the girl threw a knife, and Shoomud sat down heavily to die.

"Can I help?" Kengee asked.

"It's too late. Gerto-Kasumi is finished. Get out of here fast. I'm going north." As the girl died, Tanee escaped. Kengee was angry for a moment that Tanee had abandoned him and kicked the body of the Zabo girl. But then he was immediately sorry for doing such a silly thing.

He saw the guards closing in as the moon suddenly broke through the mists exposing him in brilliant light. Kengee jerked the spear out of the dead girl and then placed his foot on Shoomud's body and shouted the upper Ta war cry: "Yanzoo, Yanzoo, Yanzoo." The guards drew back in fear of this warrior who they believed had just slain the mighty Shoomud. When the mist dimmed the moonlight again, he turned and ran, staggering toward the grove, and he only slowed down when he crashed into heavy undergrowth.

Orders were shouted in the plain and the barbarians

179

mustered to avenge the death of Shoomud. But the warriors were slow in resuming their pursuit of Kengee. He stumbled on through the grove, wondering how he could ever reach the water and the boats. He was sure he would never make it and again cursed Tanee for doing such a bad job of rescuing him. Already the sky was beginning to lighten. Kengee tripped and landed in the midst of a huge plant. He heard a female morning yawn.

"Not before breakfast, Kengee," the plant said in a teasing voice.

"Not what before breakfast?" Kengee felt the leaves of the plant begin to stroke him, leaving behind a warm, sticky substance.

"It was a girl joke," Takusa laughed.

"You'll laugh harder than that I suppose when the guards catch me."

"Now just stay where you are. No one is going to hurt my Kengee." He sat still allowing without resistance the plant to gently rub up against him.

"Why do you all know me?"

"All? Oh I see. I should explain that there is only really one Takusa. I'm just in a lot of places at the same time. I pop up wherever I please and you're such a traveler, Kengee."

"Not by choice. And why do you know English?"

"It's as good as any other language, and you taught it to me. You've taught me a lot. I've absorbed your thoughts and your sweet self."

"Why pick on me?"

"Well, we're sort of distant cousins. Kissing cousins." She giggled and he winced.

"You're from New York, right?"

"Right. But how did you know?"

"I just told you that you can keep no secrets from me. I was born in New Jersey myself. I never liked New Jersey or New York, even before the ice ages and they've gotten progressively worse since then. Don't you agree?"

"I don't know what they were like way back then. But how did you get to Ta?"

"I came as a seed with a lot of other seeds, but I was the only one who survived the trip. I won't tell you

180

how we made the journey since that might frighten you. Back in New Jersey my parents were insignificant plants, and I still have relatives on Earth. Pretty dumb relatives, and very homely ones, too. Anyway I made the trip and got bombarded by all that radiation and crap out in space and then I got planted. The soil here is unusual and I grew quickly, but I grew as a strange mutant. I became the biggest plant in all Ta and the most goddamned important one, too. And I'm still growing, growing everywhere. My roots are all over this stinking planet."

"Not in upper Ta."

"Don't be too sure about that. You see I'm one of those girls with a voracious appetite. I'm really eating too much —devouring all the minerals and anything else edible underground."

"But you give something back."

"Of course I do. I'm a very proper plant. But not enough, Kengee, not enough. I'll eat this planet up someday, although fortunately for me that day is a long way off. I'm destroying the ecology, but I can't help it. A girl's got to live, hasn't she?"

"And now you want upper Ta."

"I don't want it really, but I must have it. Oh, I'll try to stay underground as much as possible and try to diet. I want Ta to last as long as possible, naturally."

Shouting men were moving through the grove, jabbing their spears into every bush and behind every tree. Kengee began to shake.

"Interruptions. Everytime you are with an interesting man, there are interruptions. Close your eyes, Kengee."

"And make a wish?"

"You are amusing, aren't you? No just close your eyes." Takusa then began to spray the grove with her nozzles. Takusa's vapor drifted with the morning breeze into the faces of the barbarians who screamed and ran. In a few moments, the grove was quiet and peaceful again.

"I didn't hurt them much. They'll all be able to see again in a day or two."

"Thanks. But I can't understand why you have been helping Lornz."

181

"Are you jealous, Kengee?"

"No, I'm not." He meant that.

"I'll tell you. I'm helping him because I'm bloody bored."

"Aren't you helping him because you want to liberate the plants in upper Ta?"

"Heavens no. I'll coexist with them but eventually I'll have to put my survival above theirs. I prefer to coexist on my own terms with people. Plants are rivals, but people and plants are complementary if they both behave. To be a little gruesome, people fertilize the soil, and that's good for plants, good for old number one here."

"So you intend to start a war to make fertilizer."

"I wouldn't put it that way, Kengee. There won't be a big war anyway. The men of Ta just don't have it in them anymore. All I'm doing is playing around, honestly. I don't have any purpose. Why should I have one? I already told you that I just want to survive as long as possible and live well, but a girl also has to be entertained."

"Then why are you withholding your milk from upper Ta?"

"Oh that. A game, only a game. If you wish, I'll give it all to you and you can become the wealthiest man on Ta and I'll forget about starting a little war. It's not that important to me. I can do a lot for you, Kengee, much more than those dogs you used to go to bed with on Earth. Yes, I know all about your past. . . . After all we Earth types ought to stick together. What do you say, Kengee?"

He said nothing. He knew a tempting proposition when he heard one and he knew propositions such as this always had their price. What did she want in return?

"Rest your head against me and think it over. I'm in no hurry for your answer. Take a week, a month, or even a year. Or are you in love with Tanee? If you are, go ahead and live with her. She's a freak and she has to live in a cave. I'm sure you'll be very happy in your poverty. Maybe you will be happy for a year or so. That's about as long as human love lasts with any heat.

182

And then what happens? You'll find yourself stuck in a cave full of screaming brats. And then what does Tanee do? She gets tired of you and the cave and the brats and starts running around at night in her strange way, leaving you with the kids. If you want all that, go ahead. I won't try to stop you."

"And how could I live with you?"

"I could turn you into a plant."

"No thanks." He started to get up.

"Sit down. I wouldn't do that against your will. But you don't know how nice it is to be a plant. Of course, you could just be Kengee and I could just be your loving Takusa."

"And sex?" he snarled.

"I could arrange something. I'm very inventive." One of Takusa's nozzles nudged him and he shifted away from its moist, hot touch.

"How about Lornz?" He was trying to change the subject.

"He's just a big baby, my baby. He had a terrible mother, you know, never gave him a minute's affection. I am just giving him a little motherly love. He's a petulant man-child and I spoil him, but I certainly don't feel about him as I do about you. I think it's because we share common ancestors. Don't you, Kengee? That must be our bond. Here we are on this crazy planet of Ta, far away from our home. Strangers in a strange world. And then bang, we meet. And then bang, it happens."

"Bang, it happens," Kengee muttered.

"You're hard to get and I like that about you, Kengee. But remember, I'm a very stubborn female. Do you want a martini?"

"I never drink before breakfast."

"I didn't know you had a special time for martinis. But I'll remember. Do you like them best at the end of the day? I'm sorry I can't produce ice, but I can make 'em cooler."

"And drier."

"And drier."

Several nozzles began stroking him. "You couldn't find a better wife than I. I can whip up something that tastes

183

like steak and French fries, although they won't look like steak and French fries. Tanee couldn't do that for you."

"Forget Tanee."

"With pleasure. I never liked the bitch. I kept her ass out of lower Ta because I couldn't stand her."

"She's been here and gone."

"I let her come just this once to get you out of that horrible cage."

"Couldn't you do that?"

"No. I can't bore through solid rock, no matter how much I love you. I'm soft and tender and I have some limitations. But damned few."

"Sun's up," he said too cheerfully. "No mist. A beautiful day."

"A beautiful day for traveling, I suppose," Takusa said sulkily.

"Well, honey, it isn't safe for me here in lower Ta, and I can't spend the rest of my life sitting in this grove. I should be on my way while the guards are still blinded."

"I don't really mind if you go, Kengee. I'm not the type of female who's going to tie a man down. You're free to come and go as you please. I'm not the overly possessive type. You're free to move about as you wish, Kengee. You always will be. And I'll always be waiting here or somewhere for you when you return. Waiting with a dry martini and love." One of Takusa's nozzles poked him playfully in the ribs. He did not bother to move away. He had been mauled by women before. He remembered others in his past who could not keep their hands off him . . . touching his hair, rubbing his back, fingering his fingers. But then Takusa didn't have hands. She read his mind.

"I could try to grow hands, Kengee."

"Don't bother. I love you the way you are."

"Bye, love," Takusa said as he rose to leave.

"Bye," he shouted back as he hurried from the grove.

He did not feel really safe or free until he reached the highway. If he ever got back to upper Ta, he would never return to the south again, no matter what. A few guards were lying in the middle of the road, rubbing

184

their eyes and moaning out desperate pleas to Lornz. He stepped over them and kept walking toward the harbor. It was early morning and only a few women were up and moving about in front of their chalk cave homes. There were hungry baby wails coming from the caves.

He found his boat without difficulty and started up its engine. When the put-puts were strong and regular, he headed up the waterway toward the north, steering close to shore to avoid the onrush of pilgrims whom Lornz had called for that day.

"Lornz is we and we are Lornz," a woman shouted to him across the water.

"Yeah," he shouted back in English. The bewildered woman smiled and waved at him.

TEN

It was not a happy homecoming. Kengee was very worried. As he tied up his swamp-stained and battered boat at a pier, he sensed the gloom in the capital. The docks were deserted and empty barges were rocking in the water, straining against ropes as if they were trying to escape from the city that was doomed to economic ruin. It was twilight and the godowns, dark gray in the fading light, looked melancholy. They seemed about to leap in the water and end their misery. It was all very depressing to Kengee who had his own troubles.

On the long voyage back, Kengee had tried to balance the successes against the failures of his mission. He had despite betrayal reached Lornz's miserable capital, and he had come back through the hostile swamps. Shoomud, the greatest of the barbarian warriors, was dead. But Lornz was not, and there would be no Takusa milk for the industry of upper Ta; there would be none unless Kengee accepted Takusa's proposal. This he dreaded to do.

Dressed in his muddy, tattered clothing, he walked toward home. He was shunned by the citizens of the

185

capital, both swordholders and the lower classes alike. He looked like a loser and most wondered why he was showing himself on the streets while there was still light in the sky.

At the gate of Denzo's house, Gijo met him with a disgusted look and promptly rushed him upstairs to bathe and change his clothes. Gijo informed him that his sister Macha had secluded herself in her mother's apartment since the old woman's death. Denzo attended his committee meetings, visited the pillow houses, and showed no sorrow over the death of his wife or concern over the behavior of his daughter.

As Kengee lathered his body, Gijo repeated the rumors and gossip of the capital. Since Kengee's departure, the crisis had worsened. Factories were closing down daily and the traders were in despair. The rich gathered each day on the docks, desperately hoping for the arrival of full barges of Takusa milk. None came. They were grumbling and complaining and whispering threats against Mako. There was talk of a need for new leadership. As Kengee was drying himself, Gijo whispered that there was also talk of raising Denzo to the directorship. If Mako was in trouble, Kengee thought, then he was in worse trouble.

The next morning, he sent Gijo to the Director's office to announce his return. When Gijo came back to the house, Kengee strapped on his sword and walked unescorted to the shabby offices of the Director. If Mako was worried, nothing showed on his smooth, smiling face. He displayed all the refined, basic courtesies one swordholder extends to another. With studied restraint, he did not come to the point quickly.

"How did the steam engine on your boat perform?" Mako asked. "It is a new design, made to conserve fuel, and, of course, we must conserve fuel these days."

"The engine did its job," Kengee replied and at once realized he had left himself open for a sarcastic remark by Mako. But the Director disdained such an easy opening.

"And how are the barbarian women? In my youth, I had many sexual adventures on the fringes of lower Ta.

186

I remember them vividly to this day. Those women are like animals—hungry, direct, and wild. And they wrestle like men. I emerged from these encounters of love bruised and bleeding but completely satisfied."

"There was little time for women," Kengee said.

"There should always be time for women. You must learn to set aside an hour each day for women. They are one reason for living."

"Interest in women comes when danger is passed, but the danger was always present in lower Ta."

"Danger is food for a swordholder."

"It has a taste, I admit."

"And how did you find Lornz?"

"I found him calling his people and left him half dead."

"Half dead," Mako repeated.

"His brother, the great warrior of lower Ta, died at my feet, and with Shoomud dead, Lornz is half dead."

"Yes. It is true that he is half dead but then he is also half alive."

"Certainly, he is half alive."

"If he was three-quarters dead, I would be more pleased, and more pleased than that if he was nine-tenths dead, and deliriously happy if he was totally dead."

"Your feelings are my feelings."

"But it is something to have slain Shoomud."

"Thank you."

"It is something but not enough."

"It would have been much better to have killed Lornz too."

"Kengee, you and I agree on most things. And truly you have brought honor to upper Ta. You epitomize all the ideals and virtues of a swordholder. I am sure children for generations will reenact in their childish games the great duel between Kengee of the North and Shoomud of the South. Your name will be remembered for a century at least. I know you are a modest man, but I would like to have a statue cast commemorating your great feat of arms—your holding a bloody sword with your legs astride the giant body of Shoomud. I would like to do that but, of course, we have no Takusite now with which to cast a statue. It is my hope that you will live long enough to see this great memorial."

"It seems to me," Kengee began, dropping his trembling hands out of sight into his lap, "that it makes little difference if Lornz is alive or dead as long as Takusa milk reaches upper Ta."

"Good thinking. If that were possible, I suppose there would be no objective to allowing a fellow like Lornz to continue to exist in lower Ta. We in upper Ta never kill without reason. If our industry and commerce are prospering, we are a very peaceful, warm-hearted people. But this is only talk. We don't really believe that the milk will flow as long as Lornz is alive, do we?"

"I learned much in lower Ta. There may be a way."

"That would be very nice. Could you manage to start shipments in say about three weeks? We are rather in a hurry right now." He did not believe Kengee. He was almost certain that he was stalling, but then three weeks was very little time and it was Kengee who was gambling.

"I could try."

"Try very hard. If you succeed, there may be an even greater reward than just a statue."

"Like being allowed to live."

"Something like that, Kengee. Three weeks, agreed. We shall prepare a convoy of a hundred barges and it will be ready to leave in two days. Take that time to relax and enjoy yourself. You must be very weary from your victorious duel with Shoomud and the long trip home."

Out on the street, Kengee felt the full horror of what he had promised. He had been backed into a corner and now there was no escaping Takusa and her desires. The only satisfaction in the interview with Mako was his growing feeling of contempt toward the Director of Ta. Mako thought he was Director of Ta but in reality Takusa was the director. Maybe he could keep her happy somehow without giving too much of himself. He felt she had a good heart, if plants have hearts, and she was pushing a fortune at him.

Gijo was waiting for him at the gate of Denzo's house.

Gijo told him that Macha had earlier stormed through the house demanding to see him. He had enough trouble without meeting Macha, but it was best to keep peace in the family and so he went directly to Macha's apartment. Macha seemed the same except for the way she studied him coolly without a hint of her former sexual interest.

"Home safe," she said flatly.

"Home, at last."

"I don't care to hear about your troubles. Follow me."

Hibee pressed her palms against the wall and the panel swung inward revealing the secret passageway. When they entered the apartment of Macha's late mother, Tanee looked at him from the hammock where she was reclining. The smile never left her lips as she slipped gracefully out of the hammock and came toward him. He noticed she was barefoot and this strangely excited him. He then felt a little ashamed of being turned on by dusty toes.

"My sister must have had a change of heart or have you tampered with her mind?"

"Your sister is no more. Hibee inhabits her brain and body now. You must remember Hibee—the little Zabo girl who you were so anxious to make love to on the boat." Hibee scowled and left the room.

"Sometimes you frighten me, Tanee."

As she explained, he looked at her with wonder. She seemed to be little concerned about having committed murder, and he considered her brain transplanting work just that. Her diabolical powers troubled him greatly. He knew Tanee did more good than bad and certainly worse crimes were done on both Ta and Earth. But it bothered him that she accepted her strange powers so naturally and never suffered from a bad conscience no matter what she did. It was as if she felt that everything she did was in the best interests of humanity. She was completely confident, completely sure of herself. An extraordinary woman and damn dangerous.

"And so Macha is now nothing but a bad memory, Hibee's bad memory," she concluded. Tanee always had a way of saying things well with a little wit, he thought.

"Was Mako satisfied with the death of Shoomud?" Tanee asked.

"No."

"What does he want?" she snorted.

"Takusa milk."

"And you promised to deliver it or you would not be here. Of course, you can, but what does Takusa wish in return? You, I suppose."

"More or less. But how did you know about Takusa?"

"When I was in the south, I had the opportunity to talk with that plant's mind. She had never let me enter lower Ta before and only allowed me to come that one time to get you out of the cave. She flaunted her superiority before me and laughed at my powers and boasted that her lousy plants would dominate all of Ta."

"She only wants to eat."

"Don't defend her. I really hate to refer to that ugly plant as 'her.' Takusa isn't human, although she is very female. And don't believe that all Takusa wants to do is eat. She wishes to replace the rule of man with the rule of plants on Ta."

"She might do a better job than Mako or Lornz."

"Don't be a smart ass," Tanee switched to English. "They're at least human and so are you, and as long as we have a chance, we humans had better stick together. Put a plant in charge and we'll be nothing but fertilizer, if she doesn't change us all into plants first."

"If she wants to do that, no one's going to stop her. And the offer isn't so bad. She'll live in the south and I'll live up north and visit her once in awhile. That's all. And as long as I keep her happy, she won't do terrible things to Ta. In a way, I'll become the savior of Ta."

"You're a fool, Kengee. You're not dealing with an ordinary human female. I know about your silly powers over sexed-up-middle-aged women, but Takusa is quite different from your former conquests. Do you think you are the only man she's taken a fancy to and then discarded after her love runs out of sap? Look at Lornz. She probably told you he was just a baby, her baby. But that's a lie. A lot more went on between those two. She now prefers you to Lornz or any other man, but for how long? You're a fool and I'm going."

"Back to your cave?"

"Where else?"

"I'll visit you sometime."

"You had better ask Takusa for permission first." Tanee stepped into her boots and went out the door without turning back.

"She's gone." Hibee had come through the passageway seconds after Tanee's departure. She had been listening to the quarrel and thinking hard about what both of them had revealed. "She's shown some good sense at last. And I have learned that you are about to depart the capital with a hundred barges. I want to talk to you."

Hibee did the talking and Kengee the listening. She offered him protection from Mako and a small share of future profits if he saw to it that Takusa milk flowed only into Zabo front companies. She offered him a lot of trouble if he did not become a partner. He bickered over the amount of his share and settled for 4½ percent. She assured him he would live a comfortable life with that amount. Life was looking up again. If Hibee began to lean on him too hard, he knew he could always ask Takusa for help. Tanee could sulk in her cave. He felt he was learning how to live on his own in Ta without her help.

After Hibee left, he wandered in the cool darkness of the garden humming an Earth tune and feeling that Ta had possibilities after all. It might be a good place to settle down. With the money that soon would flow in with the Takusa milk, he could buy a big house, bigger than Denzo's. He could fill it with pretty girls collected from all over Ta. He might even open a chain of pillow houses. He had noticed that there were none along the canal routes. Drive-in pillow houses might catch on and he knew he could handle this kind of business. He felt his worries were over.

"Hi, honey!"

It was Takusa's most sultry voice and Kengee froze. He peered in the direction from which the greeting had come, next to the garden wall under a sputtering torch.

He saw the unmistakable spiked green leaves of Takusa. The plant was small, no bigger than a basketball, but the voice was turned on full volume.

"Surprise! You don't have to go south. I'm here." Takusa had switched to her little girl voice—the one Kengee disliked the most.

"You're damn well not supposed to be here."

"Aw Kengee. I thought you'd be happy to see me. I've been underground for ever so many years in upper Ta, and when I heard you make a deal with that Zabo bitch, I just had to pop up."

"I was going to tell you all about that when I went south. I wouldn't do anything without your approval."

"Anything you do is all right with me, love. You can start loading up with milk any time. You don't have to make that long, hard trip south."

"From here? God, that's impossible."

"No, no, no. I could, of course, swell up and take over the whole garden and do the job here, but why crowd out a lot of innocent plants? No. You'll find me big and ready for you a half day's journey down the canal. You'll get Ta moving again in no time and you'll be a big man. Now sit down and touch me, Kengee. I've missed you ever so much."

He obediently knelt down and stroked her leaves and tiny nozzles, and she sighed with deep pleasure. It was disgusting to him but what else could he do? She had been so obliging.

Hibee who had been watching from the shadows near the house also was disgusted. She did not understand the strange language in which they were talking but she understood the phony sexed-up voice of Takusa and Kengee's amorous attentions. They were too preoccupied with each other to notice her as she returned quietly to the house. Once in her rooms, she strapped her dagger holsters to her thighs and went out the front door. A fast Zabo boat carried her swiftly up the canal and she was at the entrance of Tanee's cave at midnight.

After Tanee had arrived home, she spent an hour rummaging through scrolls in her library and reading. One by one, she tossed them to the floor and then she climbed into her hammock and stared hard at the rock ceiling, thinking through it into space. When Hibee entered, Tanee looked at her but said nothing. Only after Hibee breathlessly announced the arrival of Takusa in her garden did Tanee come fully alive.

"So she's already here." Tanee bounded from the hammock and began pacing nervously about the cave. "And soon we'll all be plant food with that idiot Kengee running her errands. That egotistical fool thinks he can handle any female, but this time he'll be the one who crawls. It will serve him right."

"He's already doing that. But what am I going to do about that vicious weed in my garden?"

"There's nothing you can do." And then Tanee stopped pacing with a thoughtful look on her face. "What did you call Takusa?"

"A weed, a vicious weed," Hibee hissed.

Tanee rushed to the shelf cut in the rock and took down a thick scroll. She untied the ribbon and rapidly began to unroll the scroll which was entitled: *Beyond Ta—Notes and Observations on a Place Called Earth.* . .

"Hibee, we've got work to do. I must make a long trip and we're going to need every Zabo to search Ta for what we require. Now start taking notes." Hibee just listened. A Zabo never forgot anything.

Before Kengee departed with his convoy, Hibee ordered one of her front companies to buy up the field where the Takusa had surfaced. Once the convoy arrived at the place, Takusa began pumping milk and continued to do so for three days and three nights. Kengee then towed the barges triumphantly back to the capital where traders and factory owners crowded the docks to cheer. Even Mako was there to meet him, and so was Denzo and the girl whom he thought was his daughter. The man who bought the land which was blessed by Takusa had been a small trader. But now Chobo was the most important trader in all of Ta. Chobo promised a fair distribution at reasonable prices, and many considered him a fool because they were certain that Takusa would soon flower all over upper Ta. Then Takusa milk would become plentiful and cheap, and Chobo would have missed his chance to make a great fortune. The traders and factory owners already were speculating in land, purchasing lots which seemed likely to attract Takusa.

The popularity of the Director of Ta was restored. The crisis was over. No longer was upper Ta dependent on lower Ta. Takusa had moved north and the barbarians had lost their monopoly over the only thing which upper Ta coveted in the south.

But there were a few wise traders who began to worry. Although the factories could start running at full capacity again, producing more and more Takusite products, one of upper Ta's major export markets had been lost. What did the barbarians now have to offer in trade? However, the pessimism of these few did not spoil the celebrations which went on for two days and nights in the capital.

There were small and large parties given for Kengee. The wealthy swordholders swarmed around Kengee, at times literally thrusting their marriageable daughters into his arms. Kengee got in a few quick feels, made polite conversation, and escaped without making any commitments. Mako held a large open-air feast along the main canal to honor Kengee—now a commercial success and not just a war hero. As the pillow house girls began their mass dance on one of the docks, Mako took Kengee aside.

"It was too bad that you did not discover Takusa on the lands of one of our more respected trading or manufacturing families," he said. "I don't mean to criticize, since Ta certainly will benefit from your discovery, but still it would have been better if Takusa had sprouted someplace else."

Kengee watched the dancers instead of replying. He was deliberately snubbing Mako since he felt it was time to remind the Director that he, not Mako, had saved Ta. When the dancers began to whirl and their robes spread free from their thighs, he forgot for a moment that the Director of Ta was even there.

"Do you think Takusa might grow elsewhere in the north?" Mako asked in a loud voice.

"Perhaps."

"Unpredictable?"

"I didn't say that. I said perhaps."

"It is not good for such a very small company to have a monopoly. The real wealth of Ta should remain within the great houses."

"The Chobo family may soon become a great house."

"You have been here too short a time to really understand our codes. The Chobo family is not a family of great swordholders. Five hundred and fifty-one years ago, a Chobo swordholder lost a small fight with the barbarians and was surrounded. He lacked the courage to fight to the end and ran. For three days, his relatives pursued him until they caught him and assisted him in performing the honorable last act of sitting on his sword. They say the man screamed like a woman.

"The Chobo house may become a rich house but it can never become a great house. You must remember that you are the son of Denzo, the head of an illustrious family throughout the ages. No one wearing the crest of Denzo's family ever dishonored it during the entire thousand years of warfare. If Takusa should sprout on the property of one of the great families, I would be highly pleased."

"I shall consider all you have said."

"Good. Someday soon, there may even be a place for you on the Committee of Five." Kengee grinned and then he saw Hibee watching him intently a few paces away. He greeted his sister with a kiss and she whispered in his ear, "I would not consider betraying the Zabo."

"Never," he said. "Now I think I would like to go home and take a quiet walk in our garden." Her smile was malevolent.

When he returned to Denzo's house, he went deliberately to the garden to talk to his ally against the Zabo. The first thing he saw were two gardeners lying dead on the ground with their hoes still clutched in their hands and then he noticed that Takusa had expanded. She now occupied a quarter of the garden. He was furious.

"You promised to stay small and look at you," he shouted. "And what happened to the gardeners?"

"I'm sorry. I couldn't help it. Those idiots were about to hoe me up like some common weed. I was frightened

195

and angry and just naturally swelled up with fear and rage. Then, I squirted the bastards good. Humans have no hearts. Imagine trying to kill a plant just because it is different from the rest. Really, Kengee, I have decided to turn you into a plant for your own good. Humans irritate me. Just think, together we could spray the hell out of them and then have a little peace on Ta for a change."

He looked again at the gardeners and gasped. They were slowly revolving now, screwing themselves into the moist, soft ground, and turning a bright purple. Their arms had already transformed themselves into branches and their fingers leaves. All human features were rapidly disappearing as he watched.

"See? I didn't really kill them. They'll be beautiful flowering bushes by tomorrow morning. And believe me, they'll thank me for it. No more hard labor. All they have to do now is let their roots soak up all the good things below ground. But I would make you a more splendid plant, Kengee. You would become king of all the plants with roots everywhere in Ta, intermingling in love with mine."

"Would we have children?" he asked trembling.

"Sorry, Kengee. I'm sterile. All that radiation in space, I suppose. But it hasn't affected my health or my desires one bit. And if I could reproduce, the whole damned planet would be quickly consumed. There's a good reason for everything that happens, don't you think?"

"I would have to consider very carefully before becoming a plant."

"Sure, baby, I understand. Take a couple of days. But really, I know what's best for my boy. God what a beautiful plant you'll become. I can hardly wait." He felt Takusa wink, but of course it was only a feeling since he had never found anything resembling eyes on her green body. She did not protest when he excused himself and hurried to his apartment.

Once inside his rooms, he locked the windows and doors. His hands were shaking so violently that he could not lift the wine bowl set on the table by Gijo earlier and had to lap the wine up like an animal. He considered running to Tanee, but how could she help him? Wherever he went, Takusa would pop up, and eventually she would squirt him and change him into a plant. Granted he would not become just an ordinary plant. He would be king of the plants, but how much fun would that be? He heard Takusa humming some goddamned old-fashioned, sentimental Beatles song in the garden. "Bitch," he said but only in a whisper. Later there was a knock at the door and someone pushing against it. "She's here," he gasped and fled into the closet, certain that Takusa had grown up the stairs to spray him. He heard the door open and then he heard Hibee's voice.

"What are you doing in the closet?" Hibee asked after sliding open the door. "And where are Daddy's two gardeners? He's terribly upset."

"They'll be lovely bushes in the morning, flowering bushes."

"Takusa?"

"Who else?"

"I'll fix that dirty female weed," Hibee snarled.

"I'll water you every day. I wonder what she'll turn you into. She's not fond of women. Maybe, she'll make you an onion or some kind of insignificant fungus."

"Shut up, Kengee."

"I'll let you in on a secret. I'm to become king of the plants, and when I'm king, I'll treat you very nice even if you are a lower species. I take care of my friends. I always have." Kengee then burst into tears.

Takusa began singing. "Ain't he sweet, with his green hair and brown feet? Now I ask you very confidentially, ain't he sweet?" She had filched that stupid tune from his head and was making up her own words. Kengee's sobbing became almost hysterical.

"Men always crack first," Hibee said coldly. "Learn to bite the sword hilt and keep going. I just don't know what Tanee sees in you."

"You can talk tough. No one ever threatened to turn you into a plant." He was angry now.

"That's better," Hibee said. "No one ever threatened to and no one is ever going to turn me into a plant, or you either. Now get down there and distract that over-

197

sexed plant. Hold her attention. Tanee says you are good at entertaining women. Make this your best performance."

"I don't want to go near her."

"Do as I say or I'll turn you into plant food." Hibee opened her robe enough to expose her thighs and the two daggers, and Kengee went down the stairs to the garden, fearing the worst.

"Takusa, I couldn't sleep."

"Insomnia is a human affliction. You'll soon be cured of that, dearest."

Excited spiked leaves began to caress him. It was an uncomfortable feeling since the leaves were wet and cold with dew. When he began to shiver, Takusa heated up. She was talking to him in her most husky voice but her emotions were so turned on that her normally flawless English was incoherent. He could hardly understand her words but he understood her mood too well.

Hibee slipped into the dark garden unseen with the container that she and Tanee had designed strapped on her back and a hose in her hand. The device resembled an Earth-type flamethrower and ironically was made entirely of Takusite plastics. Hibee carefully stepped between the leaves of the plant, working her way slowly toward Takusa's core. In the moonlight, she could see Takusa's nozzles quivering in Kengee's direction. She ignored these repulsive nipples and pointed her hose at Takusa and sprayed the plant.

Takusa screamed and her nozzles went limp. Hibee kept spraying for a few more moments and then went to the garden wall and brought back a torch and studied the plant intently. The edges of the leaves already had turned brown. The plant was still pulsating but the beat was weak and irregular.

"You murdered me, you fucking human."

"I don't understand."

"You murdered me, you heartless Zabo animal," Takusa said in the Ta language.

"Not all of you, but I could. I've just given you enough to make you sick for a couple of days and to make you get out of this garden."

"I feel like throwing up. What was it?"

198

"A weed-killer that is used effectively against your cousins back where you came from. Dandelions I believe they are called. They're a very common weed. Small boys dig up dandelions with garden tools or exterminate them with a spray gun. Dandelions are despised. And you are nothing but an overgrown dandelion and there is no reason why I or anyone else should respect or fear you."

"I feel awful. Humans are terrible, just terrible."

"And I suppose you think you are noble and beautiful with impeccable morals."

"Yes, I do." Takusa's voice was weakening rapidly but was still strong on self-pity.

"We won't argue. There isn't much time. But I want you to know that I can get rid of you, all of you. Any time you poke your head above ground, I can have you sprayed, and eventually your whole system will be poisoned. And I'll do just that unless you start taking orders from me."

"What do you want?"

"Get out of upper Ta for a start."

"It will be difficult. It took me years to reach this far. I've got roots all over the place."

"I'll help you on your way with a few squirts of this."

"Please don't."

"Then listen. You start shrinking. I want you to reduce your presence everywhere and I want you to stay in the south. And you will produce milk on demand within your capabilities, because if you do not, there will be no reason for your existence on Ta."

"You'll destroy the balance of nature," Takusa protested feebly.

"And what are you doing? With all your pretended love of plants, you've displaced them everywhere you have gone, even in this garden. Now get out and get smaller." Hibee kicked the plant. There was one tiny gasp and then the plant collapsed. Hibee turned toward Kengee who was standing by the garden wall.

"No tears for your lover?"

"Not tears but thanks."

"Go to Tanee. She's the only one on Ta who will want

you now and tell her the weed-killer was very effective and that I'll try to be a good tyrant. I can't promise for sure that I will be, but I'll try. I intend to make a lot of changes and I won't tolerate any interference from the men who think they run Ta."

Kengee began walking toward the house.

"Wait. I am curious. How do you manage to make so many women fall in love with you?"

Kengee thought for a moment. "Male charm, I guess."

"And what is that?"

"Above all you must have confidence and a quiet threat about you. You must appear both dangerous and vulnerable, capable of both love and violence. A victim and a victimizer. And you must be able to balance attentiveness with indifference. A woman lures with tenderness, a man with thinly disguised brutality."

"I can't believe it."

"Well, it works."

"Goodbye, Kengee."

Kengee went directly to Denzo's apartment where the committeeman was sleeping his heavy drunken sleep. He pried open a box and filled his pockets with Ta currency and several valuable jewels from eastern Ta. He knew his career had come to an end on Ta and all the wealth he would ever have was now in the side pockets of his robe. Takusa belonged to Hibee now. He went out of the house, leaving his sword behind.

When Kengee entered the cave the next day, Tanee was bent over the stone table copying the contents of several manuscripts onto a scroll weighted down by crystal rocks. She continued to write, ignoring him. Finally, she straightened up.

"Ready."

A girl who Kengee had seen sitting quietly in the shadows came forward to receive the scroll which she tucked into her sleeve. The girl smiled broadly and then strode out of the cave without even looking at Kengee.

"One of Hibee's murderous darlings," Tanee said. "I've sent her a list of formulas for weed-killers in case your beloved Takusa develops resistance to the one Hibee is now using. How is the old girl?"

"Wasting away, at least in upper Ta. And no more Takusa milk for me. I'm finished on Ta."

"And to think that you almost became king of the plants. Takusa had the right idea. I'd like to see you take roots someplace for a change."

"Hibee has exiled me."

"To where?"

"Here, I've got nowhere else to go. I can pay rent, however." He poured the loot out on the table.

"Once a house thief, always a house thief. Well maybe you're better at that than at being a warrior. But my brother would not approve of cohabitation with a deformed woman, and he's still pretty mad that I escaped from his underground prison. You would only get yourself into worse trouble."

"Where the hell do you expect me to live?" Kengee shouted. "In the desert? You brought me to Ta. You're responsible. You have to take care of me. It's your moral duty."

She smiled very sweetly at him. "How would you like to go home, Kengee? Home to Earth."

"You told me I could never return."

"I was not telling you the truth exactly. You see it is not necessary for you to return because you never left. I only copied your brain, your self. I didn't destroy you. Kengee, you're still functioning as usual back on Earth, unaware of yourself on Ta. Now all I have to do is give you poison and this existence ends and you'll continue to exist there."

"That sounds too much like dying."

"I didn't think you would like the idea. But there is another possibility. I could retransplant you back into your original self—a grafting operation. You then would be what you are here, or at least have all the memories of Ta, and also what you are on Earth. How would you like that?"

"Let's go."

"Are you so eager to leave me?"

201

"Of course not, Tanee. I don't want to leave you at all, but there doesn't seem to be much else I can do."

"I know," she said with a sad voice. "I must think of what's best for you."

"That's very nice of you, Tanee."

"And I do owe you a lot. You accomplished all and more than I had hoped for. Really, you were quite splendid."

"How?" He was honestly puzzled.

"I knew for a long time that there existed a great danger to Ta in the south, but the barrier was there that kept me from finding out what it was. Mako saw only a threat to upper Ta's economy and believed Lornz was the only enemy. But then Mako lacks my perception. He did however authorize me to import a hero and left the selection up to me. I wanted no warrior. I wanted a catalyst. While searching Earth one day, I went for a walk in the park in a borrowed body. I jumped two feet in the air when I first saw a dandelion. It produced a spark of the same great fear which I always felt when I approached the south. I sensed the relationship and knew my man must come from Earth.

"You and Takusa shared a common heritage—Earth. You were not only successful in exposing Takusa but in leading her to subjugation. She now is under control. You were the male bait in the trap. And there was much more I wanted—I desired change on Ta. I naturally despised my brother's Institute for Human Perfection. I hated it, in fact, and sought its destruction. It will be destroyed now that Hibee is in command of the Zabo. And Mako and the Committee of Five will now see their hold over Ta weakened. I don't pretend to have planned it all. I only sensed that an alien of your type would be a disturbing influence—a change maker.

"And I don't even know if Ta is going to be really better as a result of the changes—the breakdown of the old power centers and the inherited power of the swordholders. But I think it will be better."

"With Hibee in charge, I have my doubts," Kengee said. "She hates men and I for one don't want to stick around and be ruled over by a big mama who hates men.

202

She's got a very vicious streak and she's a power-mad bitch."

"I am a little worried about Hibee myself, and that's why I gave the Takusa-killing formulas also to your friend Gosho. He'll know how and when to use them to keep the Zabo from gaining exclusive rights over Takusa's milk. And if the time comes, he'll know how to destroy Takusa."

"Hibee's not going to like that and she can be dangerous."

"Thanks for worrying about me, a little bit. But I can take care of myself."

"I know you can and therefore I will be able to leave you with a good conscience."

"Kiss me goodbye first."

He did with some impatience.

ELEVEN

Kenneth O'Hara shivered under the blankets in his apartment above the warm springtime streets of New York. The late afternoon sun was like the open door of a furnace, but it could not burn out the deep feeling of absolute cold which Kengee had brought back with him from Ta. The short existence of Kengee had been grafted skillfully by Tanee to the being of Kenneth O'Hara, and there had been a total exchange and complete acceptance. The separate existences were now one and a very enlarged one. Hours before they had felt the farewell embrace of Tanee who now was gone. The chill lingered.

An hour later the cold left him, and Kenneth swung his legs out of the bed and worked his toes into the soft, furry carpet—a gift from a woman who was no longer around. He felt good, happier than he had ever been before. He had done all right on Ta and he had at the same time done well in New York. Kenneth shared the news with Kengee. While they were apart, Kenneth had profited. His aging lover had left him the night before, saying she was returning to a young Miami shoe salesman. But first she had loaned him $5,000 in cash. There had been no tears or hard words, and his wallet lying on the nightstand was heavy with tens and twenties. Kenneth waded through the furry grass of the carpet to the bathroom where he showered quickly and then shaved slowly and carefully, thinking all the while.

Kenneth felt liberated. The dangers of Ta were forever behind him and so was the necessity of making love to Debbie who had begun to demand passion beyond his abilities to fake it. He no longer had to perform but could pick and choose among the girls on the sidewalks, in the department stores, and in bars. He was free, at least until his money ran out. He thought he might even try acting again. He had learned much about acting on Ta.

Kenneth went out to meet the night, pulled by the certain knowledge that there was a great opportunity not to be missed in the early hours, someplace. Without knowing why, he told the taxi driver to take him to a midtown hotel that he had visited only once before. He had spent two hours in its bar with a girl from New Mexico who hated New York because the dirt under her fingernails was black instead of red. He settled down on a bar stool. This was home at last for the Kengee part of him. He ordered a martini, remembering the ones Takusa had tried to make for him. He wondered how Takusa was making out in her unfair contest with Hibee and her deadly spray gun. When the glass was set before him, Kenneth lifted it to eye level. "To the king of the plants," he said aloud. The bartender began wiping the far end of the bar. He didn't mind eccentrics. He just avoided conversation with them. But a girl, whom Kenneth had not noticed until then, tilted her head and smiled down the bar at him. The smile warmed him to his knees.

"You think I'm fooling."

"If you wanted to be king of the plants, I'm sure you could be just that, and I'm sure you would be a good king, too," she said. "You look like the kind of man who could be anything he wanted to be." The girl's hair was black and long. Her words came from her throat with husky slowness. He thought she had a slight foreign accent. He liked her long legs. But her large tits pushing against her blouse pleased him more. He had the urge to tear open her blouse and grab, but this dirty thought went away when she smiled again. She checked out O.K. and he shifted to the stool next to hers.

"If I became king of the plants, I'd make you queen, and we could mingle our roots in love," he said. The bartender watched them, wondering how long the girl could put up with such stupid shit.

"Oh I really wouldn't want to become a plant. I love to move around too much." Her breasts wobbled to make the point.

"I'd like to plant you," Kenneth said. Her eyes never left his nor did the slight smile vanish from her lips. She was a woman, he decided, who could not be jolted by directness.

"You talk like a man who has just come off a ship or out of the woods."

"I've been away but not in the woods or on a ship."

"Vacation?"

"No, secret mission. Interplanetary stuff."

"You're crazy."

"No, just wild. Do you like wild men?"

"I adore them. Let's go." The bartender shook his head as the two rushed out of the bar, hand in hand and laughing.

They went directly back to Kenneth's apartment where he intended to have a real homecoming celebration. Two martinis were quickly made and the stereo put into action. He lit his pipe and they exchanged looks. A contract, he felt, had been signed.

"Do you like my home?"

"With a few changes, it would be all right."

"Changes?"

"Changes certainly. A woman wants to create her own home. You must know that. Dark orange drapes, really, and a pipe rack on the coffee table. And these ugly phony leather chairs. It's a dwelling for a bachelor and done with indifferent taste."

205

"Hold on, sweetie. I didn't invite you up here for life. Just relax and we'll enjoy ourselves. By the way, what's your name?"

"Tanee. Couldn't you guess?" She began giggling.

Kenneth kicked the pipes across the room and then collapsed into one of the phony leather chairs that Tanee said were ugly. He felt like crying but instead glared at the girl.

"Now as soon as you get over the shock, you'll be happy I came. How do you like the body? Believe me, I shopped all over New York to find a body that would please you." She stood up and spun around like a woman exhibiting a new fur coat. He groaned.

"Who did you kill to get it?"

"It was an act of mercy. The poor creature swallowed a bottle of sleeping pills at 4:31 A.M. this morning. I made her throw up and drink coffee. If I hadn't intervened, she would have died then. She really didn't want to live anymore and so we made an agreement. I took over. Of course, if you don't like the body, I'll go out and find another."

"It will do," he said hurriedly. "How long do you intend to stay, Tanee? I hope long enough for me to show you around New York."

"I'm settling down at last. I couldn't live on Ta anymore either with Hibee in charge and I knew you would need me even on Earth. I'm here to stay and stay, and I don't miss my former self at all. That's funny. But I suppose it's because I at last have found a compatible human to occupy."

"I've only got a few dollars and no prospects. There's a lot of rich guys on Earth. Why don't you look around a little first. I don't want you to make a mistake."

"You've got five thousand dollars, minus taxi fares and two drinks. I arranged that she give us that much before I kicked her out. But you'll have to find some kind of respectable job. Maybe you ought to take up accounting."

"Accounting, for Christ's sake!"

"Well why not? You've always been interested in money and I could help you. I'm good at numbers. And

206

I'll work too. I think I could make a lot of money on the stock market. I could get the best advice in my own way. We won't have any children for a couple of years, not until you're established."

"Tanee, no."

She ignored this and began slipping out of her skirt and blouse and then she slipped out of everything. He eagerly followed her into the bedroom.

"I'm sorry the bed isn't made."

"We won't have to make it for several days."

They kissed.

"I feel so puritanical suddenly, now that we're going to live together for the rest of our lives. Maybe we shouldn't be doing this before we're legally married. But we can take care of that quickly enough. I've looked up the regulations."

When they were resting later, Kenneth drowsily asked her why she had been considered a freak on Ta.

"I thought you knew, Kenneth. You see I was very much like I am now. My breasts were too big and my hips too wide and, well, I had a little too much behind. I was outsized all over compared to the acceptable standards for girls on Ta. I never realized that I was not a freak until I came to Earth."

"At least this beats living in a cave."

"It surely does, Kenneth." She pressed her outsized body against his and he forgot about wanting to be free.

the tip of the spear with her finger.